DATE DUE

Oc 8 80			
GAYLORD			PRINTED IN U.S.A.

THE HOUSE OF POWER

THE HOUSE OF POWER

SAMI BINDARI

TRANSLATED BY
Sami Bindari
and
Mona St. Leger

HOUGHTON MIFFLIN COMPANY · BOSTON

1   9   8   0

ORIGINAL EGYPTIAN TITLE

AL-SARĀYAH

FIRST AMERICAN EDITION

DESIGNED BY DANIEL EARL THAXTON

Copyright © 1980 by Houghton Mifflin Company

Library of Congress Cataloging in Publication Data

Bindārī, Sāmī.
  The House of Power.

  Translation of al-Sarāyah.
  I. Title.
PZ4.B5994Se [PJ7816.I527] 892.7'3'6 79-24665
ISBN 0-395-28540-2
PRINTED IN THE UNITED STATES OF AMERICA

TO MY WIFE WHOM I LOVE SO MUCH

PUBLISHER'S NOTE

The Pegasus Prize for Literature provides recognition for authors writing in languages other than English, whose work is deserving of wider attention. Prize winning works are then translated into English, thus making them available to a wider audience.

The first Pegasus prize for Literature was awarded in Egypt in 1977, upon the advice of a selection committee of Egypt's leading literary figures, to two Egyptian writers. One of them is the author of *The House of Power* and a leading Egyptian novelist, Dr. Sami Bindari. The portrayal of the corruption of bureaucracy, and its failure to sympathize, much less help, poor people, is one of the qualities that earned this novel its high reputation when it was first published in Arabic in 1971.

The chairman of the Pegasus Prize selection committee, Mr. Yahya Haqqi, is one of the great men of Arabic letters—a lawyer, diplomat, writer, and editor, a recipient of the Egyptian State Prize for Literature, and a member of Egypt's Supreme Council for Art, Literature, and Social Sciences.

The other members of the selection committee, who were chosen by Haqqi, are also prominent in Arabic literature. Dr. Louis Awad, formerly head of the Department of English Literature at Cairo University, is a distinguished writer and a cultural and literary editor of two Egyptian newspapers, a past Fellow of Princeton University and a past Professor of Comparative Literature at UCLA, and the author of more than forty books. Dr. Suhayr al-Qalamawy, who has been a visiting professor at a number of universities in the United States, is Professor of Modern Arabic Literature at Cairo University, Secretary General of the All Arab Federation for Women, and Vice President of the Egyptian Society for Writers. She is the author and translator of many critical literary works. Dr. Morsi Saad al-Din, a journalist, author, professor, and former Under-secretary of State for Culture, is currently Secretary General of P.E.N., the international writers' organization, and Deputy Secretary of the Afro-Asian Peoples' Solidarity Organization and Afro-Asian Writers. Denys Johnson-Davies is a Canadian scholar who has translated many works from Arabic into English. Dr. Fatma Moussa Mahmoud, previously head of the English Language and Literature department of Cairo University, has published translations and surveys of both Arabic and English novels.

Although the first true Egyptian novel, *Zeynab* by Husayn Haykal, was not written until the beginning of the twentieth century, Egyptian writers are not newcomers to the craft of fiction. In the twelfth and thirteenth centuries, Arabic writers expressed themselves in *qasas*, anecdotal tales and stories. Oral fiction, which produced such tales as the famous "Thousand and One Nights," captured the imagination of listeners in the East and West. *Siras*, or prose romances in Arabic, are believed to have influenced the fifteenth-century romances in Spanish and French literature.

The appearance of *Zeynab*, in 1914, is generally considered to mark the birth of the modern Egyptian novel. The form has evolved rapidly since then, moving quickly through a period of close imitation of European novels—especially Russian and French—into its current stage which has a distinctively Egyptian character. Novels published in Egypt over the past sixty years have moved from classic to colloquial Arabic, from external descriptions of country life to views-from-within of peasant psychology, and from realism to the exploration of abstract themes and innovative techniques. In doing so, they have also provided a record of the tremendous changes that have occurred in Egyptian society in this century.

Arabic, with its rich vocabulary and complex grammatical structure, is an extremely difficult language to translate into English.

The spellings of the Arabic words are like all transliterations, close phonetic approximations of the original words. "Sheikh," a title given to a respected older man or man of religion, is sometimes spelled "Shaykh." The reason for this confusion is that there are only three vowel sounds in Arabic, and their English equivalents are a matter of how the English ear hears them and how various Arabs choose to pronounce them.

On behalf of the author, we would like to express our appreciation to Mobil Oil Corporation, which established the Pegasus Prize and provided for translation into English.

THE HOUSE OF POWER

CHAPTER

I

T he eyes are immediately attracted by a flock of flying doves. They look up, and their gaze is rapidly drawn, through layers and layers of luminous blue sky, to catch up with the white wings that flutter in the transparent light. The mind is overwhelmed by all this brightness and swift movement. Then the flock of doves turns back and the eye follows it, till it meets the delicate graceful palm trees whose heads are raised as if in prayer to the sky. The doves circle over the colored fields of patched green and gold with the ornate lace and shining silver of a small river between them. Suddenly, the eyes drop to a dark dense forest of casuarina trees and discover above it the high walls of a mansion . . . and lower down appears the village with its little mud huts covered by hay and straw roofs. The narrow tortuous streets thrive with life like a beehive. The small canal passes by it and bulges to form a laughing pond where kids, geese, and ducks play together in its water. The doves circle over the village and then turn toward the towers of the white pigeon house . . . which is an altar of cleanliness, purity, and peace.

The time was about noon. The sun glared and nature was glittering . . . but something strange had taken hold of this black little village . . . a strange stillness. The women at their doors whispered with each other. Even the children at the pond stopped jumping and playing in the water, their naked bodies shining and their round bellies protruding above thin legs. Their enormous organs bulged from bilharzia, which gave them an appearance of abnormally mature development at an early age.

At the corner of an alley the men stood in a crowd. Some of them looked at the entrance of a certain house as if waiting for someone to come out. Eyes looked steadily ahead yet were empty. Hard faces toughened by the wind were full of dignity. From the hut rose an inhuman cry, which made the men shudder. It was followed by the wailing of women. At that moment, the coffin appeared. Elders of the village moved with slow steps behind it. A woman darted from the house, trying to follow. Her face was wrinkled with deep furrows of sorrow and age, and her blind eyes were shut with the grief of weeping. She staggered, stumbling against the supporting men around her, weeping and moaning. The hard faces around her were affected by her sorrow. Some hands grasped and stopped her, and the women dragged her back inside the hut.

While the wailing and weeping continued, the funeral procession headed toward the hill which had served as the village cemetery for generations of the village people.

The general manager of the estate, Chief Abdul Meguid, and his assistant, Hassan Effendi, rose reluctantly when they saw the procession coming. Chief Abdul Meguid looked regretfully at the cane armchair that had comfortably embraced his posterior. The chair was under the wooden awning that covered the terrace at the entrance of the estate office building. It was his favorite spot, having a cool breeze, and there he usually received the greetings and curtsies of the passing peasants. However, death asked for respect, so the two men joined the procession, though they were indifferent about it.

Heading the procession marched a young man who could still be considered a boy. He had large dark eyes and fine delicate features. He was so handsome in fact that he looked more like a beautiful girl with kohl around her eyes. His face contrasted with the coarse faces around him. Near the high wall enclosure of the mansion, the casuarina trees threw their cool shade on the procession, which slowed down as the mourners were drawn irresistibly to look up toward those high walls and trees, as if the house had a power of its own which could be imposed even on death.

When the procession reached a clover field which had recently been mowed, it stopped and the pallbearers laid the coffin on the ground. Prayers for the dead were recited. Saleh, the boy, repeated the words as if they had no meaning. His mind wandered, incapable of attention. He kept asking himself what was the meaning of it all. Did his father really lie in this coffin? . . . Dead . . . he did not understand yet all the implications that such a word carried.

He saw everything as being destroyed and perishing every day around him. Crops grew, then withered. Animals were fattened, then were slaughtered as he watched. They would simply kick their legs, then shudder, before stretching quietly forever. Exactly as his father had done in the early morning. He kicked, then shuddered, then lay quietly in peace. His mother had not cried and wailed when their dog died from eating fish last winter as she did today. His father had thrown the dead dog in a deserted place and his fellow dogs ate him . . . how terrible!

Who would eat his father? With difficulty Saleh erased a smile that was forming on his lips. Of course people don't eat each other . . . they say it's worms that eat them. He grimaced at the thought, so that a man put his hand on his shoulder to comfort him. That aroused his attention to what was going on around him.

The coffin was raised again on the men's shoulders. Saleh saw the chief, Abdul Meguid, and his assistant, Hassan Effendi, and the Head Foreman, Mahrous, quickly returning to the estate offices while the procession moved in the other direction. He noticed that the steps became faster. Everyone wished the ordeal to end as quickly as possible. A corpse in this warm weather rapidly decomposed. Already a nasty smell began to creep into the air. They arrived at the top of the hill and saw the grave diggers sitting at the edge of the grave, laughing and joking as they finished their work. They immediately became solemn and rose in attention when they saw the procession. Everything ended hastily now as the shrouded body was taken out of the coffin and covered with earth (in the Moslem tradition), Saleh watching in bewilderment as if all this did not concern him. He was still too shocked for sorrow or tears to blur his vision.

Then he was left alone, facing the grave. Everyone had departed after shaking his hand and giving their condolences. An awesome anguish racked him as he looked around the deserted hill with its many graves and the understanding suddenly burst into his mind like a gun shot: his father had left him. Never again would he stand beside him or smile gently, when Saleh returned home. Never again would he interrupt his work by throwing his hoe in the corner of the wall to greet his son.

A painful despair grasped his heart . . . squeezing it hard. Suddenly his face shrivelled in a fearful grin that opened his mouth widely, showing his teeth. Kneeling at the grave, he pulled back his head and from his very soul, deep from his entrails, rose a cry that filled his lungs and throat, making him sound like a young wolf, echoing the frightening howl of the wild.

The men who had been in the funeral came hurrying back and tried to take him back to the village, kindly at first, then by force, but unsuccessfully. He struggled fiercely, escaped, and hid among the graves. The villagers shook their heads sadly and let him be.

Saleh returned to the grave and lay across it, weeping and moaning. He fell asleep exhausted and continued to sleep until nightfall. The dew awakened him. Darkness had crept in among the graves, and a new hidden world had come to life, with strange soft sounds all around . . . hissing . . . purring . . . rustling and rattling. The shadows of the tombs seemed to take shape and move. He realized where he was and shivered. Then he began to run. Only when he reached the road leading to the village did he stop. There, as his heart pounded in his chest, someone rose from under a tree as if he had been waiting for him.

"Is that you, Trunk?" Saleh asked.

"Saleh? Thank God, it is you. Where were you?"

Saleh's friend was older, shorter, but much broader, powerfully built, with huge muscles. That's why the village people had given him the nickname of "the Trunk."

Saleh gave no answer, and the two friends strode silently along between the rows of trees. From far, the village lights appeared, in particular the glow of the kerosene pressure lamp which hung from the straw roof of the wooden shed that had been quickly erected at the entrance to the village, not far from Saleh's hut, to receive the mourners.

Once in the village, they parted. When Saleh came to his hut the angry shouts of women stopped him at the door.

"Where were you, Saleh? You left your blind mother alone, shame. No one was here with her to receive the mourners".

Saleh looked at the wrinkled faces of the village women. He had not expected to see so many of them. They filled up the hut. They had come to express their condolences, bearing the usual trays of food on their heads. He straightened up and walked among them. Sensing his grief, they patted his shoulders with their hands as he made his way out of the hut to the shed.

He advanced into the light of the kerosene lamp. No one gave him a glance. He hesitated for a minute. Men were sitting around the trays of food and eating quickly and heartily. Saleh asked himself for the second time what was the sense of all this. The eyes around him gleamed with pleasure, the mouths opened and closed, the throats moved, and black flies—awakened by the light and the smell of meat—flew around the lamp and struck against the shining faces. Outside, in the dark, the village dogs barked frantically as if they had gone mad. It was traditional that a feast, lasting two consecutive days, be made to honor the dead. It was incumbent upon each hut owner to contribute one tray of food. It seemed ironic to Saleh that these poor villagers would order their wives to cook rice and kill a chicken or cook a piece of meat, although they spent most of the week surviving on peppers and bread. Yet he knew that appearances were as important in this village as everywhere else, and that thrift on such an occasion would be tantamount to sacrilege.

There sat Abdul Sabour al-Kallaf, the cattle feeder, hastily gorging himself as if late for an appointment. A few rice grains clung to his mustache and his face shone in the glow of the lamp. Next to him Saleh's Uncle Atiya Fawas closed his eyes as he ate, as if he enjoyed some heavenly music. Both had been friends of the dead man, like him they were poor, and like him they labored daily until the muscles along their spines cried with pain. Near them sat other neighbors, and their expressions, as they looked at Saleh, showed how grateful they were to Saleh's father for dying and affording them this feast. There in the center sat Chief Abdul Meguid; next to him, behind a tray, was Sheikh Maamoun, the chanter of the Koran. The rest of the mourners were at a respectful distance. Sheikh Maamoun bit into the breast of a duck, while Chief Abdul Meguid fiercely struggled with a wing. Even Guirguis Effendi, sharing a tray with Mahrous, the Head Foreman, ate as if in a race. Saleh observed it all silently. What concern of his was all this? Uncle Atiya opened his eyes and glanced at Saleh. He immediately recognized his nephew's perplexity and said, "Saleh, come here and eat with us."

Saleh responded to the invitation and sat cross-legged in front of the tray near Atiya. He reached for the rice and put some in his mouth. He immediately felt nauseated. A loud powerful belch rose from the stomach of Chief Abdul Meguid, announcing that he was full, so immediately some peasants got up to fetch pots of water to wash his hands. Saleh wanted to help, but Atiya told him to sit still. Then Sheikh Maamoun told a few jokes, as the dark lovely tea was poured. Chief Abdul Meguid put his hands on his belly and dozed. Sheikh Maamoun stood up, put his hand on his cheek, and cleared his throat, to attract their attention and call for silence. He lifted his head for the prayer of the evening.

The mourners repeated the prayer after him, then Chief Abdul Meguid said in his gruff voice, "Tell us, O Sheikh, some of the wonderful verses God has offered us." Sheikh Maamoun put his hand on his cheek once more, raised his voice, and mournfully chanted prayers from the Koran.

Late that night, Saleh walked with Sheikh Maamoun to the house of the Head Foreman, where Sheikh Maamoun had been invited to spend the night. On the way, it was difficult for Saleh to keep the dogs from attacking Sheikh Maamoun and tearing up his elegant clothes.

The Sheikh patted him on the shoulder and said, "Your father was a good man, Saleh. God bless you, Saleh. . . . Give my regards to your mother, my son." He stopped for a minute, kindly patted Saleh's back again, then said, "Tell her to send me two pounds tomorrow," and he patted Saleh gently, with affection, once more.

His mother was lying in a corner. She lifted her head and immediately smiled. They embraced each other for a long time, silently, tenderly.

"Sheikh Maamoun wants two pounds," said Saleh. She frowned.

"He left no money?" asked Saleh.

"No."

They sat quietly for a while, until he noticed the tears streaming down her cheeks.

"Don't cry, Mother."

"If it had not been for the neighbors, I would have been so ashamed. I could not prepare a single food tray," sobbed his mother.

"Mother, poverty is no shame. They all know we are poor."

"True, but how shall we live now?"

"I'll take care of that." He answered in a firm, strong tone of voice so as to make her have confidence in his words.

"How? Will you leave school?"

"I will find work, by God's will."

"Like what?"

"Don't worry about it, Mother. I will find something."

She lamented as if her husband was still in the room. "How many times did I tell you, Suleiman, that it was not necessary for Saleh to learn to read like the wealthy children, but you never listened to me . . . you should have taught him to labor with the hoe instead, and earn his daily bread."

"Mother, you mustn't have any regrets."

"How? You are so thin, what can you do? I am sorry for the weak way your father brought you up. . . ."

"Don't worry, Mother. I will find something. I promise you."

Saleh took his straw mat, lay down on it, and fell into a restless sleep. He began to sweat, and in his nightmares it seemed to him that he was in a room full of square-headed people. They pushed toward him, surrounded him, crushed him.

His mother's voice woke him up. He was still shivering.

"It is so cold," he said.

His mother covered him with some old rags. Suddenly he felt hot . . . his lips were parched.

"Water . . . Mother . . . water. . . ."

She gave him the jug and he took a long drink to quench the fire inside him. He became quiet and, before dawn, slept. His mother sat beside him, looking like the shadow of her son by the subdued light of the kerosene lamp. Through the small rounded window the gentle grey light of dawn entered, and a patch of illumination fell on the face of Saleh. It was a handsome face, with its delicate regular features. Its pale complexion had the glow of youth and puberty, with the shadow of soft black hair here and there above the full lips and on the contours of the cheeks and chin.

Saleh's mother felt the coming of dawn and heard the call to prayer. She went to the wall and felt her way along it till she found the kerosene lamp and put out its flame. Then she made her ablutions and prayed.

Umm Saleh, Saleh's mother, had been young and pretty when she was married. The beauty of her black eyes had been the subject of evening songs and poems by the young men of the village during Ramadan. But her first three children died, and her eyes became severely infected and she lost her sight. Saleh was her fourth and last child; God must have wanted to make her dark plight easier by giving him to her. And her husband had become more and more attentive to her. He was her sight and her light until she accustomed herself to blindness and learned to live and work within her own darkness.

The rising sun introduced fingers of light into the room, touching things, coloring them, spreading a glowing, shining carpet on the floor.

Umm Saleh took a deep breath in front of the window, then woke up Saleh.

"Saleh, get up, and go meet Sheikh Maamoun before he comes to the shed."

"Mother, I feel exhausted. My legs won't even carry me."

9

She gave him tea and a piece of bread. He smiled and thanked her. Three small birds flew in through the door and hopped a few steps, looking at him. The sight of them cheered Saleh up considerably and he laughed. He threw a piece of bread among them and watched them peck at it. Saleh rolled up the mat, said good-bye to his mother, and left.

He stepped outside in full daylight, and looked up. He was dazzled by the bright blueness of the sky and its infinite width. Its purity gave him confidence that he was entering a better world. Light always came again after darkness. Was it possible that all this beauty hid evil in its depth? No . . . life was good and he would take his share of it.

He had matured overnight. The boy of yesterday had become the man of today. The flock of doves passed just over his head. With a flutter of wings, they circled in the clear blueness, then went rapidly in the direction of the white towers of the pigeon house.

Saleh inhaled deeply in the warmth of the sun. He walked by the little canal and smiled at the geese and the ducks. He washed, then went to the shed, and after praying he sat cross-legged and waited for the Sheikh.

When he heard the fierce barking of dogs, he knew that Sheikh Maamoun was coming.

"God damn these dirty vile animals," said the Sheikh. Then seeing Saleh he said, "God's peace, grace, and blessings be with you."

"And to you as well," answered Saleh.

The Sheikh sat under the shed, took out of his pocket an elegant small silver box, and put some snuff in his nostrils. He sneezed and, looking obliquely at Saleh, asked, "Did you give my message to your mother?"

"Yes," said Saleh, blushing.

"What did she say?"

"She will send you what you asked for shortly."

The Sheikh took a deep breath and played with the beads of his chaplet. Some villagers came over, which gave Saleh an excuse to ask for permission to leave. He went in the direction of the estate offices, thinking of various ways to find some money to pay the Sheikh's fee and to support his mother. He felt sure Chief Abdul Meguid would help him, if only in remembrance of his father.

The Chief was sitting in the strategic bamboo chair on the

shaded terrace from which he supervised the goings and comings of the villagers. To his left extended the row composed of an office building, storehouses, personnel cottages, and then the village. In front of him stretched the vast empty yard where harvests were heaped, to his right was the main road of the estate and the mansion. When he saw Saleh coming from the village a dark shadow passed over his face. Squeezing his lips together in scorn, he said "Bring the payroll ledger, Guirguis."

Guirguis Effendi stuck his owl head out of the office window and looked over the Chief's terrace with slightly raised eyebrows. His stone-hard features registered some astonishment.

When he saw Saleh he quickly brought a ledger to the Chief, who made a show of studying it. "Guirguis, has Suleiman Hawari received full payment for his work, God have mercy on his soul?" said the Chief.

"The ledger is with your Excellency."

"Do we owe him any money or don't we?"

"We owed him for two days' work, but then he was absent for two days, and you ordered me to deduct the whole from his wages, as punishment for his laziness as you said."

"But he is dead."

"The ledger could not foretell his death. Your Excellency ordered the deduction."

"Then, let it be. We owe him nothing."

"Yes."

Saleh came up the stairs and approached with great deference, as he had seen other peasants do when they approached the Chief.

"Peace and God's grace and blessing be with you, sir."

He received no answer. The Chief seemed to be totally unaware of his existence. Saleh thought of attracting his attention in some polite way, but instead looked even more profoundly at his feet. At last the Chief spoke:

"How are you, young Saleh?"

"Fine thank you," answered Saleh. He knelt in front of Chief Abdul Meguid, kissed his hand respectfully, and said, "Sheikh Maamoun asked us for two pounds, but we have no money."

Chief Abdul Meguid's face became red as if he had been personally affronted.

"Two pounds! Is he crazy? Did you hear that, Guirguis Effendi? Two pounds! Don't give him more than one pound, Saleh!"

Saleh took a step backwards. "But," he began.

"Go immediately and tell him he has angered me," said the Chief.

"But we don't even have one pound!"

"Stop muttering and go!" The Chief half stood up as if on the verge of hitting the boy. Saleh ran until he reached the village. He cursed the Chief inwardly.

As Saleh passed the village he could hear the voice of Sheikh Maamoun chanting prayers from the Koran. He cursed Maamoun too. He walked on and reached the cotton fields. He saw the bent backs of men hoeing there. The Head Foreman, Mahrous, was officiating, shrieking the usual curses and insults at the men.

Finally Saleh came back to the village. The sky shone like a knife's blade. A dog barked near Saleh and he threw a stone at it. That made him feel better.

He went under the awning and sat near Sheikh Maamoun. He listened to the Sheikh's prayers, and said "Amen" automatically with the rest of the people.

The mourners departed one after the other until only Maamoun was left. He coughed and asked Saleh, "Where is the food?"

Saleh stared back, and was about to burst into a loud laugh at Maamoun's fat worried face, when he saw it suddenly relax with pleasure.

Saleh turned, Atiya's wife was arriving with a tray of food on her head. Saleh stood, took the tray from her, thanked her, and placed it in front of the Sheikh.

At dusk he went to the end of the village, to the estate canal, to think. He took pleasure in watching the retreating army of red waves, running away from him, when he touched the water. His friend "the Trunk" joined him and Saleh related to him the news of his meeting with Chief Abdul Meguid.

"You will have that pound tonight."

"How will you get the money?"

"Don't worry!"

"God keep you, Trunk."

With the call for prayer at sunset, Saleh hurried back to the shed to receive the mourners. The same joyous proceedings repeated themselves, the delicious wrestling with the trays of food that ended with the loud belch of Abdul Meguid and the chant of Sheikh Maamoun reciting the Koran.

Later, at the evening prayer, Trunk did indeed arrive with the promised pound for Sheikh Maamoun. Uncle Atiya, Trunk, and the Sheikh haggled over the fee, with the Sheikh accepting the pound in the end.

At last everyone left and the shed was dismantled. The village had celebrated the funeral of Saleh's father. They had prayed for his soul; they had eaten up a quantity of food in the form of ducks and geese, the amount of which the deceased had never eaten in his life; and it was they who had paid Sheikh Maamoun one pound for his prayers.

C H A P T E R

2

S aleh woke at dawn at the sound of the morning call for prayer. He went to the canal where he washed as usual, then prayed, then sat cross-legged in the small dried-mud elevation on the bank that served as a mosque. He enjoyed this hour of the day and this particular place. The canal mirrored the sky, and beyond it the fields shone with morning dew.

Uncle Atiya, Ali Keilani (Trunk's father), and some neighbors came into the mosque. They were not surprised to find Saleh there, since he was the one youngster in the village who prayed with the men, mainly because of the fact that Saleh's father had felt it was important to educate him. Because of that, some of Saleh's playmates used to call him mockingly "Sheikh Saleh" or "Professor."

The men prayed and sat cross-legged in silence with Saleh. Uncle Atiya then looked at Saleh and asked in a hoarse voice:

"What are you going to do, Saleh?"

"I will do my best, Uncle Atiya."

"Your mother is blind, Saleh. You are responsible for her."

"I know, Uncle Atiya, I know."

"You have to support her."

"I shall."

"How?"

"I don't know yet, but I shall ask Sheikh Ahmed, my teacher."

"Why don't you ask for work at the estate offices?"

"At the estate offices?"

"Why not? Your father lived in their service and died in their service. It is their duty to give you a job. You're well-educated. You could be an assistant to Guirguis Effendi or Younes Effendi or Hassan Effendi."

"Is that true?"

"Sheikh Ahmed will be of no use to you. Go to Guirguis Effendi and ask him to intercede for you with the Chief."

"I'll go today."

"Goodbye, and God be with you."

"And with you, Uncle Atiya."

The men stood up and left him to take their places in the

workers' queue in front of the estate offices; Saleh stood up too, in deference, then sat again.

He rejoiced in observing the awakening of life around him, and the little changes that made dawn turn into day: the chant of the cocks on the roofs announcing sunrise, then the sun's first glance from over the trees as it flowed into a fountain of colors across the fields, lighting every dewdrop. The sunrise demanded a greeting from the different farm animals. A formation of geese marched toward the canal and a flock of doves circled again in the sky. On the road in front of him silently passed the men going to the fields, dressed only in their underwear, their hoes on their shoulders, with deep-lined, hard faces, ready for a long day of hard labor. Women and girls passed also, talking, followed by younger laborers, boys and girls, playing, quarrelling, running, laughing, till the sting of the canes at work made them cry.

When the groups of workers had disappeared from sight, Saleh stood up, passed the village, and went to the estate offices. Chief Abdul Meguid was not there yet, but Guirguis Effendi was behind his desk.

"Good morning, Guirguis Effendi."

Guirguis did not reply, but this time Saleh paid no attention. He stood his ground firmly and decided to stay there until Guirguis looked at him. Finally, after a long time, Guirguis Effendi said, "I am busy now."

"I have only one word to say to you. Please let me speak."

Guirguis interrupted him by a gesture of his hand and bent over his papers, muttering to himself that the boy was there to ask for money and the best thing to do under the circumstances was not to give him an opportunity to ask.

"One word," said Saleh. "I wish to work as a clerk or an assistant at the estate offices."

Guirguis Effendi lifted his head quickly and glared at Saleh.

"My brothers died before I was born," continued Saleh. "I have no one but you, Guirguis Effendi, and God of course. My mother is blind, but I have learned to read. I am your servant, Guirguis Effendi. Please give me a job."

Guirguis Effendi said nothing. Saleh begged, his lower lip trembling. "Please, Guirguis Effendi, please, answer me. Don't leave me like this."

Still the hard face before him did not move or reply. So Saleh left the office and went down the stairs quickly, with tears in his eyes. He slowed down, on the main road of the estate, his heart pounding in his chest as if a steel hand was squeezing it. The dense high casuarina trees cast their shade on him when he passed the walls of the mansion. He immediately stopped crying, and felt a sudden dread. He threw a frightened glance at the top of the high walls that hid behind the trees. His steps slowed down in submission. He started to run again when he left the shadowed coolness.

After a long march he followed the curve of the main road away from the hill that served as a cemetery for the peasants. The corn fields here extended on vast stretches of land. The stalks, still green, were beginning to raise their hands to the sky, swaying with the breeze. Saleh felt better looking at this sea of quiet green, full of goodness. He decided to visit his teacher, Sheikh Ahmed, as he had planned to do before. He reached the railroad tracks that divided the estate's land into two; there was the train station, some shops, a few houses belonging to merchants, the market, the mill, and the small hospital. The domain comprised two villages. The upper one, where Saleh lived, was near the general managerial offices and the mansion called the "Palace" by the peasants. The other, smaller village, west of the station, was where Younes Effendi, the second assistant, lived and from where he daily rode his horse to the estate. There also was a small mosque, a real one, not a stretch of dried mud on the canal bank.

When Saleh reached the mosque, he heard the voice of a young boy asking for mercy. Saleh smiled. Sheikh Ahmed was punishing a boy with his cane. Saleh went in and saw the Sheikh sitting cross-legged, with his students facing him, the smaller ones in the first row. The Sheikh looked at him with dismay. Saleh sat silently in the last row. Sheikh Ahmed's face was broad and shaped like a triangle, with huge flattened Negroid nostrils above a wide mouth shaped like the slot of a post-office box. His long beard obscured the rest of his face. His slim, short body was stooped, carrying an enormous hunch back.

Sheikh Ahmed took out his frustrations on the children, especially if they were good looking. He caned them on the slightest pretense if they were lax in their studies, and he enjoyed hitting them hard across the bottom of their feet. But he was a good teacher. With him, the children learned the prayers of the Koran, the principles of religion, reading, writing, and mathematics.

Saleh waited until the end of the lesson. When the students left, he approached the Sheikh, who stared at him coldly and concentrated on putting together his papers. In spite of the Sheikh's harshness, Saleh looked upon him as his teacher, respected and even liked him.

"Why did you come today, Saleh?" asked Sheikh Ahmed.

"Sir, my father died."

"I heard about it. However, at the first opportunity, you must pay me back the sixty piastres that he borrowed from me."

Sheikh Ahmed then turned his hunch on him and left.

Saleh went to the canal to have his ablution, then returned to the mosque for the noon prayer. Later, he saw Sheikh Shaban, the senior Sheikh of the mosque, sitting at the entrance in a halo of light. He knelt in front of him, kissed his hand silently, and sat down. The Sheikh was pleased.

"How are you, Saleh, my boy?"

"Fine, sir."

Saleh attempted to get up, but the Sheikh put a kind hand on his cheek and said:

"Sit near me, my boy."

Saleh marvelled at the soft, velvet-like touch of the hand . . . so gentle.

Saleh sat near him and felt the eyes of the Sheikh examining him. He knew that his boyishness had gone, that his expression was that of a man who had aged prematurely. The Sheikh's voice was so kind that Saleh almost burst into tears. The Sheikh offered his condolences and said:

"This is God's will. His ways are mysterious. We do not understand them, and feel perplexed, but they are, in any case, for the best."

They both sat silently while the Sheikh fingered his prayer beads.

"Do not despair, my son," continued the Sheikh, "despair is the worst enemy. Life is like a wheel. Never allow yourself to be under it long, for it might crush you. Never let life defeat you. Your father died. So be it. It is not surprising that you feel like crying. But your father is now in a happier place. Do you wish him anything better?"

"I believe in God, sir, and desire only His mercy. But I need to work. My mother is blind. How can I look after her when all doors close in my face? What can I do?"

"If you are looking for a solution, have courage. Don't let the first battle be a defeat. What doors have been closed in your face?"

"Uncle Atiya advised me to look for a job at the estate offices as a bookkeeper or whatever, but Guirguis Effendi ignored me as if I were a dog before him."

The Sheikh frowned.

"Then I went to see Sheikh Ahmed," continued Saleh.

"Sheikh Ahmed?"

"Yes. He was my teacher. I only wanted his advice, but he asked me instead for the sixty piastres that my father owed him."

The Sheikh laughed, and after a moment Saleh joined him.

"Look at you . . . you are laughing heartily . . . yet a moment ago you were full of despair because of the death of your father. So do not linger in the path of despair . . . laugh and always look ahead with hope, even on your own death bed . . . but take care, do not take life lightly or it will crush you without pity as I said before, under its wheel."

They remained silent for a while and Saleh felt a strange quietness within him. He was elated with a sense of euphoria that he had never felt before. Only when he was at the small mosque on the bank of the canal in the quiteness of dawn had he felt anything like this. He wished the conversation could go on forever. He stole a glance at the Sheikh from under his long lashes and asked himself, "Is he really a saint, that man?"

The Sheikh's looks would have seemed to point to that. He had a long emaciated face that culminated in a small white beard; a large forehead; and handsome, regular features. The eyes were wide and beautiful, and always shining. Daylight could be mirrored in their amber-colored depths.

In spite of his years, he always stood erect. His presence had a calming effect on arguments and violence. He enjoyed the respect of everyone; in fact, he often served as a judge in village disputes. He came from a peasant family but his grandfather had, at great sacrifice, managed to purchase some small parcels of land. The price of cotton had increased and the Sheikh's grandfather had bought additional land the following year and more land the year after. Suddenly the matter became of great concern to the estate authorities, who attempted to get hold of the property by any means at their disposal. They schemed until they got back most of the land except for the initial three small plots—and these were still owned by Sheikh Shaban.

Chief Abdul Meguid felt immense unhappiness each time he rode past the land on his white donkey. In the midst of an ocean of cotton or corn were the few acres of Sheikh Shaban with their palm trees which pointed and laughed at him with the wind. The small mud house of the Sheikh was in the middle of one cluster of palm trees. If the Chief went too near, the dogs of the Sheikh would bark at him fiercely, and no one would prevent them from attacking him, and he would be filled with rage. What made him even angrier, was the knowledge that the village had unanimously accepted Sheikh Shaban as their religious leader. Sheikh Shaban's father had initiated the building of the mosque, and the Sheikh continued with a weekly collection to complete it. The estate managers, through government authorities, had often sent leaders and prayer readers to the mosque to supplant him, but to no avail.

Chief Abdul Meguid finally surrendered and gave Sheikh Shaban all the outward marks of respect; secretly, though, he connived to fight him in every possible way. Instead of allowing the village water to irrigate Sheikh Shaban's plantations as it was supposed to, Chief Abdul Meguid gave instructions for it to be diverted. When Sheikh Shaban protested, he pleaded ignorance, smiled, and said, "Why don't you let go of this property which is giving you so much trouble? I will buy it from you at the best possible price."

Chief Abdul Meguid ultimately discovered a weapon that would work in his favor in his attempts at acquiring the remainder of the land. Sheikh Shaban's family had increased; his children and his brothers' children had grown, many had married and had children of their own. There was nowhere for them to work except in the fields owned by the estate. The Chief knew the general principle, that if a ruler showed his anger at one of his subjects, the rest would immediately abuse and humiliate the one that had had the misfortune to fall into disfavor. Without being asked to do so, but of their own accord, all his assistants, inspectors, and foremen helped to take the Chief's revenge on Sheikh Shaban's children. It was such a pleasure for him to hear one of his subordinates say: "We have flogged one of Sheikh Shaban's children," or "We've deducted a couple of days' salary from one of them."

That is why the men of Sheikh Shaban's family had a distinctive air about them. They were all very good looking and well-built, and had a calm, distinguished personality, yet they were set apart by the miserable rags they wore proudly.

Thus Sheikh Shaban sympathized with Saleh completely, but felt sad at being unable to do anything for him.

politely. Then he went up the steps and looked at the astonished face of Chief Abdul Meguid, shocked by his boldness.

"Sir, you attended my father's funeral and I thank you, but you left no instructions to help my blind mother, or to give me work. . . ."

He stopped talking as he saw the Chief's eyes widen and his arms rise above his head as if saying to Younes: "Look at your beasts . . . to what degree of impudence they have reached . . .!!!"

This was the occasion that Younes had been waiting for all morning to ease his nerves. Saleh did not even realize what was happening, but his nose hit the wooden floor of the terrace with an explosive force that echoed at the back of his brain. He felt someone rolling him down the steps, then he cried loudly of pain when the vicious shoe, in a last kick, crushed the base of his spine.

Finally he managed to get up, half bent. Blood was trickling from his mouth and nose. When he reached the village huts, he noticed that women were coming out of their huts to stare at him. Thanks to the secret telegraph system of the village, the news had spread instantaneously that Younes Effendi had beaten him for his impudence by order of the Chief. Saleh forced himself to walk erect as if he did not care. His mother met him.

"Mother, I am fine," he said. "There is nothing the matter with me."

She hugged him hard.

"I am fine, Mother," he repeated. His mother dried her tears and went inside the house. Saleh took off his clothes and wiped the blood from his mouth.

"Why do you go there, my son?" asked his mother. He began to weep and did not answer.

"May God punish you, Suleiman Hawari, for what you've done to your son."

"Mother, please, don't say that."

She waited and then said apologetically, "It's true that your father was a good man and that he is dead, but look at us now, my son. We don't even have any flour in the house."

She went towards the door.

"I intend to go and kiss the Chief's feet until he decides to forgive you," she added.

"Don't, Mother, come back."

She stopped, afraid of the tone in his voice.

Without a word, Saleh left the room went to the small empty shed that served as a second room and returned a few moments later wearing his father's clothes and carrying his father's hoe. He felt his mother's hand on his shoulder. She sensed that he was holding the hoe even though she could not see it.

"Why the hoe, my son? . . . Do you intend to do anything with it?"

He laughed and said, "Don't worry, Mother. I'm not a fool. I will not sell my life cheaply for the sake of the fat pig that sits on the office's terrace! I intend to take it and go to work."

"Work with the hoe is difficult, my son."

"With God's help, I will manage."

In the evening "The Trunk" visited Saleh. He came running after work to see what had happened to his friend.

"How are you, Saleh?"

"As well as can be expected after what happened to me."

"Did the son of a bitch hurt you?"

"Yes."

The Trunk greeted Saleh's mother and said, "Take this, it's a bit of tea and sugar." Then he turned back to Saleh and asked, "Is it true, Saleh, that you shouted in the Chief's face?"

"No, I just asked him politely to help my mother and for a job for me."

"Now what are you going to do?"

"Now, nothing. I shall take the hoe and go to work with the rest of you."

"Saleh, you are too frail to be able to do that."

"Is this how you encourage me?"

Saleh's mother brought tea and they all drank together.

"Won't you apologize to the Chief even if you're not really sorry?"

"No, Trunk, I've had enough."

"This is dangerous, Saleh."

"Why? I've done nothing, and tomorrow the Chief will see me using the hoe. I hope he'll be satisfied."

"Maybe, but I'd feel more comfortable if you went and apologized to him. What if he reports you to the Palace?"

"The Palace?" Saleh jumped as if bitten by a snake.

"Why not?"

"What has the Palace to do with me? . . . My God! I wish I could run away and look for work somewhere else."

"No, you won't be able. . . . Take care, Saleh. The sun rises at the east horizon on the estate and sets at the west still on the estate."

"But the world is vast beyond the estate's land."

"Don't you believe it. The estate is wider than the whole world and the long arm of the Palace will catch up with you wherever you go."

They kept quiet, brooding gloomily, absorbed in their own thoughts; then the Trunk went to his house. Saleh then went to his mat and tried to sleep.

C H A P T E R

3

I t was a long time before he fell asleep, and when he did he had a strange nightmare that he was walking slowly in a deserted place. The sun was setting and it colored the sky above him with its red glow. Every now and then, he came across the skull of an animal that grinned frightfully with its protruding teeth. He reached the edge of a freshly dug grave. He struggled in vain with a power that pushed him into it. He stretched on his back, his heart pounding painfully in terror. The coolness of the grave made him shiver. He became aware that blood was dripping from the red sky. It fell on his face drop by drop, and became heavier, filling his nostrils and his mouth. The blood had a sugary nauseating taste. He trembled all over when he suddenly realized that the earth above the grave was falling on him, burying him. He tried to rise . . . but could not. The earth covered his mouth and nose, forcing him to struggle for breath, choking him. He suffered the agony of death with a sharp acuteness. So he gathered all the power he had, tightening his shivering muscles in one last attempt at yelling for help. It did materialize. It echoed in the room, awakening him and awakening his mother who rose, terrified.

He opened his eyes and saw her covering him with an old sack. His teeth snapped and chattered.

"I am dying of cold, Mother . . ."

She piled on him all the old rags she could find. After a while he felt suddenly very hot. . . . He threw the sack and the old rags away and sweated profusely all over his body. A deep sleep overtook him.

Dawn entered furtively, awakening him by gently playing its light on his face. He stretched his body, his muscles ached, and he remembered his decision to go and work hoeing the cotton. He felt a certain apprehension that he would not succeed and that he would make a fool of himself. He discarded this thought, deciding that he would hoe even if he should die doing it.

He remembered the big urn of water that his father used to fill in the canal before going to work every morning. His father was the only man to do so in the village, as his wife could not, blind as she was. Saleh now raised the urn to his shoulder, and while he went out he could hear his mother thanking him; then she raised her voice loudly, asking God to protect him and give him strength. He prayed at the river bank, filled the urn, and started back to his hut. He met some youngsters going to work, their hoes on their shoulders, and they grinned mockingly. He could not care less. His mother had prepared the tea; he quickly drank it and ate a piece of bread, said good-bye to her, then marched toward the estate offices with his hoe, his heart pounding.

When he took his place in the midst of the laborers, the faces around him showed real astonishment. The older ones nodded sadly: they blamed Saleh's dead father for the way he had educated his son; while the younger ones could not conceal their rejoicing at his misfortune. They gloated; one of them whistled. Another asked, unbelieving, "Do you really intend hoeing the cotton with us . . .?"

He did not answer but kept staring at his bare feet, ashamed, red in the face. He felt the touch of the Trunk's shoulder next to his. He raised his head and turned, and immediately received an encouraging wink. The two smiled at each other.

Suddenly, they all became silent as Hassan Effendi appeared at his doorstep, walking with his peculiar dancing gait, as if there was a soft spiral spring under each of his buttocks. He was a short round-bellied man, always moving, jumping from one foot to the other, even while standing. His face, too, was on the move. His small squinting eyes looked in all directions and one could only guess by the direction of his long pointed nose where he was looking. His small chin also fled beneath the always open, smiling mouth. The only fixed point in this face was the black hole in the midst of it, the place of a missing tooth.

With all this smiling and laughing he was popular among the men. His demeanor was in sharp contrast to that of Younes Effendi. One presented a face of optimism while the second personified pessimism. Their work methods also differed drastically. When Hassan wanted to punish someone, he smiled at him, but reported him nevertheless, while Younes would thrash him and insult him on the spot. In their simplicity, most of the peasants thought that Hassan Effendi was the better man.

Now he walked among them, smiling, until he reached Saleh.

"Saleh, welcome. Welcome, professor. Are you here to use the hoe? If all professors worked with the hoe, this would be a much better world."

He laughed loudly, a contagious laugh which the men joined; laughter shook their bellies merrily. Saleh wished that the earth under his bare feet would swallow him, while Hassan Effendi, seeing the men happily laughing, said more.

"Well, professor, handsome professor. You should wear a veil and work in a house. The hoe is for men, professor."

A loud grave voice was heard that stopped the mocking and laughing . . . Uncle Atiya's voice.

"Hassan Effendi, you have no right to speak thus of an orphan. He is our son, and we care for him."

Hassan shrugged, and began distributing the jobs for the day.

"Saleh Hawari to the cotton hoeing . . . join the others. . . . Go with them, Mahrous, make them work real hard . . . I want you to turn their intestines inside out."

Saleh thanked his uncle for standing up to Hassan Effendi, and quickly joined the group of men that were following Mahrous. While they marched along, the Trunk gave him some advice about hoeing.

"Saleh, stay behind me so that I can help you. Don't bend your knees while working, bend your back. Keep your body firm, otherwise your muscles will really hurt you. Let your shoulders move with the hoe. Don't put your weight on only one foot."

"Thank you, Trunk. I'll be careful."

The men reached the cotton fields and they placed themselves in line along the furrows. Saleh took off his long peasant gown, and hesitated. Immediately Mahrous shouted at him with the vilest, dirtiest insults.

"You Saleh there . . . son of a bitch . . . did you come to coyly show the white of your legs . . . you . . . you . . ."

The men all around laughed boisterously as Saleh, his head reddening, still hesitated about where to put himself.

"At the end you . . . the last one . . . you . . . you . . ."

Again the dirty insults followed and then the loud merry clamor.

He heard the Trunk whispering to him.

"Don't mind him, go at the end. I'll be just in front of you."

He went to the end of the line and began to imitate the Trunk and understood quickly what was expected of him.

At first, as he worked, a mixture of rage and extreme shame filled him; then he began to calm down. He was amazed to discover that he felt a certain pleasure in performing this new manual work, a sense of harmony with time and space. He raised his head a little and saw the men in line. They all worked like him, gently turning over the earth around the young cotton plants.

They danced with their shoulders and arms together with a special rhythmic cadence as if they were joining in some kind of strange quiet prayer. Later the Trunk whispered:

"How are you doing . . .?"

"My hands have begun to hurt."

They could not continue talking since one of the foremen came nearer; there was a good number of them because the area to hoe was vast, and the men working were many. As the hoeing continued, what began as a slight scorching turned slowly into an unbearable burning, and the heaviness in Saleh's arms went down to his spine. After another hour passed he felt his whole body crying in severe pain the moment he began to raise his hoe. Another hour passed and Saleh slowed down. One of the foremen came with a nasty twinkle in his eyes and a mocking smile.

Saleh jumped as the cane stung the stretched skin of his behind, he involuntarily hissed between his teeth in a shout of pain.

"Aie."

The most vile insults imaginable flowed from the mouth of the foreman.

"Aie . . . you son of a bitch . . . aie you . . . you . . ."

But the Trunk really got sore and protested, red in the face.

"What's the matter with you all? He is working hard and doing a good job . . . I am getting mad myself. . . ."

The foreman, enraged, went for the Trunk, his cane raised, but Mahrous, the Head Foreman, bellowed from the far end of the field.

"Shut up you there. You son of a bitch . . ."

The Trunk returned to his line and began to work, as did Saleh. The assistant foreman did not insist.

The hoe was heavier and heavier. His muscles were aching and his palms burning. Without being seen by the foreman, the Trunk began to work for both Saleh and himself.

"Come on, don't let the men laugh at you," said the Trunk.

Saleh tried, until it was time to drink and rest. He sat in the middle of a furrow.

"Why are you sitting there open-legged like a prostitute, professor?" asked the foreman.

Everyone laughed. Saleh got up, crossed the furrows, and went to join the Trunk at the shaded path that bordered the field. He walked past a group of young laborers lying in the shade of the trees.

"Come, professor Saleh, and sit with us."

They needled him. Saleh did not answer and kept on walking, the Trunk following him. A young fellow named Sayed slapped Saleh, as he passed, on his buttocks, with a shameless gesture. This was too much for the Trunk. He slapped the scoundrel back on the face. The other, mad with rage, attacked him with his raised hoe, but the Trunk stopped the descending arm midway, and with his other fist, caught Sayed in the soft part of his stomach. Air rushed out of the belly with a compressed hissing sound, and the blow made the fellow double up and roll, his knees to his mouth, on the ground.

The Trunk turned now to the other young men around, who immediately began to look at the horizon, admiring the view. He asked in a threatening voice:

"Does someone want to joke with Saleh . . . ?" Of course no one answered.

Then he sat and asked Saleh to share his lunch: a piece of bread, a radish, and an onion; but Saleh refused.

"Eat a piece of bread," said the Trunk. "It will make you feel better. We still have a long day ahead of us."

Saleh looked at him gratefully, held out a trembling hand for the bread, and took a piece. Just then they heard Mahrous; he had given them only fifteen minutes. The Head Foreman began his shower of insults, and the men rose slowly.

More curses. The Trunk did his best to help Saleh without being noticed by the Head Foreman. The heat of the sun became even more intense; the effort of lifting the hoe inflicted its own pain. In a haze of pain Saleh felt as if his hands did not belong to him any more; as if they were holding on to the hoe in spite of him.

Mahrous said it was time to rest. It was noon. The men took off their clothes and washed in the small canal nearby. Saleh saw the Trunk doing the same. He tried to take off his rags but could not move his arms. Instead he went and rested under the shade of the road's trees, his mind as numb as his body.

Suddenly he realized that what he had gone through so far was nothing in comparison with what awaited him in the afternoon.

Even now he had no inkling of what was yet to come, yet he

shivered without knowing why. He urinated on himself and could not help it.

The Trunk came back, saw him prostrate, and said half sadly, half jokingly:

"What shape you're in, Saleh."

After he had dressed, the Trunk forced him to eat. Then they both dozed off, snoring. Half an hour later, Mahrous shouted,

"Get up, you loafers."

Saleh woke the Trunk, who cursed Mahrous under his breath.

"We have the right to rest longer. The Head Foreman is a bastard."

He got up and was surprised to see that Saleh did not.

"Get up, Saleh. If you don't, they'll deduct two days from your wages. All your work will be wasted."

"I can barely lift my arms."

He finally stood and walked out into the fields with the Trunk. The sun was very hot but Saleh resolved not to weaken no matter what.

In spite his resolve, the pain started once more and increased steadily; Saleh's work became lax, and Mahrous several times ordered one of his assistants to whip him with the cane, and the assistant foreman obeyed, but without too much conviction. They noticed Saleh's tears, as well as the blood on his hands. The day dragged and Saleh kept on working despite the pain. The other men's glances changed from sarcasm to sorrow, then respect and finally admiration. When the working day at last ended and the huge red sun touched the horizon, the men surrounded Saleh and congratulated him. The Trunk hugged him, and lifted him onto his shoulders. The rest of the men cheered, and Saleh laughed in spite of his pain. The Trunk put him down and they walked back to the village.

The canal beside the road had a fascinating beauty in its soft flowing water at the end of this torrid day. The willow trees on its banks dipped their branches in it cutting the current with bright red colored streaks. Near the village Saleh stopped, wanting to cross to the elevated mud platform on the bank under the willow trees that served as a mosque.

"Come with me, Trunk."

"No, Saleh, I must go to the station and the shop."

Saleh watched him leave. Like the rest of his friends, the Trunk was illiterate, and the words of the Koran meant nothing to him;

but he looked at the Book with respect and fear. He thought it had a power of its own. He knew only the prayer of the Fatiha. As for God, whose name was often on his tongue, the Trunk asked for His mercy and help in times of need, and knew He was most powerful and always present and of a dimension beyond his comprehension. He thought of him as one who inflicts punishment mysteriously. He did not feel it was up to him to understand or to question. He treated God as he treated the mansion; he kept his distance and tried not to attract attention.

Saleh smiled, walked towards the canal, and washed. In the water he swam until his muscles relaxed. He swam under water, then came out and sat naked on the grass. He wanted his body to dry before he put his clothes on again. The sky was red and gold; birds chirped, frogs croaked companionably, and on the breeze came the sound of women chattering as they came to fill their urns at the canal, peeping at him from far behind the veil of bamboo plants. They resembled slender gazelles as they knelt with their elastic bodies.

In the little mosque Saleh prayed, sat, thanked God for his "victory," and was proud of himself. His hands had bled, but he had worked the earth. He looked out at the fields. He had suffered for them and from them, but it was for a purpose. Saleh's mother was waiting for him at the door of their hut. She had heard about his feat and was proud of him. She spoke to him with respect which made him very happy. He could smell freshly baked bread.

"Where did the bread come from, Mother?"

"The baker lent me some flour when news of how you worked with the hoe spread all over the village."

He kissed her hand.

"Sit down, my son."

"Let me bring you some water first."

He took the urn to the canal. Some women were there, and one of them said to him:

"How are you, Saleh?"

"Well, Aunt Amina. Well, thank God."

"Yesterday's boy became a man," said one of the others.

The women laughed and made way for him. When he passed by them, he blushed. A fascinating fragrance thrilled him, making his heart throb powerfully in his chest, as one of them passed by him, walking with a slow voluptuous manner. He raised his long eyelashes and stole a glance at her. He was struck as if by lightning when their eyes met. Hers looked at his boldly with a magnetic intensity that came from the depth of their unusual blue-green color, and paralyzed him. He remained standing motionless for quite a while after she passed by. When he recovered his senses he marvelled at what had happened to him, yet he was somewhat annoyed with himself. He knew who she was: Yasmeen, the wife of "the Catfish" as they called her old laborer of a husband. He descended the canal's bank, filled the urn, and with an irritated jerk he lifted it to his shoulders. This made him shout from the pain of his sore back muscles. Yasmeen filled his mind.

With much effort, since his muscles and back still ached, he returned to his hut. The Trunk was waiting for him at the front door with some provisions in his arms. Saleh set down the urn and grimaced from the effort.

"Put some henna on his hands so that they can dry up and allow him to work tomorrow," said the Trunk to Saleh's mother. He turned to his friend and continued, "You have to do it. You must go back."

Saleh noticed then that the Trunk was carrying a heavy club.

"I carry it for protection against Sayed, that lad I fought on your account," said the Trunk. "Don't worry, I won't use it unless I have to." He spread some henna on Saleh's hands and then stood up to leave.

"Sit down, Trunk. My mother will prepare us some tea."

"No. I must go. Otherwise my old man will hit me for being late delivering these supplies. Goodnight."

The Trunk hurried home. His old father, Ali Keilani, was notorious for two things. He was known for his fierce piety and for an equally fierce inclination to beat his children and his wife. He would create situations that would give him excuses to hit the Trunk in order to keep him straight. The Trunk had a deep affection and respect for his father. He knew that one punch of his would send his old father sprawling, so he always accepted his punishment gracefully, yelling and crying as if he was in real pain. It was the Trunk's way of keeping his father happy.

After the Trunk left, Saleh's mother put a stool in front of Saleh with fresh bread and a piece of cheese on it. He ate while she prepared tea. He closed his eyes to savor the taste of the warm bread.

"Is the bread good, Saleh?" asked his mother, sitting beside him.

"Delicious, Mother."

He did not leave a crumb. Suddenly there was a knock at the door.

"Open up, Saleh, it is Abou Bakr."

"Come on in."

Abou Bakr, who was the son of Sheikh Shaban, entered with his cousin Ali. Abou Bakr was as handsome as his father, but he was much taller and darker than the Sheikh. He had the looks of a chivalrous Arab horseman. Ali, his cousin, looked more like Sheikh Shaban, with a gentle cheerful face and amber-colored eyes that looked at you kindly.

After the customary three servings of tea and the customary pleasantries, Abou Bakr said:

"You've become a man, Saleh. You were a good example to us today."

"I have to thank Sheikh Shaban for that. He gave me the right advice."

Abou Bakr smiled, pleased. He paused, then continued in a different, more serious tone.

"The Trunk left his hut with his club. It's not like him to look for trouble. What can we do to prevent a fight?" He added, "We heard how this came about. The Trunk tried to keep you from being hit by Sayed today, didn't he?"

"Yes, Abou Bakr."

"We should have helped you, Saleh. We're sorry we just stood by."

"No reason for apology. I know your affection for me."

"When I heard what had happened, I gave a piece of my mind to Sayed's family. I told them that the Trunk was right to protect you. Then they asked me to intercede for them. Sayed wishes to apologize and embrace you."

"I have no objection, but it's up to the Trunk to accept the apology."

Abou Bakr turned to Ali and said, "Go and find the Trunk. Tell him that I want to talk to him."

Within a few minutes Ali returned with the Trunk, who was still holding the club and wearing his cap forward on his head in ostentatious challenge.

Briefly they discussed the problem.

"Justice!" said the Trunk finally and loudly.

"You took justice in your own hands," said Abou Bakr. "Sayed still twists, doubled up, from your blow to his belly!"

"That was nothing, just a small example of what he will receive. He slapped Saleh for no reason, in a shameful way."

"True, but he apologizes now."

"That's not enough."

"What more do you want, Trunk? Sayed's people have clubs too, and they know how to use them."

"Reconciliation is blessed by God," said Ali.

"Only if justice is satisfied," answered the Trunk sharply.

"What would satisfy you, then?"

"A pound or two for Saleh. He needs the money."

"Very well. I can guarantee that. If Sayed and his family can't pay it, I'll pay it myself."

Again Abou Bakr turned to Ali and said, "Go and bring Sayed and his people."

Abou Bakr did not want to lose the momentum for reconciliation. Ali came back shortly with Sayed and three of his friends. Saleh received them courteously, but the Trunk remained aloof.

"These people are here to offer you their apologies," intoned Abou Bakr.

"I accept their apologies," said Saleh.

"Saleh accepts your apologies," interrupted the Trunk, "if you pay him two pounds."

"We can pay one now and one later," said Sayed.

"The remaining pound will be paid on Thursday," Ali interrupted.

"It is settled, then," said Abou Bakr.

Sayed embraced Saleh while Abou Bakr said to the Trunk, "It is up to you, Trunk, to kiss Sayed's head as a sign that your hearts are friendly again." The Trunk immediately kissed Sayed on the forehead and said: "I apologize, Sayed."

"Don't worry about it. It was my fault."

"The prayer of the Fatiha," commanded Abou Bakr.

All of them extended their hands and recited the prayer of the Fatiha. Afterward Saleh's mother brought tea, and they all drank and talked merrily. When all the guests decided to leave, Saleh accompanied them to the end of the street, came back, and slept.

At dawn he took his hoe and went to work. His hands bled again that day, and his back and arm muscles ached as he worked, but he went back the next day, and the day after. He began to lose weight. Each night his sleep was full of feverish dreams, but he continued to work. He continued also to go to the canal at the end of each day; the water seemed to revive him, and he hoped to see those blue-green eyes again.

Thursday night came. Saleh went with the other laborers to the estate offices. The place was full of hundreds of dusty, sweating men waiting to be paid.

Saleh overheard the armed guards talking as they stood on the terrace above him. Hassan Effendi began calling the names of the men aloud. Awad, another guard, repeated them after him. Each man, when his name was called, went up the stairs to the office. Some of them stopped at the door, blinking in the light, until one of the guards sent them in with a heavy blow of the hand on their naked necks to stand before Younes Effendi's desk. Their signature on the register was a thumb mark in front of their names. Younes Effendi enjoyed the grimaces on the faces of the men as he pressed their thumbs on the register with far more strength than was necessary.

If one of the men was not quick enough to move to the opposite desk, where Guirguis Effendi sat, then a second, more severe blow on the neck with the flat of the hand would automatically move him. Then Guirguis Effendi would rapidly count the money, and the man had better go quickly or another blow on the bare back of the neck from the heavy hand of the guard, Gaith, would be waiting for him.

The room was a large one. There was a third small desk, Hassan Effendi's, under a window that overlooked the terrace from where he would call the laborer's names. Against the front wall was a large divan where Chief Abdul Meguid was enthroned, observing the behavior of his subjects and smoking his narghile. From time to time, he passed it to the chief of the guards, who reclined on a cotton cushion beside him. At their feet sat Mahrous, the Head Foreman, cross-legged on the straw mat. He also received the narghile from time to time from Chief Abdul Meguid's benevolent hand. All around the room, on the floor, sat the guards, their backs to the wall, the long muzzles of their guns between their bare toes.

Saleh's Uncle Atiya heard his name called. Standing before Guirguis Effendi after being paid, he went through the usual procedure of counting his piastres in his mind to see if the amount was correct. He was quite experienced at it and quick as Guirguis.

"Guirguis Effendi, I have not received all my pay," he cried in protest.

"Hassan Effendi deducted some money because of your lack of interest," said Guirguis Effendi.

When Atiya started to protest, the heavy palm of Gaith hit him on the neck. He went out silently, without looking around him, and slowly descended the steps of the terrace. When he saw Saleh below the terrace, he suddenly jumped at him and seized him by the neck. "You owe me a day's wages. Pay it! Pay it!"

Saleh would have been strangled had not the Trunk and some others jumped and torn them apart. Suddenly Atiya let go and looked around him like a drunken man. He hurried toward the village, stooping, like a hurt animal.

"Has he gone mad?" asked one of the men.

"He almost killed him."

"What was the reason?"

"I have no idea," replied Saleh in a hoarse whisper, still choking.

"That is strange," muttered the Trunk. "I will inquire later on."

When all the names had been called, Hassan Effendi closed the window.

"Saleh, why didn't they call you?" asked the Trunk.

Saleh was too tired to care.

"Saleh, get up and object," said the Trunk.

Saleh forced himself to get up with the thought that if he did not, it meant certain starvation for him and his mother in the days to come. Awad, the guard, met him at the door.

"I have not been paid, Awad," said Saleh.

Awad saw that Saleh was on the verge of collapsing and his expression softened somewhat.

"Go in and inquire."

He led him to Guirguis Effendi's desk and said: "Saleh worked all last week and has not been paid."

"He is not registered in my book."

"Register him then, and pay him."

"Are you giving me orders, Awad?"

"Well, Saleh worked very hard," said Mahrous, with a note of pity in his grave voice.

"I ordered Mahrous to make him work in the cotton fields," said Hassan Effendi.

"If you gave him work, pay him yourself," retorted Guirguis Effendi.

"Since when do you take it upon yourself not to register a laborer I gave work to?" shouted Hassan Effendi.

Guirguis gave no reply. They all looked toward Chief Abdul Meguid and waited for a decision or a sign. The Chief inhaled the smoke of his narghile in silence.

"Apologize, my son," murmured Awad. He led Saleh toward the Chief's feet and Mahrous made him kneel in front of the Chief, pushing him down from the back of his head.

"Apologize, my son, and kiss his foot," he said.

Saleh could smell the Chief's feet. His lips touched the leather and Mahrous pressed harder so his mouth opened forcing the leather against his tongue. He heard the Chief say with a laugh: "He licked my foot well enough, Guirguis. Pay him."

Mahrous lifted Saleh and pushed him to Younes, who took his thumb. Saleh opened his mouth to say that he could write his own name, but he could not utter a sound. Younes pressed his thumb to the register, squeezing hard, as usual.

"Thank you, Younes Effendi," said Saleh.

Younes looked at him with surprise. He did not know whether Saleh was being grateful or sarcastic. Guirguis counted out forty piastres.

"Eight piastres a day times five days."

"Thank you."

When he left, Saleh overheard the Chief saying to the chief of the guards, beside him, "A poor boy, not good for hoeing the cotton fields, or anything else for that matter; one must sacrifice a little so that he can earn his bread."

Saleh tottered down the stairs.

"Did they hit you?" asked the Trunk.

"No. But I don't feel well."

The Trunk saw that he was trembling. He supported him all the way back to his hut, where Saleh's mother made him lie down.

"What is the matter with him?" the Trunk asked her.

"I don't really know, my son. It's some kind of fever. It comes every night from midnight on. He's had it since his father died."

The Trunk remembered how Saleh had stayed late in the evening in the cemetery where his father had been buried and had come back looking as if someone had terrified him.

"Maybe the spirits of that place took hold of his mind."

Umm Saleh prayed; her son moaned. Saleh stopped shivering and began sweating. He opened his eyes. The Trunk helped him get up to drink, and stayed by his side until he slept. Then he said good night to Umm Saleh. As he turned to leave, he was met at the door by Abou Bakr and Ali who had brought the promised second pound from Sayed.

"Trunk, what are you doing here?"

"Saleh's sick."

"Are you leaving?"

"I'm going to Atiya's house. I want to know what came over him earlier."

They all went to Atiya's house where Atiya received them with an embarrassed expression and muttered some unintelligible words.

"Please forgive this madman," said Atiya's wife, Um Saad. "He tried to kill the blind woman's son for eight piastres."

"Shut up," said Atiya finally, "and bring the tea."

She went to prepare the tea, murmuring, "Madman. It's a shame before God."

When the young men stepped out of Atiya's house they were met by the brightness of the moon in its full bloom and by the sound of music and gay clamor. They immediately started to run happily to the vast open space behind the village, where the young men enjoyed themselves every Thursday night. The few coins tinkling merrily in their pockets warmed their hearts. The flute, the tambourine, the carefree laughter made them forget all their suffering.

C H A P T E R

4

S | aleh woke up when the sun touched his face. There was a bitter taste in his mouth. He tried to rise, but his body would not obey; he closed his eyes again. When the sun entered, the big fat flies buzzed around his face. He was unable to shoo them away, so they stayed at the corners of his eyes.

That was how the Trunk found him. He had planned to go shopping with him at the Friday market. It was the recreation of all the villagers. Saleh heard the Trunk's pleasant gay greeting to his mother. It went to his heart and he felt comforted. Again he tried to rise but the iron belt around his head tightened.

He cried out in pain. The sound rose but died on his lips. No one heard it. The Trunk turned to Saleh's mother.

"Umm Saleh, he looks very ill . . ."

"Perhaps he is just sleepy." She answered hopefully, but not convinced herself.

"No, his eyes are open . . . but he can't speak."

Umm Saleh was painfully affected and knelt near him.

"Saleh . . . Saleh . . ." she whispered.

He spoke in a whisper as if with his last breath.

"Leave me alone, Mother . . ."

His mother screamed. The village women heard her and rushed to her, filling the hut. They made a real fuss around Saleh. They decided that only Sheikh Ramadan the wizard could deal with the situation. He had power over the spirits.

A delegation of babbling women shot out and raced down the road to the market to find the man there, and ask for his help.

Sadly the Trunk went out, with little hope. He was met by Abou Bakr and Ali, who were coming running from the end of the street. They had come to pay Sayed's promised second pound which they had forgotten to leave the night before. They hurried when they heard the fuss and saw the gathering of so many women in front of his hut.

"Saleh is very sick, he is dying."

They were both shocked with real grief at what the Trunk told them.

They went inside. Saleh was lying on his mat on the ground. His face was white, but with wide open bloodshot eyes. The Trunk knelt beside him and called his friend's name. He was so taken by emotion that he whispered.

"Saleh . . . Saleh . . ."

He received no answer, but he could see Saleh's face lighten with a kind of smile. That was too much for the Trunk; he started to weep. Abou Bakr shouted at him.

"Get up, Trunk . . . be a man . . . he isn't dead yet. We'll carry him to the doctor."

The Trunk raised his square face. It usually looked so frightful, like the face of a savage animal, but now its expression had melted to that of a tamed one. He gave Abou Bakr a glance full of immense hope and also gratefulness. Then quickly he went out to fetch a donkey.

A few minutes later he was galloping back on the donkey.

They faced a big problem when they tried to raise Saleh from the ground: the women in the hut objected in a fierce clamor, saying that only Sheikh Ramadan the wizard could cure him.

The Trunk and Ali shrank back as the women shouted in their faces with shrill voices. Only Abou Bakr stood firm, not impressed. Suddenly, he shouted back in such a menacing, angry voice, that they became quiet immediately, afraid. Within minutes the Trunk, Abou Bakr, and Ali lifted Saleh onto the back of the donkey and left.

They reached the railroad tracks and proceeded toward the hospital. They knocked and called at the barred gate, but no one answered.

"Today is Friday. They close on Fridays," said Abou Bakr.

"But there must be a doctor inside," said Ali.

"Ho . . . Ho o o o . . ." called the Trunk at the top of his voice. His call resembled the roar of a hungry lion in the desert.

There was no answer. The Trunk climbed over the gate and jumped down inside the hospital grounds. He had taken only two steps when two men in white appeared and ran toward him at tremendous speed. They looked more like prison guards than hospital aides, with their coarse features and huge bodies. They began grappling with the Trunk, punching him hard on his face.

"Stop, stop!" shouted Abou Bakr from outside. "Open the gate."

He showed them some money. They left the Trunk, who came back, climbing the gate quickly. Their coarse features had softened a little. One of them grinned a wide smile, showing a golden tooth, and with two fingers he delicately picked the money through the bars of the gate.

"What can we do for you?"

"Our friend is in a critical condition. We need to see a doctor or he'll die."

Both men went inside the hospital building and came back with a bottle.

"The doctor sees no one on Fridays. Take this bottle. It will help your friend until tomorrow."

"But he is getting worse by the minute," said Ali.

They simply turned their backs and vanished, closing the door of the hospital. On the way back, the Trunk and the others met Uncle Atiya coming from the market. They showed him the bottle of medicine they had been given and he tasted it.

"This is no good," he said. "It's for the stomach. I was given the same medicine once. I still have some at home."

Abou Bakr looked at it a moment with blurred eyes, disbelieving, then he walked back in long swift strides, his face violent. He threw the bottle with all his might. It exploded like a bomb against the hospital wall.

They returned to the village, walking back on the main road, and entered the cool shadows of the mansion's dense trees. Saleh started to shiver and moan. His friends looked with awe at the high walls visible above the trees. Even the donkey was frightened and started to trot. They all began to run, holding Saleh from all sides, preventing him from falling. When they left the high walls of the mansion and entered full sunlight again, they slowed their pace.

Passing by the estate offices they shouted, in one loud cry, the usual solemn greeting to the Chief, who was sitting in his bamboo armchair on the shaded terrace.

"Peace be with you your Lordship!!! Peace, the grace of God and His blessings be with you, your Lordship!!!"

And as usual his Lordship, Chief Abdul Meguid, did not answer them, but he stated loudly to Mahrous at his side, who was inquiring about Saleh's condition, "Bad seed."

The Trunk heard him, his jaw muscles contracting in helpless rage. Abou Bakr too felt like choking him, but instead he wiped his sweat and continued running, supporting Saleh.

Ali started to cry.

When they returned to the hut, Saleh's mother took her son in her arms. She felt the waves of shivering, one after the other, like rustling leaves under the morning breeze. They laid him on the straw mat on the ground. His friends sat in silence, frowning, at a loss as to what to do. The Trunk with the hem of his gown removed the sweat from Saleh's face.

A gay uproar approached the hut, and the group of women, ambassadors of the wizard, entered triumphantly, congratulating themselves and Umm Saleh.

He had agreed to come that evening, for one pound to be paid in advance and twenty piastres every week, for three months after Saleh resumed work. Then they all stopped quacking and chirping and looked meaningly at the three young men who would have to pay.

Night came and the hut was filled with women waiting for Sheikh Ramadan, the wizard. They squatted in the shaded empty space that served as a stable for most peasant families, and as a second sleeping room in large families. The three young men stood up and answered Sheikh Ramadan's greetings with great deference when he entered the hut. He was a short man, but looked taller because his body was thin. He was wearing a shiny white cotton robe and an opulent black oriental cloak. He had a small pointed face with a sharp nose and shrewd small piercing black eyes that made him look like a weasel, but a very intelligent and cunning weasel.

Sheikh Ramadan majestically walked in, accompanied by his two aides; sent a swift glance at Saleh; then seated himself cross-legged in silence. Umm Saleh brought tea which he sipped noisily while playing with his prayer beads. At a sign from the women, Abou Bakr gave him the pound. He refused with a gesture of the hand and asked for more, pretending that the condition of Saleh had been badly described to him. The spirits here were very strong, requiring more effort to exorcise them, and so more money should be paid. In truth, he had realized at a glance that Saleh's disease was a serious one and that the boy was dying, so that the best the Sheikh could do would be to take as much money as possible on this first visit, then disappear. The angry grunts from the Trunk, half astonished, half menacing, made him change his mind, and he accepted the pound. Then he raised his opened palms in a begging prayer. The Fatiha. All those in the room murmured it with him. Strange words followed that only the spirit of the other world could understand. Everyone in the room was attentive, and somewhat frightened.

One of his aides took out a tambourine and placed it in a firm grip between his bare feet. Suddenly the Sheikh cried, "Allah is great!!!" and the aide beat the tambourine so loudly that it frightened everyone.

That was followed by a strange enchanting melody, played by the Sheikh on a bamboo flute; the aides gave it rhythm with their tambourines.

The audience was spellbound as Saleh's cheeks began to take a rosy color, his lips parted into a smile, then he began to move. Everyone caught their breaths and opened their mouths, their eyes wide in disbelief.

At that particular moment Saleh was dreaming. In his half conscious mind, he had heard the women enter the hut, and that special fragrance filled his mind with its fascinating charm: Yasmeen. He understood that she was in the room, probably looking at him now, with the rest of them, watching him boldly, a strange gleam lighting the depths of her blue-green eyes. Then he started to dream. He saw himself lying on his father's grave, but it was night, the full moon pouring its light on the white tombs in that desolate place. He felt frightened and a tightness in his chest kept holding him.

Then in the dark two blue-green eyes sparkled. When they came nearer, he saw that they were those of a black dog with a lolling red tongue. He was panting, crouching on the ground on his hind legs, then advancing a few steps toward him, wagging his tail. Then it became two black dogs, advancing from time to time with their blue-green eyes shining; then three more came. Though they looked friendly, he was terrified. The eyes now surrounded him from every side. Then suddenly the crash of the tambourine sounded, making them disappear. He saw them again, far off, as if dancing around a fire, and a slow melody reached him from an enchanting flute.

The dogs danced to the rhythm of the tambourine, their eyes gleamed with their peculiar blue-green shine. Their tails wagged in friendliness. Then he saw himself completely naked dancing with them around the fire, his naked body glowing from its red warmth.

In the room Abou Bakr, the Trunk, Ali, all the women and men present, saw Saleh rise up until he was sitting and with his neck, shoulders, and extended arms, begin to move to the rhythm of the melody.

Abruptly the melody stopped, and with a sudden high-pitched

bang of the tambourine, the Sheikh cried again loudly, "Allah is great!!!"

Saleh opened his eyes, looked around him, and collapsed again in an unconscious state. His friends went to him. Umm Saleh burst into tears and tried to revive him, when she realized he moved no more. All the women began to talk in a frightened way and disappeared. In the confusion, Sheikh Ramadan quietly slipped away with his aides.

Abou Bakr's grave voice comforted, "He is not dead, tomorrow we will take him to the doctor. Ali, go now, and come back in the morning with a donkey."

Ali looked down at Saleh's pale face and left, after the customary farewells. Abou Bakr lit the lamp, closed the door, and realized that the Trunk had gone out without saying good night. Saleh's mother seemed to be preparing herself for death. Abou Bakr lay near Saleh and dozed off.

Ali reached the hut at the first sign of dawn. The dew had dampened his clothes and mud was showing between his bare toes. His face was red, and he breathed as heavily as the donkey he was leading. When he entered the hut, it pleased him to see that Abou Bakr was helping Saleh eat a piece of bread dipped in tea. Then Abou Bakr washed Saleh, dressed him, and left him on his mat while he and Ali went to pray. When they returned, they put Saleh on the donkey's back with Abou Bakr sitting behind him, holding him tight. Then Ali took his hoe and left for work.

The dew continued falling on their faces as the donkey trudged ahead. In front of the estate offices, the laborers, who were gathered as usual, eyed them with apprehension. Sickness in the village is a frightening thing. Far worse than death. It's like famine. They passed the walls of the mansion feeling the humid breath of the dense trees.

Abou Bakr felt Saleh tremble. He held on to him more tightly.

"Don't be afraid, Saleh," he said; his voice echoed strangely.

He wondered at the sudden tightness that gripped his chest and asked himself: "Why do these stones and these trees, feel as if they have an evil power, inherent in them, that threatens and frightens?"

They left the mansion's high wall behind and light and warmth filled the air again.

"My God! How beautiful are those colored windmills!" Saleh exclaimed happily, excited. Abou Bakr frowned; he knew that his friend was hallucinating.

The hospital gate was open when they reached it. Abou Bakr dismounted and carried Saleh into the hospital. He saw without surprise that there were many people already waiting.

He took his place in the queue of miserable patients, and saw some of the same people he had seen years ago. One was an old man with an overswollen leg. Apparently he still came to the clinic, not knowing where else to go. He saw the same pale, ugly, sick faces, the same swollen eyes. The flies were everywhere, and they increased in number as the day went by.

He was surprised to see the Trunk suddenly appear before him like a smiling bear. He had a black eye and a bruise on his cheek.

"What happened to you, Trunk?"

"My father hit me when I decided not to go to work today."

"On the face?"

"It was my fault. I didn't duck fast enough."

"You must send someone to talk to him, someone to tell him to respect you and treat you in a better way."

"Forget it. Leave the old man alone. Who else would bear him but me?"

Abou Bakr patted the Trunk on the shoulder as if to show he understood the situation. The man behind Abou Bakr, noticing that their attention was temporarily diverted, tried to step in front of Abou Bakr.

When Abou Bakr objected, he frowned with a nasty grin; he was ready to fight, but the grin faded into a sweet smile when the large hardness of the Trunk's body faced him. "I am sorry, gentlemen," apologized the man.

The Trunk did not even answer him but looked at him scornfully. The other turned his head, interested suddenly in a view far away.

"Did you take a ticket?" the Trunk asked Abou Bakr.

"No."

The Trunk went toward the ticket window and elbowed his way to the employee in charge. He paid no attention to the protests of the people around him and came back within minutes with the required ticket.

The doors finally opened, and the people in the queue began to go in one by one. No patient remained inside more than a minute.

When Saleh's turn came, the doctor sent him a hard evaluating glance that went from the emaciated face to the feverish, bloodshot eyes and the wasted trembling body.

It had been some time since the doctor had first come to this country hospital, carrying a small cardboard suitcase and with much hope in his heart. He had surveyed, in one powerful glance, the hospital, the fields, the villages, still hearing in his mind the laughter of his colleagues on the day he had departed. How he had said: "I shall milk this country dry, and you will see me in a year or two very wealthy and living like a king here in town." The happiness and expectations he had known that day made him take a deep breath, filling his lungs like a hungry lion on the move, falling suddenly upon a land full of game. But he made a slight mistake in that first diagnosis, at the beginning of his clinical practice, and so after years and years he remained behind the small desk, in the hospital clinic, as he had done the first day he had arrived, his shirt open because of the heat and sweat, chasing away heavy flies that collected on his large plump face. He gained weight, and the extra pounds made his features look heavier than they really were. His lower lip took on a droop because of his immense, always unsatisfied, lust.

A month after his arrival he decided to open a small private clinic of his own, in one of the huts close to the hospital. Some time later, an Inspector from the Ministry visited him, and after close scrutiny of the procedures in use, discovered serious illegalities and mistakes and warned the doctor about them. He even suggested that the result of his inquest might be referred to the police. The nurses and aides, having much experience in the matter, intervened on the doctor's behalf, and among them they managed to bribe the inspector in order to get rid of him. The Chief Inspector of the Ministry arrived a short while later for the same reason, and the doctor realized that he was not the first to have had the idea of milking this country. He reached an amicable agreement with the Chief Inspector for a sum to be paid monthly. After this, the Inspectors who came to see him merely paid courtesy calls. The doctor found out quickly that the wealthy did not pay their bills, and neither did the police officers or their aides. As for the estate staff, it did not even occur to the doctor to request payment from them. On the contrary, he decided, in view of their far-reaching influence, that to serve them without charge was in fact to his advantage. Consequently, he had only the peasants to lean on, and he squeezed piastre after piastre from them. With time, he became one of the country doctors most expert at transferring to his own pocket the little money that lay hidden in the pockets of the rags which covered the naked bodies of the peasants.

The doctor examined Saleh and realized from his clothes that he was poor. He had already noted Saleh's bare-footed friends.

"What's the matter with him?" asked the doctor.

"He is feverish, and then he shivers for no apparent reason," answered Abou Bakr.

The doctor wrote down the name of a medicine and called, "Next."

As they emerged with Saleh, Abou Bakr looked at the prescription and read "Rawend."

He could hardly believe it.

"What did he write, Abou Bakr?" asked the Trunk.

"Wait here," answered Abou Bakr.

He went toward the window where medicines were sold, presented the prescription, and nearly went mad with rage when he received the same bottle as on the previous day.

"Rawend? Rawend? Rawend!?! The boy has a fever! Don't you understand?" he shouted.

The male nurse shrugged his shoulders.

A husky voice, trying to be smooth, whispered by his side. "Don't tire yourself. There is no other medicine in the hospital. Go to the doctor's own clinic in an hour and let him examine Saleh privately."

Abou Bakr turned around and saw the same huge male nurse that he met the day before, the one with the golden tooth, who took his money.

"How much will it cost?" asked Abou Bakr.

"Twenty piastres."

"We have only seventeen piastres."

"That's all right. The doctor will take that."

When the Trunk saw the bottle, his eyes bulged.

"My God, yesterday's bottle!"

The Trunk suddenly lost his temper. He clenched his fists and moved toward the aide.

"Wait, Trunk," said Abou Bakr, "fighting won't help."

But like a railroad train the Trunk was hard to stop once he was in motion. Abou Bakr seized his sleeve.

"Trunk," he said, "I'm asking you to wait. We'll go to the doctor's private clinic and request a special consultation."

That did it. The Trunk stopped in his tracks.

"Is that a promise?" he asked.

Abou Bakr nodded. So the Trunk lifted Saleh effortlessly and carried him to the doctor's clinic behind the station shops. Abou Bakr followed with the donkey. Once again they stood in the queue, part of which had been waiting earlier at the hospital. The heat and the flies had increased considerably.

The murmur of the people who were still at the hospital turned into shouts and screams. Abou Bakr and the Trunk saw the white uniformed aides hitting and kicking a patient and dragging him through the gate where he fell and rolled in the dust.

"That would have been your fate if we'd let you start a fight," Abou Bakr said laughing.

The Trunk spat.

One hour later, the doctor appeared on the threshold of the hospital building, and moved slowly toward his private clinic. He walked with exaggerated dignity. He walked like Hassan Effendi, more pompous but with the same coiled springs under his heavy buttocks, although in a softer, slower motion. The queue came to life. The doctor went in after answering the greetings of the patients with a sweeping gesture of the hand. His male nurse, the one with the golden tooth, followed him, carrying his bag.

When at last it was Saleh's turn to see the doctor, Abou Bakr gave the male nurse the seventeen piastres he had.

"I shall pay the difference myself for the time being," said the nurse. "You can pay me back next time."

Abou Bakr nodded. He laid Saleh on a bed behind a screen which had been white once upon a time. The doctor asked many questions. The Trunk answered most of them. The doctor's face became very serious when he discovered Saleh's financial state of affairs: an orphan with a blind mother, a worker in the cotton fields. He examined Saleh thoroughly, although in reality he had lost interest in him. He sat behind his desk, unbuttoned his shirt, wiped his face with a dirty grey handkerchief, and said gloomily:

"His condition is very serious."

"What's the matter with him?" asked the Trunk.

"Malaria, difficult to cure."

"Please cure him, Doctor," begged the Trunk.

"He will die if he does not get the proper treatment right away," stated the doctor.

"If he does get it will he live?" asked Abou Bakr.

"Yes, but it is very expensive."

"We are all poor, Doctor."

The doctor nodded his head as if to say that was their problem, not his.

"How much will it cost?" asked Abou Bakr.

"Fifteen pounds."

They were stunned. They looked at the Doctor and then at one another, aghast.

"Next," said the doctor.

But the male nurse intervened.

"No, Doctor. They are poor people. This boy is a relation of mine."

The nurse and the doctor argued for a few minutes. Finally the nurse smiled triumphantly at Abou Bakr.

"God is with us! The doctor will accept only eight pounds."

"I'll absorb the cost of the medicine myself," said the doctor sadly.

Abou Bakr and the Trunk found themselves outside the clinic. They put Saleh on the donkey's back, and took him home.

Their faces were grim, their minds blank. Everything was over; their friend had been condemned to die; there was no escape. It did not occur to them even to consider the possibility of finding the required funds. Saleh's father had died for lack of treatment, and so would Saleh. They must accept his fate.

CHAPTER

5

A bou Bakr and the Trunk took Saleh back to his hut, where his mother was waiting. They left, not answering her questions. Night fell on the little village, and inside the hut Saleh felt it. He opened his eyes and realized that his mother had not lit the lamp, as she did usually. She had stopped her crying and quietly waited, seated on the ground, leaning her back against the wall. Why light the lamp? For whom? She believed that Saleh would not live through the night, so she was waiting, her blind eyes turned towards the door, as if death would come furtively slipping through that way. She wanted to be near him when his time came.

Saleh himself knew that the end might be near. He remembered a poem he had learned in the mosque:

> They entrusted me with a responsibility I could not hold.
> Although I held it, I remained astray,
> The men came and taught me how to carry it.
> I was given a responsibility which others could not hold.
> I talked to the moon in the presence of God, and the Muse
> came to me,
> And I suddenly saw my soul in the land of God.

Saleh asked himself whether it was possible to die without agony as in the poem. Or would he shiver and kick in convulsions like his father? Finally, as Saleh prepared to accept death with resignation, he heard a knock at the door. His mother did not rise to open it, she did not ask who was knocking, but Saleh heard the door squeak open and he felt a sudden draft of cooler air.

"What's the matter, Umm Saleh? Why do you leave Saleh in the dark?"

Saleh's heart began pounding madly in his chest: Yasmeen's merry voice filled the room, her special fragrance reached him. In spite of his fever, in spite of his pain, he lifted his head, and saw Yasmeen's green eyes shining in the dark.

Saleh's mother got up and lit the lamp.

"Welcome, Yasmeen, welcome," she murmured sadly.

"My God, what's happening? He can't just lie there. You can't just leave him like that without treatment. Where's the tea? We can't just leave him to die."

"What can I do? Sheikh Ramadan came and . . ."

"Sheikh Ramadan is a quack. What did the doctor say?"

"He asked for eight pounds."

"I know. What happened next?"

"Nothing."

"Does that mean the matter is at an end? Listen, we must outwit these thieves at the hospital."

"How can I do that? I am an old woman. All I have is a pair of blind eyes and my old body."

She burst into tears. She felt overwhelmed and somewhat invaded; she didn't know how Yasmeen could be so well informed about what had happened at the clinic. There had once been rumors of a relationship between Yasmeen and the male nurse, the one with the golden tooth, but those rumors had never reached the ears of Umm Saleh.

Yasmeen said to her gently: "Everything can be solved. Saleh is young and strong. Go to Mahrous, the Head Foreman; he will know that I sent you. Take three pounds from him to give the doctor as an advance. I will get Umm Saad to accompany you there before I leave. The doctor will come and save him, I promise you."

Saleh heard Yasmeen leave; he became angry and cursed her. She had made him even more feverish and now he was no longer resigned to death. He wanted to live.

Mahrous's wife, Khadra, received Saleh's mother and Umm Saad courteously and kindly served them tea.

"I was so sorry to hear of your son's sickness," said Khadra; "We're all proud of how he worked in the fields."

Saleh's mother nodded but said nothing. She was embarrassed to ask for money.

"Tell me, is there anything I can do to help?" asked Khadra.

"We came to ask Uncle Mahrous for an advance to give to the doctor. Saleh will repay it when he goes back to work," said Umm Saad.

Khadra nodded and took Umm Saleh by the hand, and they entered the corridor that led to Mahrous's room. She saw him at the far end, trying hurriedly to escape from the house. He must have heard of the visit of Umm Saleh; he knew that she came to borrow money.

"Mahrous!!" called Khadra angrily.

He immediately stopped and came back, embarrassed but smiling. If there was anything this powerful, harsh, hugely built man, so ruthless with the workers, was afraid of, it was to have to face the anger of the head of this house, Khadra, his third wife, with her strong personality and the power of her many sons behind her.

"Welcome, welcome," he said to the visiting women. "How is Saleh?"

Saleh's mother took his hand and tried to kiss it, but he withdrew it in time.

"Umm Saleh wants a loan from you to pay the doctor to treat her son," said Khadra.

Mahrous did not like to lend money. He regarded the request as an insult to his honor, but he put his hand in his pocket and took out a pound and, hesitatingly, another.

"Here are two pounds," he said.

"Yasmeen said three pounds," Saleh's mother said innocently.

Mahrous began to sweat at the mention of Yasmeen's name. He looked sideways at his wife, like a dog that has pissed on the rug.

"What business of Yasmeen's is this?" he blustered. "Here are three pounds anyway," he said, and vanished.

"You dirty man," Khadra remarked.

"Did I do anything wrong, Khadra?" Saleh's mother asked.

"No," said Khadra. "Take the money. I hope it's of use to you."

"Was it necessary to mention Yasmeen?" asked Umm Saad, when they left Mahrous's house.

"Why, what's wrong with that?"

"Nothing, I suppose."

Amid a boisterous clamor of dogs' fierce barking, the old Ford arrived at the entrance of the village and stopped in a clatter of all its loose parts. All the doors of the huts opened, stunned faces appeared from everywhere. The secret telegraph of the village spread the astonishing news: "The doctor in person came to the village to treat Saleh."

The heavy hand of the male nurse, the one with the golden

tooth, started smacking the children that tried to climb over his car. By striking right and left he opened a path for the doctor. Yasmeen led the way to Saleh's house.

The noise and light that flooded the hut were like explosions in Saleh's ears and brain. A thick strong hand took off his clothes, examined him, palpated his naked body, tried to open his mouth and force things in between his clenched teeth. It turned him ruthlessly on his face and it pushed something in from behind. Hot tears of shame came to his eyes, as he imagined her now, looking at him mockingly with her blue-green eyes. Worst of all was the soft haggling he could hear in the empty space next door to his hut. It sounded more like an exchange of sweet loving words than a bargain about money. Yasmeen and the male nurse were arguing about the doctor's fees.

"Four." "No, two." "No, four." "No, two." The argument ended on "Three," with laughter, a quick kiss, some talk of meeting later, and more laughter, then light, escaping steps in feigned coyness. Finally she remembered Umm Saleh.

"Give us the money," Yasmeen directed, and Khalil, the male nurse, handed the three pounds over to the doctor. The doctor and his retinue left, and the hut became quiet.

"The dogs!" That was Yasmeen's voice.

Saleh's mother found her way to her, caressed her cheek and kissed her hand. Yasmeen tried to pull her hand away, but Umm Saleh would not let go and held it to her face.

"Don't kiss my hand. I am a whore." And Yasmeen went out, laughing, leaving Umm Saleh astonished behind her.

Yasmeen actually had two personalities that determined her actions.

A long time ago, when she was a child of ten, she had been left alone to care for her prematurely aged mother. A cholera epidemic had almost wiped out her whole family.

She helped pick the cotton and weeds in the fields and with her little earnings she barely supported herself and her mother. Always on the verge of hunger and death, she clung to life. With the passage of time, she changed into a strange maiden with a very thin, elastic body and broad shoulders, all bones, nerves, and long steel-hard muscles. Her sunburnt face was dominated by a pair of two wide blue-green eyes that glittered like the eyes of a hungry cat. From the time when she was still a young girl, she had to face the attacks of the village young men, since she had no father or brother to defend her. Many times the youths fell on her, struggling with her in silent rape, between the corn stalks or behind the bamboo spikes at the canal bank; panting, mad with desire, thrilled by the fires of her strange eyes, their loins blazing under the scorching sun. She resisted fiercely at times, but gave way completely at other times, even though she was not at the age of puberty. However, no one asked to marry her, because of her strange looks and her poverty.

She was very grateful when the old laborer "the Catfish" asked to marry her; he wanted her to take care of him and his three children after his first wife died. She accepted and she gave birth to children who looked like their father, with that peculiar ugliness that characterized the features of the famous fish. Then she had other children with delicate, fine, fair skin and handsome regular features. With the appearance of this new progeny, her shoulders and breasts became rounder and her body bloomed into soft, elastic contours. Lust and fulfilled desire illuminated her complexion, making it fair and transparent. She was so beautiful that men, looking at her, caught their breath in astonishment, while a thrill of desire descended quickly down their spines. Richness, too, came with the blossoming of her beauty, but the Catfish still went in rags. That was his way of protesting his disapproval.

Then Yasmeen gave birth to a blond child with golden hair and blue eyes who resembled Yani, the Greek grocer who owned the big grocery store at the train station where liquor was served in the backroom cafe.

Gossips in the village babbled a lot. However, this new affair gave Yasmeen a new status of power and respect. Many courted her; she refused no one; all received their share; yet their longing for her took fire again the moment it was satisfied. Khalil, the huge male nurse with the gold tooth, became her client. Lately, her position had advanced a step further: the latest gossips reported that Mahrous had fallen under the spell of her lovely eyes. Thus, she became part of the administration.

The male nurse Khalil came daily to care for Saleh and give him his medication, and so did Yasmeen. She began enjoying her visits to the hut to help Saleh's mother with her household tasks, fill the water urn for her, and prepare some simple meal. She also enjoyed seeing Saleh come back to life. Happily she watched his bloodshot eyes regain their shining transparency and saw the color return to his cheeks. Saleh became accustomed to Yasmeen's presence, her fragrance, her smile, her glittering glances with their blue-green shine, and the whispering with Khalil, the male nurse, in the back room. He enjoyed watching the movement of her lithe body as she knelt to prepare tea, as she sat, as she stood, as she walked. Every time she looked at him, he felt his pulse quicken.

When news of Saleh's improved condition spread, the women began visiting his mother during the day and the men came to visit him in the evenings. Abou Bakr and Ali came frequently. Even Uncle Atiya paid a call on him. As for the Trunk, he came after each day's work in the cotton fields, trying to measure the degree of improvement in his friend's condition on a daily basis. After dinner, he came back and sat silently beside him like a guardian.

Five days later, Saleh was able to go to the canal and wash himself. The brightness of the light in the canal and the reflected motion of the trees gave him vertigo. He smiled at the world, nevertheless: at the sky, at the dogs, at the ducks. He wanted to think of God with his previous piety, but he could not, and wondered why. He found that he simply did not feel like thanking God sincerely. Was this because of his desire for Yasmeen? Nevertheless, his nightmares had turned to pleasant dreams these past few days. In so many of these dreams he saw himself running towards his father's grave, sitting on it, watching black dogs dance in front of a fire; and when he approached them, the dogs would wag their tails, mouths open, red tongues lolling, green eyes shining, and he would dance with them around the fire. He was completely naked and he felt the warmth of the fire on his body. Basically a simple boy, Saleh asked himself whether this dream had been sent by a devil and if the devil had also sent Yasmeen to corrupt him.

When he returned to the hut, he was aloof toward her, even rude. She inquired, sincerely worried, "How are you?"

He passed by her silently, going to the corner of the room.

"By the grace of God, why don't you answer?"

With a harsh irritated gesture he turned. "How can you possibly utter the name of God, on your lips."

She reddened as if he had slapped her hard. "Thank you!! I helped a scorpion without knowing!"

His mother shouted at him, really angry.

"Saleh!!"

He muttered an apology in a trembling voice, tears jumping to his eyes.

"Mother, I could not pray this morning!"

Yasmeen's hearty mocking laugh echoed loudly in the room.

"And I am the cause? You small devil! You're right, I am a bitch!" Laughing again, she went out, banging the door.

She came again the next day. Actually Yasmeen had developed a sincere affection for Saleh's mother and discovered in the help she was giving her a pleasure which she herself did not understand. It was almost as if she were serving her own mother. Also she enjoyed watching Saleh's radiant, comely face coming back to life with the innocence of youth still in it. One glance from her would make it redden deeply.

This morning the secret telegraph of the village spread the news that an important official from the Palace was coming to visit the estate. The word spread through the fields like wildfire. It made the laborers work harder and the foremen utter harsher insults. The Chief left his bamboo chair and hurried to the mansion to extend his greetings. Guirguis Effendi did likewise, as did Hassan Effendi and Younes Effendi. A large black car was seen on the main road of the estate. The peddlers and beggars fled the domain, while guards appeared from everywhere to insure maximum orderliness with no loafing workers around.

Saleh's mother heard the rumor and decided on a plan. While Saleh was at the mosque, she put her black veil on her face and went out alone, feeling her way by touching the walls of huts along her path. The dogs watched her but none barked.

When Saleh came back he was surprised not to find his mother at home. He thought that possibly she had gone to see Umm Saad. He prepared himself some tea. Time passed. Toward noon, he became worried. She was late. Where was she? He prepared to go out and look for her. Suddenly there was an uproar in the street outside, and the door of his hut burst open. His mother was sent sprawling into the farthest corner of the hut by Gaith and two of his colleagues.

"You, Saleh," shouted Gaith, "keep your mother away from the Palace or else."

As soon as Gaith and his aides and the crowd of watching children had gone, Saleh attended to his mother, who had been badly beaten.

"Mother, what happened?"

"It was my fault. Please forgive me."

She told him how she had made her way to the Palace that morning and waited at the gates.

When they opened, she appeared in front of the car. It hit her as it was coming out of the gate. She raised her head from the ground and got up, her forehead bloody from a cut. The guards surrounded her. . . .

"How could she come so near the Palace gates!!!" roared Chief Abdul Meguid to them.

A strange smooth voice with a foreign accent said:

"What's the matter? Is she blind? Did she get hurt?"

"No, I am all right, your lordship, it was my fault. I threw myself on the car. I came to plead for my son, his father worked during his whole life for the estate. I am blind and useless. . . . My son is the light of my eyes. Please give orders so that he may be given some work. He can read and write. He can be useful as a clerk or a storekeeper."

The young man's face reddened. He turned toward Chief Abdul Meguid and asked:

"How is it that this poor woman's son is left jobless? Work is both a duty and a right."

"I . . . well . . . she . . . he . . ." stammered the Chief Abdul Meguid, his face pale and sweaty.

The thing that frightened him the most, this tyrant full of arrogance, was to have to account for something in front of anyone from the Palace. His behavior toward the Palace people was always obsequious. Now he could not lift his head.

Hassan Effendi saved him, jumping from one foot to the other as usual, his ever-moving features quickly showing their largest smile.

"Don't listen to this senile peasant," he said. "The estate administration opened their doors to her son when he asked for work. We need men in the plantation fields. But he worked two days and ran away. He is spoiled, he does not want to work. Does she want us to put him in an office when the cotton needs every strong able hand? The boy is lazy. If we favor him, it will have an adverse influence on the rest of the men."

The young man regarded Saleh's mother sternly. The magic words, "the cotton needs every strong able hand," had affected him. It was proper that these people had a sense of responsibility toward the cotton, that they didn't let themselves be swayed by emotions. Without further ado he climbed back in the car with the driver, the Chief, and Hassan Effendi, and they drove off. After they left, Gaith shook Umm Saleh.

"You miserable old bitch. Do you want to put me out of a job?"

He hit her again and again until two guards intervened.

"Leave her alone, Gaith. You should not hit an old, blind woman."

The three of them dragged Saleh's mother back to her hut.

After she had told Saleh her story, she wept bitterly. Saleh comforted her, kneeling by her, drying away her tears with his clothes. He was racked with anger and despair.

"I deserved it," said Saleh's mother. "I should never have tried to go to the Palace."

There was a loud knocking at the door and the voices of the village women asking to be admitted.

"Don't open, my son. I don't want them to see my bruised face."

Their continued knocking angered Saleh and he shouted, venting his wrath at them. The women finally left, and Saleh attended to his mother.

C H A P T E R

6

O n the following day Saleh stood in front of the estate offices with his hoe on his shoulder. A thick white mist like cotton permeated the air. Nothing could be seen through it except the tops of the trees and the edge of the mansion walls. The moisture in the air, the dew, and the damp earth under his naked feet sent a shiver down his spine. He rested his back against the wall and placed the hoe beside him. He shifted his weight from one foot to the other, rubbed his hands, and looked at the horizon. Then he lowered his gaze to the mansion, which seemed to be lying in wait for him. He looked away and wished the other men would come soon.

After a while some laborers emerged from the dense fog, greeting Saleh, and waited beside him in silence. Then, one by one, others came. Most of them seemed to remember Saleh; they came close to him and looked at him keenly. They found him feeble and emaciated, with a pale face which moved them deeply. Hassan Effendi appeared, prancing, and assigned the jobs for the day. Saleh found himself walking with the hoe on his shoulder toward the cotton fields.

Saleh became accustomed to this new life. The hoe left its imprint on his body. His hands bled, but were healed by the Trunk's prescription of henna and gradually became hard and strong.

Now that the disease had left him, his body was not withered anymore. On the contrary, he became broader and more developed, with rounded powerful muscles that were envied by many young men in the village.

Every day that passed placed on him a new layer of hard muscles. His body responded very quickly to the stress of hard labor, though he entered his ordeal at a bad time: summer came early that year. The sun poured its scorching heat over his back and loins, the earth reflected the heat to his blazing thighs.

As Saleh's body became stronger, so did his resignation to the incessant insults. Like the rest of the men, he developed an immunity to the daily humiliations; he learned to consider his body the property of the estate and to work without letting the Head Foreman out of the corner of his eye. He, like the others, doubled his energies when the Foreman came by and relaxed them when he went away. Saleh became an example of good behavior. Neither Mahrous nor his assistants could find a reason to punish him.

When Thursday nights came, he stood before Younes Effendi at the estate offices. On one particular Thursday, he refused to put his thumb print on the register and asked, "May I sign my name, Younes Effendi?" His heart leaped with joy but his face was mask-like, serious, and cool, as he noticed the sullen aloofness with which Younes Effendi gave him the pen. Even Gaith showed a look of grudging respect and refrained from trying to slap his bare neck as usual.

"Eight piastres a day, times seven is equal to fifty-four piastres," said Guirguis Effendi as he counted out the money.

"Seven times eight is equal to fifty-six, not fifty-four," Saleh corrected.

Boisterous hearty laughter shook Chief Abdul Meguid. He said to Guirguis:

"You should have taken him with you as your clerk. Now he has caught you red-handed."

Guirguis's face darkened and he handed Saleh the two piastres.

That was how he cheated some of the laborers out of part of their earnings. Profiting by quick counting and the heavy hand of Gaith he was able to commit his petty thefts. The Chief never allowed it in his presence, possibly because Guirguis kept it all for himself.

Saleh and his friends went running to the open space behind the village where the music and dancing was going on. Saleh clapped his hands without feeling any pain in his palms, as Sayed, with a belt around his waist, danced to the music of the drums. Later, accompanied by a flute, a boy named Hameed sang one song after another.

> When the wind of youth rises, all those in love gently sway.
> Although they are the victims of love, we pray they
> remain that way.

They all forgot the memory of weeks of misery. They laughed, danced, clapped, and sang until the moon rose golden in the sky.

Friday was a day of rest. The sun was hot and Saleh's small dark hut was boiling. Saleh woke up still exhausted from the preceding evening.

The pain in his muscles had eased except for a pang at the small of his back every now and then. He looked toward the window and the brightness of the sky hurt his eyes. When he looked around, he saw his mother beside him, kneeling on the straw mat.

"Good morning," he said.

She caressed his face with her hands, kissed him, and then touched his cheek again. She got up and felt her way to the small wooden trunk; she took from it a razor which had belonged to her husband, a small piece of soap, and half of a broken mirror.

"Do you want me to shave?" he asked, taking the razor. She smiled and nodded.

"You've become a man in every way, my son. Yes, you should shave."

Saleh put the mirror on the window sill, while she brought him some water. He shaved easily. He compared both sides of his face in the mirror and examined his whole head. He smiled at himself but could not see the whole smile because of the small size of the mirror. He looked at his features one at a time. It was a pleasure. He gave each equal importance. He smiled at his muscles the way a girl would have smiled at her newly formed breasts. He was satisfied with what he saw and told himself that he was "handsome." He washed his face, then reminded his mother to make tea for breakfast. She should have prepared it by now as she always did.

He was worried about his mother. Ever since the day when she had been brought back from the mansion, she had had fits of absent-mindedness which puzzled him. Frowning, he drank the tea, ate a small piece of dry bread, then took the woven straw basket and met the Trunk for a shopping trip at the market.

"Take your father's club with you," said the Trunk. "You're a man now, and the market is not a safe place."

Saleh hesitated, then returned to the hut for his father's club.

The people swarmed in the market like bees around a hive. Near the railway, the merchants displayed an assortment of grains, dry goods, and vegetables. The clamor of arguments and bargaining filled the air. The Trunk and Saleh elbowed their way among the people in the narrow alleys. The Trunk, like the rest of the village men his age, was happily examining all the women's eyes without any shame and without any rebuke from them. As a matter of fact, some of them returned his stare with a smile. His arm touched a bosom here, a buttock there. The crowd was an excuse for anything. The Trunk let himself be stimulated by the presence of the women as well as by the colors and variety of the merchandise in the shops.

Saleh filled his basket with tomatoes, onions, lentils, and salt, all the necessary foodstuffs for a week. He lounged about with his friends for two hours, looking at all that was displayed. He stopped near the meat market but found the prices too high for his meager earnings. He could not afford even a small piece. However, he let himself bask in the enjoyment of moving among the people. One thing marred the pleasure of the day, however, and it was the sight of a soldier on a horse, moving slowly, with a Sudanese whip in his hands and meanness in his face. The soldier, like an evil, cruel statue of tyranny, reminded Saleh of suffering and oppression, the real dimensions of his world.

On the way back, on the main road of the estate, they saw a man riding a donkey. He ignored their greetings and rode on.

"That was the Catfish, Yasmeen's husband," said Saleh.

"He acted as if he wanted nothing to do with us."

They stopped briefly at the canal bank to pray with some of the village men, then shared and ate a tomato, an onion, and a piece of cheese, and drank tea.

The Trunk suggested that they go fishing, and Saleh agreed. They decided to fish at a small drain that was far from the village, between the cotton fields.

Once there, they took off their clothes, built a dam across the drain, blocking a section, and started to empty it of its water by throwing it out with their cupped hands. They looked like two shining black devils in the sun with mud on their naked bodies. The fish, feeling the danger, tried to jump over the dam. They caught them in their hands one by one and threw them on the bank.

The sun was getting low on the western horizon. Saleh, on the bank of the drain, was gathering the catch in his old straw basket. His hand reached for a big fat fish, the pride of their catch, when suddenly his hand stopped midway in the air. A bare foot had stepped near the fish, a human foot, large, ugly, with broken yellow nails and black contours of dry dirt. At its side protruded the disgusting excrescence of a sixth toe. Saleh shot a glance at the owner of this foot. Abdul Dayem, the guard, was looking at him with murderous eyes. Saleh had acquired experience by now, and his powerful lithe body responded with a swift recoil, and avoided the rapidly descending club of the guard, aimed at his spine. As quick as a wink he had gathered the large fish and crossed to the opposite bank with the basket. A flow of the vilest insults shot one after the other at him with tremendous speed from the guard's mouth. But the Trunk, an experienced diplomat, stopped it by a soothing suggestion.

"Why do you get angry? We were just going to look for you to give you a present of some of the fish before offering the rest to the Chief . . ."

The guard's ugly face became radiant and smiled. "Well, well, show me what you caught." Saleh crossed again and put the basket at his feet, keeping at a safe distance.

"I will just take this one. Keep the rest for yourselves and enjoy them. The Chief does not really need any, he receives so many presents."

They saw with broken hearts the guard hurrying away on the road with the large fat fish, the pride of their catch, dangling from two delicately closed fingers.

Late in the evening, Saleh, the Trunk, Abou Bakr, and Ali gathered in the empty small barn of his hut. The glow of the fire was reflected in their eyes while they sat around it happily laughing and waiting to eat the grilled fish.

Saleh labored in the fields, mainly hoeing cotton. He was given extra work, though he was not paid for it, like loading fertilizer sacks from the storehouses to the trailers, then going with the trucks to the fields and unloading the sacks again. He would then join his fellow workers to hoe the cotton for the rest of the day.

The men sensed that this was Hassan Effendi's cunning revenge. He would choose for Saleh the hardest of jobs, then lie in wait for him, waiting for signs of weakness or failure to carry the jobs out. Saleh silently puzzled over the reason for this hatred while he was running to the trailer, his back bent under the fiftieth heavy sack, his thighs trembling from the weight. He came to the conclusion that behind Hassan Effendi's ever-smiling face was a mean, frustrated, evil soul. He did not know that Hassan Effendi had volunteered to affirm that he was a good-for-nothing lad in front of one of the Palace men; Hassan Effendi did not want to be proved wrong, and secretly he was hoping eventually to break Saleh's spirit. On the contrary, as time passed Saleh's muscles developed smoothly. He even experienced an almost sensual pleasure when he stood in front of a heavy sack that he had to load. He felt like a boxer in the ring, meeting the challenge. As his chest broadened, every seam of his underwear split at the shoulders, under the arms. His muscles were like hard stones breaking through the fabric.

His father's clothes, that had originally been too large for him, were torn in every place.

He really had nothing to wear any more except these rags.

He became even more aware of his strength when the Trunk one day tried playfully to dump him in the canal. He could not budge him. Instead, Saleh threw the Trunk in the water; he coughed, swallowed water, and nearly sank, since he did not know how to swim.

"I have to watch out for you from now on," said a pleased Trunk, after Saleh held him tight and swam with him back to the bank.

The Trunk was not the only person to be surprised. The rest of the village was as well. As they saw the bulk of Saleh's work, they started to have some compassion for him. They had expected him to die from malaria, but this "bad seed," as the Chief had called him, had blossomed into a beautiful and powerful youth. News of Saleh's daily achievements became the village gossip, spread by the secret telegraph. "Do you know that Hassan Effendi was terribly upset when Saleh, the son of Suleiman Hawari, lifted the loads he, Hassan Effendi, gave him as if they were feathers?" The villagers were delighted, experiencing a vicarious revenge on Hassan Effendi. They identified with Saleh's youth and courage. With the change in his body came a change in his face; it became the face of a man. Sunburnt, it took the color of red brass, peculiar to the young men of the Delta; its regular features combined in harmonious, yet manly, hard-cut lines, and the coming of manhood gave his complexion a special inner glow. Now, men and women alike would spontaneously turn around to look at him astonished when he passed by them.

One morning Hassan Effendi admitted his defeat. He sent Saleh back to the cotton fields without any other additional burdens for the day. From then on, he concentrated on another plan to break him, but a more far-reaching, more cunning plan.

His mother's condition continued to mar Saleh's happiness. She had changed gradually since that day at the mansion. It was as if something had been destroyed within her. She sat for hours without speaking or eating. She seemed unaware of her surroundings. Her hearing, which had been her substiture for sight, began to fail. She no longer recognized her son's footsteps unless he came and touched her. Then she would merely look at him tenderly with blind eyes and return to her dreams.

Another person noticed this drastic change in her: Yasmeen noticed, too. At first she believed that Umm Saleh was merely becoming lazy, and admonished her about it in a kindly way on more than one occasion. But Yasmeen soon discovered that the woman was failing. She began to assist her more and more.

Saleh, for his part, began relying on Yasmeen almost completely. He went to her house to give her all his earnings on pay day and was received by her children as one of them. He often encountered the Catfish at home and greeted him uncomfortably. The Catfish never answered and invariably went to his room. At first this would make Saleh uneasy and he would be tempted to leave, but Yasmeen always intervened.

"Stay, Saleh. Leave the old man alone."

She behaved like his tutor. He could not keep any amount of money from her. He knew she was concerned with his welfare and was infinitely grateful. One day, he attempted to keep five piastres for himself. He was discovered.

"Have you learned to smoke?" she asked.

He blushed under her scrutiny. She shrugged her shoulders, but she agreed to let him have the price of a small packet of tobacco. She was right about his smoking. A few days previously, Abou Bakr had brought some tobacco and some cigarette leaves and shown him how to roll one and smoke. The Trunk joined them, and cigarette smoking became a habit during rest intervals at work.

They enjoyed inhaling the smoke. As a matter of fact, Saleh enjoyed it so much he decided to buy his own cigarettes. If Yasmeen refused to give him the money, he used lunch money for cigarettes that day. But she guessed his needs and made no great fuss. Saleh accepted her tutorship with pleasure, although he did not always understand her moods: at times she was angry with him for no reason.

"Get out, Saleh. I'm busy. I am waiting for someone."

He would leave, furious, cursing her and her lover, her "I am waiting for someone."

He wondered who "someone" was. Khalil, the male nurse?

Mahrous? He suspected that she probably said these things just to annoy him, and she certainly succeeded. Why? What business of his was it anyway?

On nights when Yasmeen had angered him he could not sleep in spite of his exhaustion after a hard day's work. He would toss and turn and groan and moan as he saw her with her lovers in his dreams.

The following day he would find her sitting with his mother, while her youngest played nearby in the dust. He would greet her coldly and go into the hut to find the food cooked and prepared on the small table. Then, of course, he would turn back to thank her and find her staring at him and laughing.

"Are you angry with me, Saleh?" she would ask.

"No, Why should I be? I am grateful to you for saving my life."

She would laugh and then leave without another word.

It never occurred to him to treat her as the male nurse did, to whisper to her, kiss her, embrace her, or be one of her lovers. He still had no word for what he felt for her. The effect she had on him was partly due to his physical development, to his new and unacknowledged need for sex. If her moodiness sometimes annoyed him, if her sensuality was too obvious, if her promiscuity was too pronounced, he felt a jealousy which he still could not identify. She excited him as she did all other men, especially those in the prime of their youth. But as his working days lengthened with the arrival of summer, the time he spent with her each day shortened. He saw her only when she brought his food and filled their urn with water or when he turned over his wages to her so that she could buy the essentials for his mother and himself.

C H A P T E R

7

S summer came to the valley, carried on by the khamasin winds, the sandstorms that blew in from the desert. They passed over the village and the fields, making the corn quiver, the stalks ripening under the hot breath. Every living thing in the valley longed for love and was burning with desire.

The young men became irascible, sighed without reason, suffered from insomnia, sang in the evenings (with varying skills) the song that was repeated with its echo.

When the wind of youth rises, all those in love gently sway:
Although they are the victims of love, we pray they
remain that way.

When the reaping season started, it found many men and women working in the fields. They were scattered here and there under the clearest of blue skies. The dunes of harvested corn grew higher by the day, and the estate trucks carried them to the grain silos.

Saleh woke up one morning before dawn at the sound of someone banging at the door. He opened his eyes, puzzled; it was still night. Then he realized that the Trunk had promised to come wake him.

Their work now consisted of reaping the corn, then loading it on the trailers. They worked from before dawn, with a pause at noon when the sun was hot, and worked till late in the afternoon, when the sun dried the stalks. Most of the other laborers slept in the fields to save time. In order to insure fast delivery, the estate paid by parcel of reaped land and every able individual helped, aware that laziness meant hunger for the whole village. In spite of the miserable wages, harvesting corn was considered a luxury in comparison to other work. No Mahrous, no foremen, no insults, no thrashings. There were only friends and laughter. The young ones had energy and speed, and the older ones, experience. That meant freedom in work.

When Saleh and the Trunk left the hut, Saleh was not surprised to notice in the subdued aura of this starlit summer night, men and women filling the streets and going towards the corn fields. They passed by the mansion and entered the darkness of the shadows of the trees. Here there were no stars glittering above their heads. Their hearts jumped in sudden terror when a fierce hoarse barking sounded near them; the Palace had strange hounds. They calmed down, reassured, when they realized that the high wall separated them from the dogs. They hurried nevertheless along the road, leaving the mansion area as fast as they could.

As the Trunk had expected, they found Ali, Abou Bakr, and others already at work, and Abou Bakr chided them for being late. Saleh apologized and worked industriously. Dawn came, shedding its light gently on the fields and illuminating the bent backs of the young people. The dew evaporated from their damp garments in white ascending vapor. The call to prayer was heard and they stood up, wiped their foreheads, left their sickles silently, and went towards the stream for the necessary ablutions. They recited the prayers of the morning. Then they went back to the fields. Someone shouted from far, "He is the only one." They answered, chanting in unison, "He is one . . . there is no God but one God."

Hameed's beautiful voice rose in song and everyone intoned the couplets' delightful choruses.

A young maiden challenged him by chanting also in a lovely crystal clear voice, so they interchanged singing, the men and women echoing the refrains.

Suddenly, the first sun's rays colored everything, making the laughing faces shine, and the corn stalks sparkled with drops of dew.

The corn harvest was also an occasion to get acquainted. Languid eyes with kohl around them met their fiercely bright opponents from afar. The sun cast its blazing rays on the bent backs of the youth, lighting their loins, pushing deep inside their flesh, warming up lust and mad desire. Occasions were numerous during the day for whispers, touches, quick kisses; and then later, before dawn, night covered up the silent pursuit, the struggle, and the violent rape.

Many births had their beginnings in these moments of madness, many marriages were sealed among the corn stalks.

Saleh shared the general excitement. He too eyed the women and was surprised with quite a few tender glances sent his way.

The girls paid a great deal of attention to him; it made him want to laugh.

A jealous voice came across the field, mocking in pretended friendliness, but full of spite.

"Good morning, Saleh. Did you leave the fragrance of the jasmine in your house, today, to compete with us and make the other flowers in the field jealous?"

"Shut up, Shaglouf, or else we will give you a lesson you won't forget," shouted Abou Bakr, seeing Saleh's angry face.

"Did I say anything wrong? I only said that the jasmine flower has a lovely fragrance," Shaglouf said sarcastically.

Then Abou Bakr turned to Saleh and asked, "Well, what is this story with Yasmeen?" (Jasmine in Arabic is Yasmeen.)

"There is no story."

"How? It is said that she stays at your house day and night."

"She helps my mother. There is nothing between her and me, I swear."

"Is it necessary for her to be there all the time? People gossip."

"Listen, my mother is blind, and she seems somehow to be losing touch with life. She can't even eat unless someone is there to remind her what to do. Yasmeen has been kind enough to help, cook, fetch water. I don't know what I would have done without her."

"I am afraid that people won't leave you alone. You should find another way of helping your mother."

"I really have no choice."

"I guess you know what you're doing." Abou Bakr, by that statement, ended the discussion.

But rumors about an affair between Saleh and Yasmeen spread like wildfire.

One day the Head Foreman came to the usual morning gathering of workers in front of the estate offices. He was limping; he had injured his knee the day before, jumping over a drain between two fields. Hassan Effendi seized the opportunity and pointed his nose at him, laughing loudly.

"Ha . . . ha . . . you've become an old man, Mahrous . . . ha . . . ha . . . why don't you leave the women to the younger ones? . . . This one for example . . ." and he pointed his nose at Saleh. "He looks so sweet . . . and he seems to have surpassed you in doing . . . ha . . . ha . . . you know what I mean. . . ." He winked a dirty, gloating wink at Saleh and stressed his point further with a shameless flutter of his middle finger. Mahrous's face darkened deeply in violent but well controlled anger, while Saleh lowered his head and gazed at his bare feet, his face red and hot from shame and embarrassment.

The rest of the men enjoyed the scene in silence. They could not laugh outright for fear of Mahrous's retaliation. Of course, village gossips spread the story and the women assured each other that Saleh was, in fact, Yasmeen's latest lover.

The days passed alike, one after the other. In spite of it all, Saleh was fairly carefree. He heard the whispers concerning his alleged relationship, and would occasionally blush, but more often shrugged his shoulders. Hassan Effendi fell ill for a while, and Mahrous took charge. He seized the opportunity to send Saleh to the estate's huge barn. Saleh was surprised, since he had no experience in cattle breeding and care.

The villagers understood the unspoken conflict between the two men because of Yasmeen. They sensed that Mahrous was doing this to keep him away from Yasmeen. Saleh realized that he would be a prisoner at the barn, with permission to leave only a few minutes a day. Working at the barn was like working in a huge penitentiary.

After saying farewell to his mother, Saleh went to Yasmeen's house to inform her of the latest development. She was baking and looked so ravishing that he stood there speechless. Her children flocked around him playfully.

"Well, Saleh, what brings you here?" She asked him. He told her. She shrugged.

"Mahrous is a cunning devil. But it is better for you. Many try to get that job because it lets you earn a living in winter. Don't worry about your mother. I won't leave her alone."

He looked at her gratefully and nodded his head in agreement, then quietly went out.

The huge wooden doors of the barn were partly opened, so he slipped in. He hesitated; a subdued light filtered between the great arcades, just enough to differentiate the color of the different animals: the light yellow, dark brown, orange, and white of the bulls and cows; the black of the water buffaloes; and the grey of the donkeys. Hundreds of large eyes peered at him curiously. He felt his heart pounding in awe. He turned his head at the sound made by Mahmoud, the foreman of the barn, who came out of his little cell near the entrance. He was a short, very dark man, a negro, all nerves, with knotted hard muscles. His eyes sparkled in his black face and he looked menacingly at Saleh. Saleh swallowed hard, frightened, then gave a deferential greeting in a quivering voice.

"Peace be with you, Uncle Mahmoud . . . Uncle Mahrous ordered me to come and work at the barn."

"I know. Why are you late?"

Without waiting for an answer Mahmoud leaned down and grasped a long cattle whip made of knotted cord that was lying on the ground near the wall. Saleh jumped high in the air and arched his body sideways at the same time like a bow that has just shot an arrow, and the whip cracked near his waist but missed him. He cried out, protesting in real anger.

"I swear . . . I came immediately."

"All right, I'll forgive you this time, but beware!!! At the first mistake . . . I'll skin you alive. I intend to skin you in any case. I mean it. Don't you ever leave the barn without my permission."

"Yes sir . . . yes sir . . ." stuttered Saleh, who was really frightened.

That is how Saleh entered the barn world. It was an isolated world of its own where one lived a strange life in the midst of a completely different society. He was given ten bulls, ten cows, ten calves, and four horses to care for by Mahmoud.

Saleh soon found out that Mahmoud knew his job perfectly, and that except for his nervous bad temper and harsh ways, he was a good man, dedicated to his work and the welfare of the animals. Saleh received from him all the advice he needed and he learned from him quickly.

Also from the first day he made his acquaintance with the other workers in the barn, who were mostly young men like him, patient, hard workers. Warm, merry friendships were tight bonds among them all. They were jolly fellows too, anything would make them laugh heartily.

Probably those were the things that made their lives bearable in this penitentiary. They lived and slept in the barn; Mahmoud would not allow them out for more than a quarter of an hour at sunset to have dinner with their families, but that did not leave them enough time to drink tea. So they usually gathered to drink it after Mahmoud left for his house and locked the door from the outside. They sat together in the wide space near the entrance, where the arcades began. They would sit around a small glowing fire, drinking tea and merrily cracking jokes. That night they made a really joyous feast out of Saleh's arrival.

One of them, called Saber, laughed loudly when he consoled Saleh mockingly; but really he meant no harm.

"My poor fellow, you are now chained to the pillory and they've made you leave your beauty . . . what a pity."

"By God . . . I never had a beauty . . . as you say."

Saber interrupted him, laughing heartily and happily but a little hysterically too.

"Don't get angry . . . we'll present you to the barn's beauty . . . you'll join us and take from her as much pleasure . . ."

Saleh, puzzled, asked naively, "Who is this beauty?"

They all laughed in wild uproar, their bodies contorting and shaking in hysterical merriment. When Saber finally answered, he had a certain difficulty in getting his breath.

"The beauty . . . ha . . . ha . . . she is the white she ass . . . The Chief's she ass . . . you fool . . ."

The crazy clamor was stopped abruptly by the squeak of the key turning in the lock of the great barn's door. Mahmoud had returned.

Everyone fled to his corner, pretending to care for the livestock allotted to each of them.

"Saleh, prepare the tea! Saber, come and massage my back."

Mahmoud was certainly a small tyrant in his way. He was the king of the barn and all the young men his slaves. Even tea was paid for by them. They all helped, using it as a small bribe to keep him happy and quiet.

Saleh revived the dying glow of the fire's coals. He placed the small kettle to boil over it, and watched from the open door of the small cell. Mahmoud lay extended on his face, naked to the waist, on his bed, which was a wooden board placed over two empty barrels. Saber went over the knotted black back of Mahmoud with his white powerful hands. Saber winked at Saleh and started to press with more effort on the back, making Mahmoud moan with pleasure.

In the evening Saleh sat at the edge of the straw-filled manger between the pillars of the barn's arcades, in the midst of the livestock allotted to him. The manger he had chosen would be his new bed, the place where he was to rest and sleep from now on. He rolled a cigarette, inhaled it deeply, then sent the smoke toward the ceiling with its slanting black dusty wooden boards, its rafters with spider webs everywhere. A dim yellow light fell from the small kerosene lamps between the pillars, their wicks lowered.

Where were his friends now? Probably in the corn fields. Saleh sighed and cursed Mahrous under his breath. Then he heard someone whisper his name again and again. He turned toward the sound and saw the Trunk peering in at him from one of the small windows close to the ceiling. He left his place, glided noiselessly to the wall below the window, and like a cat climbed up, using his fingers and bare toes in the small holes between the bricks till he reached the window. He touched the Trunk's hands between the iron window bars.

"Welcome! Welcome, Trunk my friend."

"How are you, Saleh?"

"In jail as ygu can see."

"Don't let that upset you. This is good work. Think of tomorrow. Think of the winter."

The work at the barn was considered a favorable, steady job, continuing through the winter season when most men were jobless.

"Let me live today and die tomorrow."

"No, Saleh, hunger is an ugly thing, especially in winter. Don't take that lightly."

"Separation is difficult."

"But you are in our thoughts and we all miss you."

"Thank you and give my best to Abou Bakr and Ali."

"Good-bye now. Take care of yourself."

"I'll try."

The Trunk left. Saleh went back to his corner to sleep. Suddenly something pricked him, again and again, all over his body. It was red lice. He cursed Mahmoud, Mahrous, the barn and everything it contained. He took off his rags and at the same time heard a movement in the stall beside him. The white bull was trying to loosen its rope. Mahmoud had warned him about this. Saleh rushed to the stall and retied the bull; he slapped him on the belly and cried at him with a trembling voice, on the verge of tears.

"You too!! You want to torment me!"

"What's the matter?" asked Saber, approaching to help.

"Nothing. The white bull almost cut loose. I fixed everything."

"You are so hot you have removed your clothes?"

"No. It's because the bugs were eating me alive."

"Don't scratch yourself. Bear it. Soon you will have developed an immunity against them."

"God help me from now until that time comes."

"You hate the barn, don't you?" Saber paused. "I don't blame you. Can I have a cigarette?"

They both smoked silently while Saber studied Saleh in earnest.

"You have a nice body; it looks strong," said Saber. Then he whistled in admiration, with a malicious wink, glancing lower down. "I also know why she found it sweet, the most lovely female of all."

Saleh blushed, smiling. "No, this is all wrong. I don't have any lovely female. . . . You are all causing me a lot of harm by this nonsense."

"Do you say that because you care about the Catfish," answered Saber disdainfully.

"No, because it's not true, that's all," stated Saleh in a stern matter-of-fact voice. He lay down again in his manger, avoiding a discussion that was getting on his nerves by pretending to sleep.

Saleh adapted to his new life quickly, even began to enjoy it. The work was not too hard, and there was no scorching sun to endure. Saleh developed an immunity to bugs. He discovered a great similarity between animals and people; they all had their own emotions, moods, and idiosyncrasies. The animals liked Saleh instantly, afd the feelifg was mutual.

Even Sabah, the white mare, accepted him, though only after a display of temperament. Sabah was one of the horses kept for the officials at the mansion. Each day Saleh had to enter the mare's stall and change the straw. The horse neighed and tried to jump and Saber advised Saleh to be careful. She had nearly killed someone before. Saleh talked to the animal quietly. Gradually the mare quieted down and after that she allowed Saleh in without protest. She accepted him as her servant; later she even showed him signs of affection.

Saleh soon learned to treat each animal differently and learned to understand their needs. He often felt an affectionate moist nose touching him as he slept, or a rough tongue licking him. Saleh washed the animals, cut the straw and hay, took them to the water troughs and waited until they had their fill. He left the barn only at certain set times, and then only very briefly to go to his hut for fifteen minutes in the evenings. He liked this orderly soldier-like life, and his body rested and filled out under this new regime. Mahmoud noticed his genuine love for the animals and his industriousness and liked him for it. He authorized him to go daily to the canal to wash the horses: Saleh was overjoyed at being allowed outside the barn in the daylight. The four horses followed him, prancing, as he took the road leading to the estate offices. Because he had gotten accustomed to the relative darkness of the barn, he found the sky too bright and the dust too hot at first.

He passed by the estate office building, going in front of its terrace, and automatically raised his hand near his head, shouting the usual greeting at the top of his voice.

"Peace, God's grace and His blessing be with you, your Lordship!"

He expected no reply and received none. He continued leading the horses with a contented heart. Mahmoud had indicated a place, past the mansion, where the horses could go down the bank of the canal. It was an enlargement of the canal, forming a sort of pool with a gently sloping bank, similar to the place where he used to sit and pray but on the opposite side of the village. Here he could avoid the noise and the barking of the dogs, which would have frightened the horses. After he passed the estate office buildings, he marched along the high wall of the mansion. The horses calmed down and paced behind him in the humid shade. Saleh's gaze wandered, beyond the top of the mansion's walls, to the high trees, slowing his steps in uncomfortable respect. When he left the mansion's shaded area, he resumed his happy stride. Even the horses behind him started prancing again.

He gazed at the eternity of fields, golden under the sky, and noticed an unfamiliar sight, a herd of sheep, grazing quietly on the empty, newly harvested corn fields. He had never seen these sheep before. They were different from the estate's red-brown sheep. These were white with black heads. Next to them was a tent, probably belonging to some nomads. Summer had come early that year and the desert was barren of weeds, and the nomads came down to the valley in search of grazing grounds. Saleh stopped at the side of the canal bank, stripped, and led the horses into the water to bathe and drink. Sabah was first, since she was the mansion's special mare, and she was proud and haughty. She would never have forgiven him if he had made her wait. Then he swam until it was time to dry and brush the horses. Afterward, he stood in the sun so that it could dry his own body. Suddenly he saw a young maiden filling an urn on the bank, across from him. He could tell from her clothes and the red sash around her waist that she was a Bedouin. She stood perfectly still when she caught sight of him. Her white face, her perfect features, her long hair had a beauty that Saleh had not known before. Her eyes were the color of corn wet with dew, her cheeks were pink, her breasts high and well-rounded. Their eyes locked for a moment. Then she blushed and turned away and it dawned on Saleh that he was naked. He saw her lift the filled urn and walk quickly away.

That night, Saleh lay smoking and observing the smoke rise towards the ceiling. He smiled. If anyone had seen him at that moment, naked, hot, sweating, and wearing a happy smile, they would have thought that Saleh had lost his senses. Saleh was thinking of the pool at the canal bank, the sky, the trees, the brightness of the sun, and in the middle of all this, the pretty Bedouin girl with eyes the color of corn wet with dew. Suddenly Yasmeen's picture came into his mind, with her daring looks and her sarcasm and her green eyes. He stopped smiling and his heart skipped a beat. He tried to take her out of his mind but without success. He heard her laughter in his ears. He confessed to himself that she too was beautiful, especially with that fragrance of hers. Images of Yasmeen and the Bedouin girl competed for his attention, Yasmeen looking at him brazenly and the girl watching him tenderly. The one made him aware of lust and passion and the other of innocence and desire. One had blue-green eyes and the other eyes the color of corn wet with dew. One had full breasts and a mature body and the other had little round breasts and a young, graceful body. The cigarette burned Saleh's fingers and shattered his dreams. He drifted into fitful sleep.

Saleh felt melancholy all the next morning, until at last at noon Mahmoud gave him permission to take out the horses. Once at the watering hole, he glanced across to the Bedouin's tents in the fields. Then he looked at the opposite side of the river and the adjoining bushes, but he didn't see the Bedouin girl. Later, while he washed the horses and waded into the water, he knew that he was being watched. He stepped out of the water, put his clothes on his still-wet body, and sat down. After a while, the bushes moved and she appeared. She knelt as she had done the previous day, filled the urn with water, and stole a glance toward him. Saleh smiled and she smiled back.

From that moment on, the young Bedouin girl obsessed Saleh. He worked, ate, and slept with her image in his mind. He lived only when he saw her; all the rest of the day was waiting. He lost weight and had fits of insomnia, but he lost his sadness, too. He laughed often and for no apparent reason. His eagerness and yearning for her lent a different brightness to his eyes.

The next Thursday, after Saleh received his pay, he went into the village. Abou Bakr, Ali, and the Trunk noticed his paleness and asked him:

"Is work at the barn that hard? Does Mahmoud beat you?"

"Not at all. Everything's fine. Thank God."

Then he inquired about the corn and their work, and asked them who owned the new herds of sheep he had seen grazing in the fields. He was told that they belonged to a tribe of Arab nomads from the north, who had emigrated from lands beyond the deserts and the mountains, fleeing from the foreign conquerors of that area. They wanted only peace and grazing land for their flocks. Abou Bakr assured Saleh that they were honorable people and that Sheikh Kataan, their chief, was one of the noblemen of his country. He added that Chief Abdul Meguid had exacted an exorbitant sum of money from the nomads for grazing rights, and had sold them some corn at an equally prohibitive amount. The Bedouin chief had been shocked, but since his hungry exhausted animals were on the verge of death, he was obliged to accept these conditions.

After he left his friends, Saleh hurried as usual toward Yasmeen's house with his salary. She too noticed his pale face and asked him if he was feverish again. He said no. She looked at him as if trying to read his mind as well as his heart. She felt that there was some change in him and in his behavior toward her.

"How are you?" she asked.

He answered quickly and then hurried toward his own hut to pay a short visit to his mother. Then he headed back to the barn.

On pay day Mahmoud carefully locked the door of the barn from the outside, imprisoning his workers inside as usual. He did not return on this particular night because he always went home to spend this night of the week with his family. By the end of the week the boys noticed from his increasing nervousness how much he needed his wife. This was not like the usual ordeal he went through when he was at home all week looking at her coarse features: she would appear lovely to him after he returned drunk from a merry evening at Yani's backroom bar.

After Mahmoud left the barn, Saleh and the others danced and sang around the fire. Saber tied a belt around his waist and danced to the clapping of hands and the beating of a tambourine.

The knowledge that Mahmoud was then either drunk at Yani's cafe or loving his wife, stimulated the young men beyond normal, as did their youth, the heat, their prison, the laughter and companionship. The fire gave a strange color to their faces and stimulated them further. But Saleh protested, laughing, when he saw Saber take off his clothes and run naked, joined by the others, throwing their clothes in every direction, the glow of the fire coloring their naked bodies.

"No, no, you mustn't!" objected Saleh. "It is a sin . . ."

They did not care, and they shouted and laughed.

"Come, you beauty!"

"Come on, Saleh, come and forget it all with the barn's beauty."

They tied the legs of Chief Abdul Meguid's white she ass and lifted her tail.

"No, don't, don't," protested Saleh again, laughing loudly.

The braying of the Chief's she ass rose higher and higher in the midst of the clamor.

One morning as Saleh was preparing to take the animals to the pool, he was startled by a sudden unusual movement from Saber. Someone was coming between the arcades.

Hassan Effendi was walking along with Saeed, the young man whom Mahrous had ousted from the barn for Saleh to replace. Saleh kept watching Hassan Effendi from the corner of his eye. Finally, Hassan Effendi approached Saleh and shouted, "Out!" He pointed a dirty finger at the door.

Mahmoud, who was working nearby, objected.

"What's the matter? Every time I get a good industrious boy, you take him away from me. How can I carry out my responsibilities at the barn like that, Hassan Effendi?"

"Saeed here was a good boy. Why did you throw him out?"

"I never did. It was Mahrous who did; but he was lazy."

"It doesn't matter. Saeed is taking Saleh's place."

With a quick stroke of his cane Hassan Effendi scorched Saeed's face because the boy did not retreat quickly enough. Saeed grimaced in severe pain; a red mark showed from his forehead to his chin; while Saleh fled from the barn, carrying in his hand the rest of his few rags and a piece of bread. His departure was given silent farewells from the eyes of his colleagues, who stood by quietly, disappointed and sad.

CHAPTER

8

T he secret telegraph system of the village once more spread the news immediately. The peasants enjoyed the action, happily gossiping. They realized that Hassan Effendi wanted to spite Mahrous, who was beside himself with anger. When the villagers stole quick, frightened glances at his hard, sullen, now darkened face they would feel their hearts lift with silent laughter. People usually laugh much more at the man who has two horns on his head, if he is generously built, huge, and powerful. The Head Foreman had all these qualities. The women, who were aware that Saleh could not have seen Yasmeen for more than a few minutes at a time while he was at the barn, now imagined the many opportunities the two would have to meet.

The whole village waited with an excited anticipation for the second round. Yasmeen laughed when Saleh went to see her. She had the thoughtlessness and frivolity peculiar to all beautiful women, who are flattered to see how men are behaving over them, without realizing how dangerous the situation could be.

"You are free now," she said. "Go to the fields. I'll wait for you this evening."

Next Saleh went to his mother, whom he had not seen in the daylight for a long time. She was so pale that he was shaken. He patted her shoulder.

The pathetic old body brought tears to his eyes.

"My son?" she said.

Saleh kissed her hands and her face. Slipping back to her dreams, she said no more. Saleh located his sickle, left the hut, and went to the corn fields. His friends received him with shouts of joy. The Trunk embraced him tightly.

"Easy, Trunk. You're choking me."

He related the latest sequence of events. When he finished, Abou Bakr murmured, "This worries me. I think Hassan Effendi is preparing something nasty for you."

"Well, I'm glad to be back. Let's forget Hassan Effendi for now."

"Well, be careful. Stay away from Yasmeen and keep her away from your house."

Saleh said he would take no chances. The sun was bright and there were no shadows anywhere. Abou Bakr signalled that it was time for noon prayers. Saleh was startled to realize that he had not prayed, or even thought of praying, since he had entered the barn. Anyway, back when he used to try to pray, the thought of Yasmeen had made praying impossible. Now he shrugged his shoulders. He walked to the canal, which was so calm it looked like a mirror. He associated this image with that of that other place near the barn where his horses used to drink. He turned to his friends and said, "I'm going home for a bit. I'll be back shortly."

They were surprised but asked no questions. Saleh hurried toward the village. Just before he reached it, he turned aside along a short-cut and headed for the watering place near the barn. He sat on the grass in the shade and waited. Then the Bedouin girl appeared. She filled her urn, looked at him longingly and lengthily, and went away.

"Where were you?" asked the Trunk when Saleh returned to the fields.

"Nowhere in particular."

Saleh avoided the Trunk's stare. Abou Bakr wanted to question Saleh but refrained. When the rest period came, Saleh lay with his friends and tried to sleep. He had a smile on his lips as if he were in a world of his own. How could his friends know that he was watching the black tents of the nomads? How could they know that he was smiling at the girl with eyes the color of corn wet with dew? They had not seen her in the sunlight as he had. Abou Bakr finally asked,

"What's the matter, Saleh? If something is worrying you, let us share it with you."

"No, no. There is nothing."

Saleh and his friends walked home at nightfall.

As he passed by his hut, Saleh hesitated. Should he go to see Yasmeen, as she had requested that morning? He remembered Abou Bakr's advice. He shrugged his shoulders, turned, and headed for Yasmeen's. As he passed between the huts, the light illuminated him clearly. "So the lover is back," thought the neighbors, with varying degrees of envy and amusement. When Saleh came into the house Yasmeen was shouting at one of her children.

"Look at this devil of a boy! He spilled the milk." She ran after him, but the child hid behind Saleh.

Yasmeen loved her children, and they returned her affection. Her anger was a kind of teasing. The boy who had spilled the milk played the game of someone who had made a mistake and was defending himself, knowing full well that she was not really angry. Saleh found himself in the middle of the entertainment, then the extent of his desire for her hit him. He had tried to catch the boy and instead found himself holding Yasmeen. She twisted away from him, laughing, her eyes taunting him. Tears filled Saleh's eyes and he hurried out, avoiding the stares of the neighbors.

The moon was high up in the sky like a large orange sun in the middle of the night. Saleh was passing near the mansion walls when a rough voice spoke.

"Stop! Who goes there?"

"Saleh. Saleh Hawari."

The dogs increased their barking. Saleh cursed under his breath. He knew this guard, his name was Abdullah. He remembered the unpleasant face of Abdullah and hoped he would have no problems with him. Abdullah's young wife had had an affair with a boy whom she had known and loved before her wedding. She continued to see him after her marriage because Abdullah spent most of his nights away from home as a mansion guard. At least, this was what was rumored. No one knew for sure and no one had actually seen them together. One day the boy simply vanished, and it was said that Abdullah had something to do with it. In any case, the boy was never seen or heard of again. Two days later, Abdullah's wife also disappeared. The police came, but Abdullah charged that his wife and the boy had run away together. The police found no evidence of crime and returned to the city. The investigation was closed. The truth of the double disappearance was never discovered, but it was believed that Abdullah had taken both the boy and his wife to the mansion, killed them, and fed them to the dogs at night.

After that episode in his life, Abdullah lived in a small room by the mansion's gate as a complete misanthrope. He spoke to no one and had no friends. He never went out except at night. Even his food supplies were brought to him by his colleague, the guard Gaith. The high walls had molded his personality, and the evil, hidden, crouching in them, passed on to him. Maybe it is always thus, that the guards and the men surrounding the absolute ruler quickly acquire a fierce and cruel temper.

Saleh hurried away, his bare feet making very little noise on the road's smooth black dust. He looked at the fields, shining with a soft silver glow under the moon. Some yellow lights danced far away . . . the tents of the Bedouins.

He smiled happily as he thought of something: why not send her a message of greeting in the form of a song, as Hameed did sometimes, imitating the Bedouins? He tilted his head back, and at the top of his voice, sang a strange couplet. The sound rolled and rolled over the fields like the howl of a young wolf, the echo answering its calling cry.

Ah . . . the patience I need; who will console me!
My love departed . . . Oh pity! . . . and left me!

He laughed, a short pleasant laugh, congratulating himself. He was sure that she must have heard him.

He repeated the song again, and once more at the top of his voice. The echo answered this young wolf's howl. When he reached his friends, they surrounded him menacingly.

Abou Bakr rebuked him in anger.

"Was it you . . . singing? What's happening to you?!!!"

"And why has it made you angry? Is singing forbidden now?"

His friends grabbed him and started beating him. He protested violently.

"Leave me, Trunk . . . What's the matter, Abou Bakr!!!?"

"You are mad . . . you want an open scandal!!!"

"Why? Don't hit me . . . just tell me, I want to understand, why is singing a scandal?"

"You are a rude, shameless fellow, and you will disgrace all of us. Every single one in the village heard you! What cheek! Sending your love to Yasmeen by singing loudly; you have no family to punish and make you learn good manners; well! We'll do it instead."

In a flash Saleh understood and protested sincerely that he did not mean Yasmeen; in any case, he promised that he would not do it again. They left him, slightly puzzled; the sincere note in his voice had won them.

By the time it was noon the next day, the sun was so hot that the corn became dry and wilted. So they stopped working and went to rest under the big trees along the main estate road. Saleh at first pretended to sleep like the rest of the men. Then he slipped away. He walked quietly so as not to disturb them, continuing along the bushes as if he wanted to go behind them to relieve himself. He looked back and noticed that one of the laborers, Shaglouf, had changed his position and now faced him. Saleh knew he was watching him from behind his closed lids, but he had to go on.

He passed by the mansion and walked slowly, still feeling Shaglouf's eyes on him in spite of the distance. Then he took a quick side turn and disappeared among some small trees until he reached the bank where he had seen the young Bedouin girl. He sat there quietly, waiting, his heart beating wildly. It seemed a long wait. The minutes passed slowly, too slowly.

At the sound of a rustling among the leaves, followed by soft footsteps, he turned, and there she was. She almost screamed. He begged her silently to be quiet, but she turned around as if to leave.

"Please, wait," he said.

He took her urn, went to the pool and filled it. She followed him and knelt down beside him as if she had known him for years, as if she had accepted him as her master and put her destiny in his hands.

"My name is Saleh," he said.

"And mine is Zeina." She smiled at him.

"Zeina. We cannot meet during the day. It's too dangerous."

She nodded that she understood.

"Can you meet me at night here? Could you come? I will imitate the cry of a fox, and we could meet here."

There was fear in her face, but she did not say no. He helped her load the urn on her shoulder and watched her leave. The bushes closed behind her as if she had never parted them.

Saleh sat on the bank for a while and smoked. He smiled at his reflection in the water, then walked along the banks for a time and chose a place among the bushes to sit. When he was sure that no one was in sight, he hurried back to the field where the workers were still asleep.

In the afternoon, the work was done in silence. Saleh smarted under Abou Bakr's thoughtful gaze and Ali's reproachful glance. Even the Trunk muttered disapprovingly. Saleh longed to convince them that he was not seeing Yasmeen, but he did not want to talk about Zeina.

Contrary to his custom, Saleh did not go to visit Yasmeen that evening but sat on his doorstep drinking tea and eating a piece of bread.

Next to him, his mother sipped some tea whenever he

reminded her to. He had seated her by the open door to catch a bit of breeze and hear the noise of the street. Suddenly Yasmeen was there, her fragrance preceding her. She carried food on a tray and put it on the table. Saleh did not get up to greet her.

"Aren't you going to offer me some tea, Saleh?" she asked.

Saleh filled a small glass of tea and handed it to her. She drank it quickly, then asked, "Why are you so quiet?"

"It's my nature."

"Why don't you eat what I have on the table?"

"I'm not hungry."

"Isn't your mother hungry?"

"She had a piece of bread with me, and that should be enough."

She sensed his antagonism and kept still for a few moments.

"Why don't you talk to me?" she asked.

"Because the rumors about an affair between you and me are all over the village."

"Is that all?" asked Yasmeen and laughed. "Is it bad for your reputation if the people believe that you are my lover? Well, you're not the first or the last they'll accuse." She paused. "You don't have to worry about Mahrous. I'll keep him away from you." She paused and added, "This means that you don't want to see me."

"You know that I care for you more than anything in the whole world, but what can I do? I feel that all the village is against me and that something nasty is in store for me. I have to keep away."

"Very well, Saleh," she said with a note of resignation. "I will send you your food with my son Ahmed, and I'll help your mother when you're working. As for money, give it to Ahmed also, on Thursday evenings. By the way, I have saved a pound for you. If you work hard, I will be able to save some more for you. Then you won't starve this winter."

"I need something to wear, Yasmeen."

"No, patch your clothes as much as possible. You will need every piastre when summer is over. Save some money to buy a small sheep." She rose and he quickly took her hand and kissed it.

The moon was taking its time to rise, but this did not stop the work in the fields because a strange brightness from the horizon lit up the fields.

Saleh felt restless. The night seemed darker than it really was, in spite of the presence of the stars and the light of the moon. He cut the corn nervously; after a while, he left his sickle and walked toward the main road. He knew that his friends probably had stopped working and were watching his shadow, but he went on, avoiding the clearly lit areas as much as possible.

After a while he could not linger any more, but started to run like the wind, not caring; the gay, sweet desire of youth made his heart pound joyfully in his chest. He forgot about his friends, thinking only about the young Bedouin girl and his anticipation of meeting her shortly. He slipped through the high bamboo stalks at the canal bank. When he reached the place, he crouched silently, hearing all the sounds that reached him with an attentive tenseness: the frog's croaking, the crickets creaking and chirping. Thousands and thousands of little noises filled the quietness of the night. None resembled the smooth gliding of bare feet on rustling dead leaves.

So he threw his head back and stretched his throat, he cried out a short barking yelp, the bark of the fox. The echo repeated it many times and the Bedouin sheep dogs answered angrily . . . and far off the mansion's dogs answered with their hoarse bark, then the village dogs went mad for a while. Saleh smiled, waiting. There was a faint rustling and a shuffle of bare feet. His face went hot, tears of thanks and emotion jumped to his eyes, the beloved shadow came into the moonlight and the stars lighted her face and placed sparkling dots in the depth of her eyes. He took her hand between his two cupped hands and felt it quiver, like a warm small dove. It wanted to slip away when it felt the smooth touch of his lips, then it surrendered, lying quietly in his grasp. He whispered softly.

"How are you, Zeina."

"God bless you, Saleh . . ."

"Let's go to the other bank . . . away from the road."

They went together. He gently pulled at her, holding hands. Her heart painfully throbbed in her chest with fear; it whispered silently within her, explaining what her agreement to follow him meant, and trying to frighten her with the consequences. But her overwhelming love for him moved her deeply, overpowered all resistance, and drove her to follow him quietly in sweet submission. They passed over the small wooden bridge, walked a little on the other bank, and sat in the darkness of a willow tree.

The leaves rustled gently and the long branches fell like curtains hiding their first embrace.

The stars twinkled. The moon danced gaily in the canal water.

A passing night bird uttered a loud sharp cry, high above; its last notes quivered many times.

Saleh could find his friends nowhere when he returned. At first he thought he had gone to the wrong place. He greeted Ragab and Ismail and inquired about his friends' whereabouts.

"They were here. Weren't you with them? Where were you? Is it a secret?"

They laughed, and Saleh felt embarrassed and terribly lonely. He found his sickle at last, and started to work. He knew that his friends thought he had gone to Yasmeen and that isolating him was their way of trying to make him choose between them and Yasmeen.

Before dawn his tired body demanded some rest. His muscles ceased to obey him. He lay down and went to sleep instantly. He woke up at the sound of buzzing flies. He opened his eyes. The sun was high in the sky, his body had betrayed him. He looked away from the sun to protect his eyes, and wiped his perspiration. Then he stood up and saw his friends working in the distance. It was clear that they had decided to end their friendship and that he would have to get along without them. He went back to work, but without much enthusiasm. The other men looked at him and laughed.

"Well, well. The professor is working alone," said one.

"His friends have deserted him," said another.

"Saleh, if we work with you, can we share everything with you?" asked a third.

"Shut up, all of you!" shouted Saleh finally.

Sayed and Shaglouf converged on him. Saleh thought there was going to be a fight. Shaglouf started to dance and sing.

"Come, Saleh. Come, my love. Come to me," Shaglouf sang, clicking his fingers.

Sayed had not forgotten the two pounds he had had to pay to make peace with Saleh. Now the situation had changed and Saleh was friendless. Shaglouf all of a sudden stopped singing. Sayed, fists clenched, was approaching Saleh. His whole group followed, their faces frowning, announcing a fight. But Sayed stopped where he was when he looked around and saw the Trunk standing behind him.

"Sayed, did you want something from Saleh?" asked the Trunk.

Sayed said nothing.

"And you, Shaglouf? Tell me why were you dancing?"

Shaglouf opened his mouth but kept quiet.

After Sayed and Shaglouf walked away, Saleh faced the Trunk and thanked him.

"Don't thank me. I would have done it for anyone," said the Trunk, and started to leave.

"Why are you acting like this, Trunk?"

"Where were you yesterday?"

Saleh started to speak, then kept quiet.

"Did you have a date with Yasmeen?"

Saleh shook his head no. Then he told the Trunk about Zeina and his love for her. He spoke for a long time, almost compulsively. The Trunk was amazed and perplexed. Then he snapped his fingers and said, "She must be the daughter of Sheikh Kataan, the owner of this large flock of sheep. This is the end of you, my boy. They are Arabs from the west and will have no mercy on you if they find out."

"I know, Trunk. I know."

There was more silence. They rolled cigarettes and smoked them.

"Good grief," said the Trunk. "From the rumors about Yasmeen to Sheikh Kataan's daughter. One of them is enough to ruin a man's life, but two . . ."

The Trunk started slapping his own face, imitating the traditional gesture of village women upon hearing news of a catastrophe.

"Shut up, Trunk, shut up. Stop it."

"How can I? You are digging your grave with your own hands."

"What is the solution then?"

"Leave the girl alone."

"Impossible."

"Don't see or talk to her any more."

"But we promised to see one another."

"Promises between the two of you are meaningless if her parents do not give their consent. And they won't. They would just as soon kill you."

After a while, Saleh spoke up again. "If I tell Sheikh Shaban about it and put my destiny in his hands, won't he defend me, take me under his protection? I feel he is like a father to me. I am sure he'll take me with him and we'll go to meet Sheikh Kataan and ask for Zeina's hand."

"You are a peasant and one with a naked backside under your

ragged gown. How can you even have the guts to propose marrying a girl like Zeina? Sheikh Kataan will throw you out of his house. He owns more than five thousand head of sheep."

"They live a simple life like us."

"The nomads of the desert are like that. Their life is hard no matter how wealthy they may be. But they think of themselves as lords. There is a large gulf between them and you. Nothing will stand between you and death, believe me. They will not hesitate."

Saleh knew that the Trunk was right, but he also knew that Zeina loved him in spite of his poverty. He couldn't accept defeat yet.

"Don't worry, Trunk. There must be a solution."

They went back to work with the feeling that they had rediscovered each other. Abou Bakr and Ali still kept their distance.

"Shall I call them over?" asked the Trunk.

"No, no. Please don't tell my secret to anyone."

"This is a dangerous game. You won't enjoy it long."

"Why? If Yasmeen has one or more lovers, what business of the village is it? There is nothing between us. And even if there were, so what?"

"She has a husband, and the village would refuse to accept this relationship between the two of you."

"Why me in particular? Does the Catfish refuse to accept Yani, Khalil, and Mahrous, and the others?"

The Trunk could not answer, and they went on talking and speculating. In point of fact, it was not as strange as it seemed. They both knew that poverty was so much present in the country that it determined every relationship, including human relationships. It defined them, it put boundaries around them. Men and women married to beget children and to serve each other materially. Frequently the woman was simply bought by being given food and shelter. She never forgot that she was her husband's servant. She had to work for him as he worked for others. She surrendered her body to him and did her best to satisfy him as he surrendered his body and muscles to the estate. She expected insults and blows and a harsh beating for failing to give him pleasure or for being lax in her housework, for negligence in bringing up her children, or for squandering money. She received the same treatment as he did if he was lazy or failed to please the estate. There was no place here for emotions or for love. The girl usually married a cousin or relative, because he had priority, or else someone from another village, whom she did not want but who had paid the required dowry. She often met her husband for the first time on her wedding night. Love was a luxury that the village could not afford. The villagers sang its praises in the evenings to the music of the flute, but, like the melodies and the words of the songs, it went with the wind and had no impact on daily life. Mad, uncontrollable passion and lust flourished in secret, but like a fire it quickly burned out, and any rumors about it were quickly hushed. The villagers accepted this as the order of things, while love and feelings could not be allowed to survive, because they presented a threat to the existing foundation of society. When Yasmeen was young, her behavior at first had attracted much attention, but as it had followed a predictable pattern, it had become accepted. When she was thrown on her back with young men on top of her, that had aroused laughter rather than anger. At most, gossips dismissed this with a shrug, a wink, or a laughing remark. Her marriage to the Catfish gained her the respect of all. Her sudden wealth, with rumors of her prostitution, inspired admiration rather than condemnation because it was a matter of payment for services rendered. Respect for money and a desire to improve one's condition were commendable qualities. The first affair with Yani, the Greek, and the second with Mahrous, the Head Foreman, improved her position in the village. She became part of the administration and had an influence that none of the other women did.

Where could Saleh fit in all this? How could this boy share the bed of the Head Foreman, this simple young laborer in rags with no underwear to hide his naked backside? He was setting a bad example to all the young men. The sighs and rumors multiplied, and phrases like "poor Catfish," meaning really "poor Mahrous," were on every tongue.

CHAPTER

9

D uring this period Saleh lived the most beautiful and happy days of his life.

Every human being has such intervals of true happiness, no matter how short, in his life. He remembers them always for years to come, turning his mind to their glow. One may suffer cruelly, strengthened by the faith that those days may return again. Saleh continued his work with his friends, especially the Trunk. Each night he would meet Zeina. Even the rumors, threatening troubles for him, had quieted temporarily. Maybe this was due to the fact that he no longer saw Yasmeen, either at her home or at his. That made Mahrous state loudly and firmly, while slipping out of the small back door of Yani's bar with Khalil, the male nurse, and Mahmoud, the foreman of the barn, that Saleh never was Yasmeen's lover and that there never had been any affair between them. Even Yani felt relieved and drank a bottle in honor of this news.

Saleh went to the market with the Trunk on Friday. He had shaved for the occasion and was happy. People greeted Saleh, and some of the women looked at him admiringly. Even the Catfish returned his greeting for the first time.

Saleh stopped as he passed a herd of black-headed sheep.

"Wait, Trunk. These belong to Sheikh Kataan." Both friends examined the herd closely under the watchful eyes of their shepherd, a young lad with a white complexion, a thin black moustache, and a bright look about him. He smiled as he said with the nomad's accent, "Be my guests."

Saleh remembered that Yasmeen had told him once to buy a small sheep. Why not one of these? He asked the shepherd the price of a ewe.

"Take this little one," said the shepherd. "I guarantee that if you take good care of her, she will be fine."

They began haggling over the price and the quality of the young ewe.

"The price is one pound and three quarters," said the shepherd. "If you wait a bit, my master will come and might give you a better price."

They sat down and waited. Saleh prepared a cigarette and offered it to the Bedouin, who declined with thanks. They exchanged polite conversation, and the Bedouin laughed when he learned that one of them had the strange name of the Trunk.

"I too have a funny name. It is Maamour" (meaning "the chief"). Saleh deduced then that he was only a shepherd who worked for the Sheikh and not part of his kin.

"What is your name?" the shepherd asked Saleh.

"Saleh, Saleh Hawari."

"You are Saleh, then?"

Saleh's face reddened.

"Your attempt at imitating the fox at night frightens the sheep," said the shepherd.

Saleh felt as if a snake had bitten him and stood up. The Trunk was already climbing the iron rail fence of the market in flight. A grave voice, greeting, stopped them.

"Peace, and the grace of God and its blessing be with you. . . ." It was the Sheikh Kataan himself.

Maamour's attitude changed into one of profound respect. Saleh and the Trunk started to leave, but Maamour spoke.

"These people want to buy a small ewe, sir."

"She was to be sold as part of the herd, not separately," retorted one of the two men with the Sheikh. They were two merchants that had just bought the whole herd.

"I asked for one pound and three quarters but they waited for you, sir, hoping for a better price," continued Maamour.

The Sheikh turned towards the two men. He had a lordly manner about him and looked comfortable in spite of the white woolen blanket on his shoulders.

"You are rich merchants," said the Sheikh. "You don't care about the price of one small ewe."

"But it is a matter of principle."

"I did not know that Maamour had already sold this small one. He speaks in my name."

"Sheikh Kataan's word is a word of honor, he never goes back on his word," said one of the merchants.

"The honor of his man is as important, and his word is final. And I give them a further reduction of a quarter of a pound," added the Sheikh grandly, and he turned his back on the two merchants.

"Take the animal, Saleh," smiled Maamour.

"The money is in my house. I shall get it to you before the evening. Do you need any guarantee?"

"No."

Saleh took the sheep and pulled it by the horns while the Trunk pushed it by the tail. They left the market, hardly believing what had just happened to them.

"Sit down, Trunk, and let's catch our breath. My feet are going to give way under me."

They both sat down under a tree.

"Maamour treated me very kindly although I think he knows everything about me."

"Don't be so sure. He still might turn on you."

"No. If he wanted to harm me, he could have done it right there and then."

The Trunk did not share Saleh's optimism. But Saleh was thinking about Maamour. He now felt he had a friend in Zeina's tribe.

Upon hearing the unfamiliar sounds that the sheep made, Saleh's mother woke from her reverie for a short while. She did not answer Saleh's greetings. The sheep did not try to escape, but she was frightened and Saleh patted her on the back; then he gave her some water in a bowl and put some pieces of bread near it on the floor of the empty space of his hut that could serve as a barn.

"Trunk, come with me to Yasmeen. If I go alone, the sons of bitches will start the gossip going again."

The sun was so bright that both young men could hardly see as they walked towards her house. The hot sand scorched their feet, but her house was dark and cool inside.

"Yasmeen," said Saleh.

Yasmeen appeared, with one cheek redder than the other and her beautiful green eyes half closed by her long lashes, as if she had just awakened.

"What do you want, Saleh?"

He was struck by her beauty; the black veil had fallen from her head, showing her lustrous black hair, falling below her shoulders. Her dress had opened while she slept, and the beautiful generous white breasts were showing. Saleh felt a shiver along his spine; was it desire or because of the sudden coolness of her house? The Trunk too stood open-mouthed with an astonished admiration printed on his coarse but gentle beast-like face.

"Well, why did you come here, to stare at me?" she asked. Saleh recovered under the whip of her ringing laughter and asked her to give him a pound and a half for the sheep. Yasmeen reached into the open upper part of her gown and brought out a knotted handkerchief. She untied it, removed a pound and a half and put it back again.

"A sheep? Do they sell them at this price?" she asked.

"A Sheikh wanted to be kind to us to annoy a couple of merchants."

"Good. Congratulations. Did you take it home?"

"Yes."

Yasmeen laughed gently again and gave him a friendly pat on the cheek.

"Boy, stop staring at me," she said to the Trunk.

The Trunk sighed with relief when he found himself back in the scorching sunlight. "What a woman," he said.

On the way back they stopped to eat at Saleh's house.

The mewing of the ewe prevented them from sleeping. They went to the dry mud elevation under the willow tree that served as a mosque, but it was filled with sleeping people, snoring in the shade. They walked along the bank, which was terribly hot. They found a grassy shaded place under a tree, they let themselves fall on the ground, and after a second they were fast asleep.

They were tired. It was full summer now. It was so hot that even the birds did not chirp with their usual energy. The fields extended all the way to the horizon and blended with it, as if forming one huge cooking pot full of water vapor. Saleh and the Trunk slept in the shade of the tree, while the sweat drops slid down the curves of their muscles. Then they dressed and left.

Saleh saw a herd of sheep moving in hues of golden dust, leaving the shade of the trees where they had rested to graze again before nightfall. He heard the whistling and voices of the shepherds. Maamour was there. He seemed to be twice his actual size; it was merely an illusion caused by the hot mist in the air.

"There's Maamour, Trunk," and they crossed, running to join him.

Maamour shook hands with them cordially, and Saleh paid him for the ewe.

"Now for my payment: kindly don't frighten my sheep at night any more," said Maamour with a mischievous smile.

"How did you know?" Saleh was embarrassed.

Maamour explained that the first time he had heard Saleh's fox sound, he saw that the sheep were frightened, but that his dogs barked loudly but stopped again, not very convinced. They remained quiet and did not attack. To him, this meant that a human being had made that sound rather than a fox. He thought that it might be a signal given by one of the local young men to his girl friend. The following evening, he wondered why the meeting place was chosen so close to the sheep. So he decided to get to the bottom of it. One night he saw a silhouette pass by the sheep and go into the bushes. After a while that same silhouette went back the same way. The sheep did not even move and neither did the dogs. He had then assumed that the silhouette belonged to some familiar being. He followed it and fell on it. Of course he was astonished to find that it was Zeina. She was terrified and begged him not to betray her. Actually Maamour had no such intention since he was in love with Aysha, Zeina's older sister. Zeina had helped them often to meet at night. As Maamour learned the whole story, he could sympathize fully with Saleh since his position with Aysha was not dissimilar. The Bedouins of the desert had very strict traditions. Maamour was only a paid shepherd and thus belonged to the lowest class in the hierarchy of that society. He was a member of a tribe which had, once upon a time, been powerful; but wars and dissensions had weakened it. He knew that Aysha was promised to her first cousin Massoud and he didn't have a chance. Cousins had accepted rights and no one, not even Sheikh Kataan, could ignore that fact. Aysha's and Maamour's was an impossible love, doomed from the start, in spite of the fact that Sheikh Kataan had a deep affection for his young shepherd.

"Saleh, it would be in your interest to stop seeing Zeina," said Maamour sadly. "She can never be yours. She will leave with the tribe at the first drop of rain. Don't hurt her, Saleh. If the Sheikh ever discovers your secret, he will kill both of you unhesitatingly."

"Well, I'll be careful from now on. I'll wait for her after midnight without uttering a sound until she comes by herself. Please deliver this message to her."

"Don't deliver the message or anything," the Trunk interjected.

"Be quiet, Trunk. Please, Maamour, don't forget."

"I'll tell her, but Trunk is right."

Saleh lived a few more days in happiness, in an Eden of love, tenderness, and friendship. The gossiping tongues of the village forgot him completely. They were now preoccupied with the fresh news that the secret telegraph of the village had thrown one day like a bomb.

Younes Effendi had fallen for the beautiful face of Haneya, the daughter of Sheikh Shaban's brother, and Ali's sister. He met her once, while he was returning on his horse from a visit to the Chief. The workers at the corn harvest were just leaving the fields. His eyes were attracted by a gay laughing face, like a small white kitten that had passed a rosy tongue over her lips. He went completely out of his wits. Every day he galloped on his horse to visit the corn reaping and watch the progress of the harvest, though these fields were not under his supervision. Once Ali slapped Haneya in front of all the other girls and sent her home after Younes had departed. Ali treated his sister this way out of respect for Abou Bakr's feelings.

Younes went blind with rage; he provoked Ali on an empty pretense and slapped him across his face with his short leather whip.

The whole village was waiting now for the results of the visit Sheikh Shaban had made to the Chief.

All this news saddened Saleh and the Trunk. Dawn found them working together in the same field with Abou Bakr and Ali. They felt that they should unite with them when they faced danger.

Younes Effendi stopped showing his face at the corn field after the village heard the terrible uproar the Chief made when he shouted at Younes. His hoarse bellowing was heard kilometers away; it could even be heard at the railroad tracks near the station. As a result, one could see lips parted and smiling here and there, and eyes winking mischievously. The secret telegraph assumed that the Chief's anger was an arranged comedy. And in fact he was delighted.

During this period, Saleh strengthened his new-found friendship with the shepherd Maamour. He often went to see him, taking the ewe so that she would be bred to the big ram of Maamour's flock. He was amazed to find that the shepherd's life was not easy, but certainly very tough. He had no roof but the sky over his head, he slept under the stars, his food was a piece of barley bread that he prepared and baked himself, some goat's milk, and tea. Yet his face was always smiling. He never laughed hysterically or cried out of anger, but he remained calm all day long. One did not notice the sharp lines which fear and sorrow marked on the faces of the village young men.

Saleh wished he could live that harsh but free life without oppression or tyranny.

The corn reaping season ended abruptly and once more Saleh

stood in front of Hassan Effendi at the early morning gathering of laborers, asking for work. The ever-smiling and moving face laughed loudly as usual as it jeered and mocked. Once more Saleh received the jet of saliva which escaped from the black hole in the open mouth where the missing tooth should have been. Hassan Effendi ordered him to work at planting the rice in fields flooded with water. This was extremely hard labor, a terrible punishment. The days were now at their maximum length.

The sun blazed, it violently radiated its scorching rays over the fields, making the water flooding them nearly boil and rise again as a warm vapor that remained suspended in the air with no breeze to move it away. The muddy earth was like hot cement, gripping at the men's legs, sticking to their skin with a thousand sucking mouths. And the heat; everything was hot, the water was hot, the vapor in the asphyxiating atmosphere was hot, the acid perspiration on the naked bodies was hot. The glare, the sharp white glare, was reflected in the water; then it jumped to the eyes, burning them, imflaming them; then it went through them, to find its way to the men's brains and to fill their minds with a blazing solid mass. The days were prolonged, they never ended. The mosquitoes, legions of small black ones, swarmed around their bodies, pricked their faces, their necks and any exposed naked skin, but worst of all, they found ways to get under the damp rags and irritate the skin in the creases, between the thighs, at the buttocks, under the arm pits. On top of this suffering was the coarse irritating shouts of Mahrous and his foremen, relentlessly yelling their vile insults.

"Bend your back . . . you son of a bitch . . . you filthy dog . . . you dirty . . . you . . . you . . ."

When he returned to his hut after his first day in the paddies, Saleh was so exhausted that he did not feel like eating; although Yasmeen had cooked for him a delicious looking plate of okra, he felt like throwing up. He drank some tea and left the hut. As usual, there was much noise in the village streets and the huts were swarming with people. As Saleh left the village, he had the distinct impression that he was being followed. Who could it be? Shaglouf? He looked behind him often but saw no one.

He passed the office building and the empty yard in front of it then entered the main road. He passed beside the huge black mass of the mansion. A light in a window, high up, seemed to observe him, peering from above the high wall fence, twinkling and flashing from behind the tree branches. He hurried along the road. The dogs barked for a much longer time then they usually did after he passed. He went to the canal, walked over the small wooden bridge and found the usual meeting place under the willow tree by the canal bank.

He sat down and prepared a cigarette for himself, then he slowly stretched his tired body, lay down, and fell into a deep sleep.

Zeina came in the middle of the night and thought at first that Saleh had not come. Then she saw him, fast asleep under the tree, and smiled tenderly. She took one of his hands, put it to her cheek, and kissed it softly. He had lovely hands, all tendons and veins, warm and strong, but rough from work. Just then she heard a noise: the sharp crack of a dead twig that cracked under a cautious advancing foot. She whispered, "Saleh, Saleh."

She put her hand on his mouth to prevent him from shouting. He immediately realized from the pressure of her hand the danger they were in, and became one tense elastic mass, all senses awakened, listening with his whole body. Suddenly he leaped, one great leap, and landed over the shadow which was crouching and advancing noiselessly, step by step. He threw his clenched fist, felt it crash into the head of the shadow on the side, crushing the ear, and heard his cry of pain. But at the same moment, Saleh received a hard knee blow in the chest that cut his breath for a second and gave the shadow a chance to slip away. He jumped after him, running, and threw his whole body in an ultimate leap that landed him flat on the ground. But his outstretched hand caught an ankle and he was on the other again, hitting the man, who twisted under him to face him. Saleh threw his fist again, splitting the lips against the teeth, but the other caught his thumb in a savage bite. It would have been cut but for a fierce, hard, vicious blow of Saleh's knee, low down, on the soft groin, crushing it against the bones of his thighs. The other, doubled up, opening his mouth wide, released the thumb, rolled with a renewed energy, and before Saleh could catch him again, he was gone. Saleh came back to look for Zeina but she had gone. He went home licking his thumb, which was swelling; he cursed the spy from his very soul, then asked himself who could it be? Shaglouf?

He shrugged his shoulders: tomorrow would reveal the spy; daylight would surely point to the bruised face. He entered the main road still cursing and insulting the dirty spy in his mind. He was received by the hoarse barking dogs of the mansion behind its wall. He looked up; the light that he had seen before had gone, and he felt with a poignant awe the weight of its formidable black mass. Because of his extreme weariness, he stooped, and with a swift movement, gathered a stone from the ground, and with all his might, threw it high up over the wall. He heard it hit the branches of the trees with a strange metallic echo. The barking of the dogs went mad, and Saleh heard the calls of the guards shouting in the dark. So he ran as fast as he could. The dogs of the village received him by barking too, and tried to bite him while he ran, leaping madly to avoid them. He leaned against the door of his hut after he shut it, panting. His heart was pounding and he was suddenly frightened. He raised the wick of his small kerosene lamp and he was shocked. His rags had gone to pieces, he was bare to the waist, with a thin band across one shoulder. How could he go to work tomorrow? He sat on the ground, knees bent, hiding his face between his arms like a child in utter despair and for the first time in a very long time, big sobs shook him.

He felt a soft caress on his head; his mother had awakened, and was tenderly stroking his hair. He was amazed when she spoke to him, since she now lived in a kind of dream, not conscious of what was going on around her.

"Are you crying, Saleh? Are you crying, my child? Why did you go to the Palace?"

He took her hand, kissing it fondly, wetting it with his tears.

"No, Mother, I didn't go to the Palace."

Her hands, coarse from all the years of working, had become so thin and smooth as a feather; they were nearly transparent under the yellow light. He knew from their sudden stillness between his hands, that she roamed again in her own world. He gently laid her on the mat, putting the straw cushion under her head.

The call for prayer was heard and dawn appeared, blotting out the yellow light of the lamp, and still Saleh was trying to patch his rags, pushing out his tongue from the effort. His coarse big hands often refused to cooperate in the delicate task of needlework.

With dawn the secret telegraph spread the news to the awakening village, from house to house, elaborating on the most breathtaking details. Eyes widened in merry disbelief and the mouths opened, showing their black rotten teeth. They related how Shaglouf saw Saleh and Yasmeen naked on the bank of the water canal, hidden between the bamboo stalks, in the most shameful position.

The rumors told how he had been caught peeping, and that the two had beaten him. The village went into a turmoil of buzzing, babbling, chirping, giggling. The secret telegraph added more details here and there. For instance, that Saleh held him tight from behind, while Yasmeen slapped him viciously, repeatedly, on the soft part between his thighs. The women, standing at the doors of their huts, showed to their neighbors across the streets with raised hands, fists together, the size of Shaglouf's calamity.

The Head Foreman blanched, his eyes narrowed, gleaming like steel, while the features of Hassan Effendi danced with joy.

The Chief laughed, heartily announcing, "The dirty fellow; he deserves to be punished!!!"

But Yasmeen herself received the news in utter astonishment, disbelieving. When so many details came to her, she kept quiet, neither admitting nor denying, but in fact confessing everything by her silence; smiling at the questions, but boiling with rage inside her. He had deceived her, this dirty lad, with his innocent sweet face, turning away his almond shaped eyes in confusion when she laughed at him, playing the pure know-nothing youth; and now she was sure that he had fornicated naked on the bank of the water canal with another woman, and Shaglouf had mistaken her for that woman.

Saleh left his hut to go as usual to the estate offices to attend the early morning distribution of work. His patched clothes showed the naked skin of his body in many parts. He had taken only a few steps, when he was met by the Trunk running to him.

"Is it true?"

"My God, the news has already reached you."

"It's true then. You were caught with Yasmeen?"

Saleh laughed nervously.

"Thank God they believed it's Yasmeen, but you know very well it's Zeina."

The coarse features of the good beast in front of him looked puzzled.

"Zeina? But even Yasmeen admits she was with you."

This was too much, his thunderstruck brain refused to work. He looked at the Trunk wide-eyed in real astonishment. Then he sighed, taking a deep breath.

"In any case it is for the better . . . at least Zeina is safe. What will be . . . will be."

The Trunk also sighed deeply, air pouring out of his lungs like vapor from a stopping train.

They stood below the office building, at the base of the terrace,

Saleh leaning as usual on one foot, with his back to the wall. His eyes were misty with tears of tenderness toward the Trunk, his friend, who touched his shoulder to Saleh's, standing beside him, while the faces of men around him looked hard and hostile. There was a shuffle of bare feet and he heard the gruff voice of Mahrous greeting the men. He answered the greeting with them. He could not prevent himself from sending a swift glance under his lashes to Mahrous's face. It looked unusually coarse, harsh, and a little pale. It turned a little in Saleh's direction and there was a swift exchange of steel between their eyes; immediately Saleh lowered his, frightened. And then more shuffling and the bodies moved in successive waves. Hassan Effendi arrived with a triumphant clamor. He greeted Saleh with a flow of the vilest insults, the coils under his buttocks making him jump from one foot to the other in a happier-than-usual dance. Then a loud boisterous uproar came from the men as they doubled up, laughing heartily, pointing to Shaglouf, who advanced in slow motion, legs wide apart, his face having all the colors of the rainbow with an enormous blue right ear.

And Hassan Effendi cackled merrily, drops of saliva jetting from his black tooth-hole. Then he suddenly turned toward Saleh, his ever-moving smiling features coming to a hard standstill.

"Out!! Get out!!!"

The Trunk protested vehemently.

"If you do not give him work, how is he going to live, Hassan Effendi!?!"

"Shut up!! You!!" And Hassan Effendi raised his cane on him. Saleh saw the Trunk duck swiftly and avoid its descending blow, so he quickly departed.

The women at their doors received him with unfriendly mocking comments.

"God punish him!!"

"Oh . . . But Hassan Effendi dismissed him."

"Of course, how can one leave such a dirty fellow in the midst of our boys."

He closed the door behind him with a bang, shutting off the nasty babble that followed him to his hut.

His mother was lying in a corner, seeming dead except for a snoring sound cmming from her nostrils.

He lay down too, lighted a cigarette with trembling hands, then relaxed.

"Oh . . . God. What can I do now?"

The sound of his voice rose in the room with a hollow dead echo. No answer. Once he would have gone to the small dried mud platform on the bank under the willow tree, the small mosque. He would have found in its quietness peace for his troubled soul. Now he just raised his voice to God, asking out of habit; but he expected no answer and none came. He asked himself if there was someone there to answer him at all. He pulled at his cigarette, filling his mind with its calming smoke, then he looked at the whirling blue-white smoke rings that ascended to the ceiling in intricate designs. He sighed . . . ah . . . life went up like these rings of smoke in meaningless arrangements, while pain and suffering closed in on him from everywhere. His mind worked uselessly . . . but came at the end without an answer.

A gentle humid touch on his cheek, and the small ewe looked at him with languid eyes.

"You too must leave now." He put a rope round her and pulled at her. He intended to give her back to Maamour. She followed him quietly.

While he walked leaving the village he was so preoccupied by his wandering thoughts that he suddenly found himself entering the vast empty space in front of the estate office building; it was now deserted, all laborers having gone to the fields. He should have left the village from the other direction, through a remote side road, so as not to pass in front of the terrace. Too late: Gaith the guard, sitting on the steps, was looking sternly at him. On the terrace itself, he saw Mahrous, with his huge body, standing in front of the Chief, who comfortably rested his posterior on the bamboo armchair, as he usually did at this hour. Hassan Effendi was there too, jumping from one foot to the other; he looked agitated as he spoke to the Chief.

Saleh passed slowly by as usual, he raised his hand near his head, shouting at the top of his voice, the ceremonious greeting.

"Peace be with you, your Lordship! Peace, the grace of God and its blessing be with you your Lordship!!"

Gaith, in answer, filled his cheeks with a ball of wet saliva that rolled in his mouth noisily, he formed his lips in a round opening, and shot the saliva ball powerfully at a distance. The large, fat spit landed on the ground near Saleh's feet with a dead sound.

Saleh met Maamour and returned the small ewe to him. He had

to explain why and saw astonishment in the other's eyes while he was doing so.

Maamour sadly promised him that he would sell it for him at the next market. He gave him part of the money. They had just shaken hands when Saleh noticed a cloud of dust on the main road, approaching rapidly. Two huge black cars were speeding toward him. Saleh's heart stopped. He started to run but too late. The first car passed swiftly in a flow of shining metal, cutting the air with a hiss like the sound of the breeze between the bamboo spikes. He just had time to glimpse sitting on the back seat the white and pink face of a man, like the face of a newborn baby, but with metal gold-rimmed spectacles on his nose. The other car stopped in a squeal of its brakes, the glass at the back door was lowered, and a coarse rough face, red and congested, bulged out of it.

The mouth, enormous with a thick dangling lower lip, opened, and whole masses of flesh quivered when he shouted.

"You animal, come here. Why are you loafing?!!!"

Saleh's lower guts griped painfully in terror and he could not move or answer.

"Answer, you damn fool?!" Why did you leave your work?!!!"

Saleh opened his mouth again to answer, but no sound came out of it. His hand, saluting near his head, stopped in mid-air, then saluted again. A dark fellow as huge as the other one seated by him got impatient.

"Leave that dumb beast now, my dear, it is not the moment . . . Drive on!"

A large shining stone flashed on his finger as he made a gesture of impatience with his hand. And the car disappeared behind whirling volutes of dust.

"Maamour, I must get away from here quickly before one of the guards comes after me," stammered Saleh hurriedly, leaving Maamour bewildered behind. In the first drain he found, he got down, and raising his rags, squatted and relieved his lower bowels from their griping cramps.

At home, Saleh stared at the ceiling. The minutes passed, and he remained motionless, crouched on the floor near his mother's inert form. The Trunk came by to see him. It was already night.

"Saleh, how are you? Are you all right?"

"I am all right."

"These are bad times, Saleh."

"It's the suspense that bothers me. I gave the sheep back to Maamour and he gave me an advance of seventy piastres, but that won't last long. I am out of work, and the price of the ewe is nothing."

"Listen to me, Saleh. Go back to work tomorrow or the day after. You are strong now and the estate knows it. If it was winter time, they could dispense with you. Right now, your strength is valuable to them. They'll disregard your morals and the troubles you are having with the village people. They are only interested in your muscles. Gaith himself will order you back to work. He'll have no choice. They need you."

"But Hassan Effendi kicked me out."

"He wanted to make trouble, but the Chief reprimanded him. They'll find other ways to get at you."

"What will happen? What should I expect?"

"Anything is possible."

Saleh walked the Trunk to his house, then turned to the stretch of empty land behind the village to relieve himself, before going to wash at the water canal. The village was sleeping, doors closed in spite of the heat; the night was moonless, and oppressively dark. He got the impression that he was being followed, after the Trunk had left him.

Saleh had just moved into the deserted place when a shuffle of many bare feet hurried behind him. On a sudden impulse he ducked. That moment a heavy club cut the air to crack his head. It caught him on the back, bruising and cutting the flesh. He cried a loud inhuman cry for help. The terror of death took hold of him. He rolled in the dust, trying to escape the many hands attempting to hold his body still so that the clubs could finish him off. They fell on his body, hurting him deeply, but none was enough to kill him as he rolled, ducked, rose, rolled again, struggling for his life. Two powerful hands got hold of his neck, burying their nails in it, strangling him. He thought the end was near, but his heart leaped joyfully and his body recovered its elastic hard-hitting power when he heard the voice of the Trunk above the fierce barking of dogs, hurrying to the rescue, his club raised: "You sons of bitches, you sons of bitches."

The tight steel grasp around his neck was suddenly released while cries of pain and sounds of blows rose around him.

He was saved. Saleh and the Trunk stopped, panting. They heard far away the shuffle of retreating feet and the shadows of their owners vanishing in the night.

"Saleh, did they hurt you badly?"

"No, I don't think so."

They returned to the village. A light showed under the door of Mahrous's house. They got the impression that it had still been open until a minute ago, and that someone was behind it now, listening. "Mahrous!! Saleh's blood will be on your hands if anything happens to him. By God I'll take your neck for it."

Saleh tried to stop the Trunk from yelling at the top of his voice, but in vain.

"You bastards, listen! Saleh's blood won't be spilled for nothing, I'll carry his vengeance!!!" The light under Mahrous's door went out. They walked along and entered Saleh's street. A shadow materialized in the dark and a gruff voice shouted.

"Stop! Who goes there?!"

Abdul Maksoud, the official guard of the village. The Trunk laughed, and imitated the voice, "Stop, who goes there?!! Do not make me laugh; as if you don't know what happened!!!"

The guard did not answer, and they left him behind, a silent dark shadow, standing.

Saleh's rags were gone. He was practically naked. Blood covered his face, and his body was covered with bruises and wounds. Yet he was smiling happily at the Trunk who was turning him around, inspecting him carefully: nothing dangerous. The wounds were covered with ashes, his head bandaged firmly with a rag to stop the bleeding of a small wound at the back of his head.

The Trunk spent the night in Saleh's hut, refusing to leave him. The night passed quietly. A cock crowed, and another, then another. . . . Some dogs barked and then were quiet.

Saleh woke; the Trunk was shaking his shoulders. He grimaced with pain all over his body.

A nasty smell filled the room; his mother had soiled herself. He excused himself to the Trunk and carried her to the small empty barn. There he washed her carefully. "You are so thin and wrinkled, oh my poor Mother." She quivered under the wet cloth, but did not awake.

He asked himself how he could go out now from the house: he was naked, his rags gone. The Trunk, alone in the adjoining room, had taken care of that. He presented Saleh with an old sack that had lain forgotten in a corner; he had opened a hole for the head to pass and two others at the sides for the arms.

"You want me to go to the morning call of workers like that?"

"Yes, you won't be the first nor the last."

He wore it. It barely covered his thighs, falling short of the knees.

"I have no choice."

Then the two friends went out, Saleh with the basin carrying the dirty water and the dirty clothes of his mother, the Trunk carrying the urn to refill it. At the canal he was aware of Yasmeen's fragrance; she was down there, kneeling near the water, filling her urn. His heart leaped and he heard the hoarse grumbling of the Trunk near him. She looked back over her shoulder, saw them, quickly put the urn on her head, climbed the few steps of the bank, and passed by them. She did not dare raise her eyes this time.

After the clothes were washed, they returned and spread them to dry over the straw roof of the hut. Saleh prepared the tea and they ate the last piece of bread that Saleh had. That is why the Trunk suggested they pass by his house to get some bread for their lunch. They went.

Saleh waited for him just on the street outside. Ali Keilani, the Trunk's father, saw his son coming, sat down his small tea glass, and went to get his club.

"Where were you yesterday? To the son of a bitch's house; and I heard that you defended him yesterday night!"

He swung at the Trunk but the club was stopped abruptly in mid-swing, much to Keilani's surprise. The Trunk grasped both his father's arms and spoke to him in an icy voice,

"Don't insult him. Don't you insult him."

Keilani found himself flying backwards until his back hit the wall. Propped there, he gaped at his son, who spoke to his mother in the same strange calm voice.

"Give me some bread, Mother, I will come in the evening for another meal. Tell the old man he must stand by me in the morning in front of the men and not leave me alone with Saleh among them."

His mother handed him the loaf as if in a daze. The Trunk walked out to Saleh, smiling broadly.

"I heard your father's voice, insulting us both. Is he still there? Did he beat you up?"

"No."

"Strange."

"Listen, he and I understand each other. He is a good man, and he appreciates the situation you're in."

Minutes later the Trunk and Saleh were in front of the estate offices. The men already gathered stared at Saleh. Their eyes were red, inflamed from working in the rice plantation.

No one laughed at his tunic that came to his knees. On the contrary, he received some swift sympathetic glances as he stood there, his head and arms coming out bare from the holes in the simple potato sack. His head was bandaged and bruises showed on his arms and legs.

Yet no one answered when they said, "Peace be with you."

So the Trunk, looking fiercely around, yelled, "I said peace be with you!!!"

They all answered ceremoniously "And peace be with you, God's grace and blessings!!!" Even Mahrous answered, a rapid twitch passing over his face when the Trunk's steely glance met his, as if he was saying to himself, "It's better not to come near this stupid beast." So now the Trunk was all smiles, trying to be friendly with everyone, sending small twinkles and sweet amicable gestures with his big paw.

Saleh heard a husky voice near him. "How are you, Saleh, my boy? How is your mother?" and Ali Keilani's rough hand was patting his shoulder.

"Thank God!! My uncle! Thank God, my uncle!!" He was so overwhelmed with gratitude that he took the rough hand and put his lips on it, kissing it, mist coming to his eyes. At that moment, from far off, came the laughing voice like the neighing of a mare, and the shuffling of bare feet on the ground.

Hassan Effendi had arrived. He pointed his nose at Saleh. The first sunrise came suddenly to a standstill.

"Mahrous, take that son-of-a-bitch group with you to the rice planting!" And with a quivering middle finger, in a shameful gesture, he included Saleh, Ali Keilani, and the Trunk.

The Trunk spent that night and many subsequent ones with Saleh, never letting him out of his sight, not even when he went outside to relieve himself. The days passed quietly. For a time, the storm seemed to be over.

CHAPTER

10

I t was a hot, windless summer day, with a white floating mist, the earth as colorless as the white sky. The warm, humid air carried a strange scent, like that of decaying jasmine blossoms. Worms were threatening the cotton crop; the strange smell came from them. The voices of the foremen were louder than usual, the cries of the children and the hiss of the canes sharper. Luxurious cars were seen driving on the estate's main road, followed by assistants, foremen, and guards, who anxiously hastened to assure the administration that they had not neglected their duty to the cotton.

For the workers, the upshot of all this activity was additional ill treatment, litanies of curses, more hard labor.

Saleh was working in the rice fields, bent, his legs in the water, when he saw the guards Awad and Gaith coming toward him. His heart sank. Everyone around straightened up, stopped working. He had expected it for a long time and now it had come.

They dragged him along; he heard the Trunk shouting and sobbing. How short the road was today; he had never known it so short. He saw the great gate of the mansion's wall open and he was pushed through. The gate closed behind him. His glance shot madly along the alley bordered with trees, and saw at the end of it the huge closed door of the mansion itself. He felt himself being pushed to a small room at the side of the gate. Gaith's voice echoed in his partly conscious mind.

"Wait here for your turn."

He stood a moment, confused, his ears buzzing, then he walked like a drunk. He sat propped against a wall, trying to find his breath, panting, with terror gripping his chest. Then his heart calmed down, and he could look at what was going on around him. He exchanged glances with everyone in the room.

A young man was standing, his back against the wall. He did not know him well. An old man was sitting cross-legged. There were two young men from the upper village beyond the station. What was their guilt? Then he saw three young men, his fellow workers at the barn; a small pitiful smile showed on the pale face of one of them, saluting Saleh. It was said that they had been eating the bull's bean ration and Mahmoud the foreman caught them. And gathered at the door, looking at the alley and the entrance of the mansion, were many young men, unknown to him. From the open door he could observe the guards sitting on the ground under the trees of the alley and part of the other little room on the other side of the gate. Abdullah's private room. Abdullah!!! Saleh had fallen into his hands and he would execute the sentence on him savagely with his whip. Terror shook him again.

His gaze left the door and wandered again in the room. He was surprised, disbelieving his eyes. Hameed was sitting there, leaning against the same wall as his, a few steps from him: sweet Hameed, the one who enchanted the whole village with his lovely voice during the corn reaping season or on Thursday night, on pay day, at the merry gatherings of young men.

What brought him there? Their eyes met. Hameed's lower lip began to quiver as if he was going to cry.

"God is one!!! Believe in him!!!" yelled the young man who was standing and reclining against the wall in front of Saleh. That was followed by the sobs of someone else. So he yelled again.

"Stop! You kid! When they stretch you at the pillory . . . cry all your soul then!!!"

Another advised: "Yes, you must attract their attention by crying loudly so they may spare you and not make you suffer much."

But the old man answered gravely: "Thou will receive what thou deserve, whether thou criest or not." Saleh crawled and sat near one of the cattle feeders, his former companion at the barn, and asked him why Hameed was there. He told him that Hameed had lately been singing satirical songs against the estate administration and the misery of men, but he had gotten bolder and even mentioned the Palace, that was why.

Gaith appeared at the door with another guard.

"Hameed."

He shrank against the wall, shaking.

All eyes were on him. The two guards lifted him up like a feather by his two hands. All the heads were turned at the door, including Saleh's, to see him being dragged along the alley. Then the huge door of the mansion swallowed him and closed again.

They returned to their places.

The young man standing in front of Saleh, reclining again at the wall, began to laugh a hysterical laugh, then yelled.

"Courage!! Let me tell you a joke . . . there was once . . ." He stopped talking, suddenly staring down at the yellow liquid which was showering on his bare feet, making a pool around them.

Time passed like an eternity. Then someone shouted.

"Here he is."

They were all at the door again, looking. Hameed was approaching in the alley coming from the mansion, completely naked. He did not turn even to take his clothes that a guard threw at him from the door and that scattered on the ground, but kept on walking with strange, short quick steps, slightly bent, like a hurt animal.

When he passed by them, they noticed tears dribbling from his eyes. His back and buttocks were colored red as if tomato juice had been poured on them. But what most moved the men looking was his continuous soft moan, like a child's cry.

The gate opened and they saw him cross the empty space in front of the estate's office building, walking toward the village with the same short quick-moving steps. Then the gate closed, and Gaith came again. They all retreated backward in terror.

"Saleh Al-Hawari!!!"

He did not move.

The two guards came to him with gleaming eyes and mocking smiles. "Come, my sweet, and sleep in the arms of your beloved!!!"

He rose, and a sudden mad powerful will took over his soul, and instead of waiting for them, he sprang at them, his fist hitting Gaith's nose hard; he was taken by surprise and fell backward silently. The other guard yelled of pain when Saleh's foot kicked him fiercely in the lower part of his stomach, sending him doubling up also to the ground. Guards poured in, unbelieving at what was happening, and Saleh found himself in a whirl of moving faces, trying to hold him, hitting him, but he punched and hit back hard. Then he felt a hand searching cunningly on his ever-moving body, finding its way low down under his tunic. It suddenly squeezed and twisted his entrails, in an unbearable torsion, as if they were bursting open.

He knelt on the floor in surrender, and as they carried him along the alley and inside the mansion, the hand squeezed and twisted, still holding.

At this precise moment, Yasmeen was running with her hair dishevelled toward Saleh's house, crying and wailing, not caring in the least about the troubled, astonished faces of the neighbors who saw her pass.

She entered the hut, threw herself at Umm Saleh's feet.

"Oh Mother. Oh Mother . . . Saleh is at the Palace . . .!"

The old woman, as usual, was dangling her head from right to left, dreaming, but she put her hand on Yasmeen's head, stroking it gently while she cried in her lap.

Umm Saleh whispered as if she had regained her consciousness.

"Do not talk about the Palace, my child, neither in praise nor in spite."

Yasmeen continued talking to her as if she was her own mother, blaming herself.

"Oh Mother . . . It's my fault . . . I am the criminal. Oh God punish me."

Suddenly Yasmeen felt Umm Saleh recoil as if her whole body stiffened. She raised her head from her lap, and saw her looking straight ahead, in the direction of the mansion, her blind eyes wide open for the first time in so many years. But they were frightening eyes, with a white shining gleam all over them and no black iris in them. She saw the old woman rise, putting a hand near her ear as if she was detecting a call coming from far away, opening her mouth. Yasmeen retreated till her back was pressing against the closed door of the hut.

Umm Saleh took a few steps in the direction she was gazing at. Her eyes widening more, she suddenly raised her palm with an arm stretched in front of her, pleading in a hoarse voice.

"No! No!!!"

She turned, slightly moving her wide white eyes as if she followed the people she was looking at along an imaginary path.

"No! No! Don't hurt him! Saleh!!! My child."

Sobs were shaking her body in a dreadful manner, tears rolling on her wrinkled cheeks.

"Please! Saleh!! Ask for mercy!!! Ask for mercy!!! Please, my child! Mercy on my child!!! Enough . . . enough!!!"

She fell on her knees, her quivering voice lowering its tone as if in surrender.

"He weeps now . . . do you see, he is crying . . . he is begging for mercy . . . enough . . . enough!!!"

And then the eyelids closed like curtains, her body shrinking little by little. She fell on the ground in a small crumpled heap. Yasmeen opened the door of the hut and fled as fast as she could.

Late that night, Saleh was lying flat on his abdomen. He raised his head a little, and said in a whisper, "Thank you." Then he resumed his soft moaning every time the Trunk touched his back with a wet cloth. The Trunk's coarse features, those of a good kind beast, happily smiling, were now lit by the yellow dancing glow of the kerosene lamp. He was really elated by the "thank you" he had received. It was the first word Saleh had spoken since he was carried in by the guards and thrown on the ground, practically unconscious. When the dawn's light gently appeared beneath the straw-covered roof of Saleh's small barn where he was lying, Ali Keilani entered the hut. He came to fetch his son and to take him to work for the estate. They argued for a while, but the Trunk agreed; Saleh needed the money as much as he did. So they got out together, father and son.

Young Ahmed, one of Yasmeen's small children, saw them coming out; he was posted there by her to give her news of Saleh, as she was afraid to go to his hut again by herself, especially when she knew that the Trunk would visit his friend, and she could not risk putting herself on the path of that savage animal in those terrible circumstances. He could well break her neck and kill her in one stroke of his big paw. She had passed the night agitated by remorse. At times she cried and moaned. At others, with an unleashed fury, she fell on her husband, the old Catfish, trying to tear his face apart with her nails, and he would squeeze himself past her, taking refuge in his room, locking himself in. At dawn she sent the boy Ahmed, and he returned quickly with the good news: the Trunk had left for the fields. She put on her long black veil and walked to Saleh's hut, erect, her head a little raised up, haughty.

There she found Saleh's mother crumpled on the floor, snoring, the way she had left her. But when she entered the small adjoining straw-roofed room, she was shocked at the sight of Saleh in that state and hid her face. Then she came nearer. He must have felt that she was there, as he raised his head a little from the ground, and turned his bloodshot eyes at her. That must have required a terrible effort from him, for he vomited. His whole body shrank and shook in an ugly contraction. She cleaned the vomited bile from the ground below his face, spread a little dry dust over it, then cleaned him, passing a wet cloth over his naked body as the Trunk had done. She remembered Umm Saleh; she woke her up, washed her in the basin, prepared tea and fed her with a little bread. Then she cleaned the house and put it in order. She went to the canal, washed the basin and the dirty rags, and filled the big urn. When she returned, she sat beside Saleh, keeping the fat black buzzing flies off his bruised, mashed skin. The door squeaked, her heart leaped in terror. She thought it was the Trunk; she had forgotten to lock the door.

But the large body of Gaith filled the entrance to the small barn. He was holding the empty potato sack, Saleh's present tunic, in his hand, and he threw it on the naked body. His ugly face smiled widely, disclosing long irregular black teeth; and his eyes gleamed with a yellow shine when he said, proposing himself, "Don't care for him any more. I believe he is finished now as regards . . . you know what I mean . . . but others are here that can serve. . . ."

He progressed toward her; she rose, facing him. He came to a stop when his face was splashed by her spit. He scowled, his yellow eyes carrying murder. Yet he calmed as he remembered Yasmeen's powerful friends. So he wiped his face with a dirty hand and silently went out. She sat again and began applying cold compresses to Saleh's now blackened back, when she heard him whisper gently.

"Yasmeen . . . please go . . . The Trunk will be here any minute now . . ."

She smiled, full of joy: he had pardoned her, he cared for her, as he was protecting her from the possible wrath of the Trunk. Then she laughed loudly, her previous merry mocking laugh, and said, "I wonder who was the bitch," laughing again. She had also pardoned him.

At noon, after the midday pause, the Trunk refused to budge, pretending to be ill. When Mahrous came to him to test him, with his cane already raised, the Trunk held his belly with both hands, but at the same time looked up at Mahrous with one eye open wide, the other closed in a suggestive message that the other understood immediately, and smiled, pleased to be able to do a small favor to this dangerous, stupid animal.

"All right, go home and I won't report you."

And the Trunk, imitating illness in front of others, dragged himself along the road, holding his belly. At the turn of the road, he started running swiftly, taking the longest way, from one side road to another, but reached the village without having to pass by the mansion, or by the terrace of the estate management offices a little further away. Saleh's face greeted the Trunk with a sweet smile that made his friend really happy, his features melting.

Then he looked puzzled when he found in a corner the jute potato sack, Saleh's rough tunic.

"Who brought you your tunic?"

"Gaith, I think," he answered.

"Who arranged and cleaned the house . . . ?"

"I don't know for sure . . . one of the women," he lied.

At night Saleh could raise himself up, and he lay on his side, resting himself on his elbow, as the Trunk presented him with a hot plate of cooked food. He could eat a little without vomiting. He felt a happy dizziness taking hold of him, his eyes getting misty again from his grateful fondness toward the Trunk, as he heard him in the adjoining room, encouraging his mother to eat with his gruff voice. Later they had a visitor. Answering to a knock, the Trunk got up and unbarred the door, and Saleh heard his ferocious mumble, half aggressive, half astonished. He leaned to look from the adjoining small barn where he was lying, and saw the Catfish standing at the entrance of the hut, an ugly short man with bowed legs. He was looking down at his bare feet, with his eyes the color of dirty water. His large pepper-grey moustache quivered when his thick lips moved under his flat nose, as he greeted with a husky, coarse voice.

"Peace be on you." They did not answer, but he entered and simply sat in silence, cross-legged.

"Hail!" yelled the Trunk, bending, nearly touching the old man's face with his fist.

"Stop it! Trunk! The man is our guest in our house . . ."

There was silence again, until Saleh cut it by asking.

"Do you know that there is nothing between me and her? Of what they accuse me of."

He nodded his head many times quietly, admitting, his face taking a dark ugly color.

"You knew that before you went to report me?"

He nodded yes.

"You knew that Shaglouf was lying and Yasmeen too?"

The Catfish raised his head but his eyes were immediately lowered again in shame.

"Yes I know . . . because Yasmeen passed that particular night with me and I did not leave her from my sight . . ."

If a huge rock had fallen on the Trunk's head it would not have made such a commotion. He mumbled, "How? How?" half rising, his fingers clawed toward the neck of the old man.

"Leave him," said Saleh. "Don't you hurt him!"

The Trunk retreated, still agressively mumbling, like a bear obliged to let his prey escape from the grip of his paws.

"Why did you accuse me then!" cried Saleh.

The old man remained silent.

"Who forced you? . . . Yasmeen!"

He moved his bent head right and left, denying.

"Mahrous? Hassan Effendi? The Chief?"

He kept silent, not answering.

"The Palace!"

He did not move or speak. From the other room came the voice of Umm Saleh: "Do not pronounce its name on your lips, neither in praise nor in spite . . ."

They remained in silence for a while. Then there was another knock at the door. The Trunk opened again and yelled in real alarm, "And there comes the second calamity!"

It was Maamour.

"Come in! Come in! Please, welcome," Saleh greeted him.

The old man mumbled a few unintelligible words and left. Maamour had come to inquire; he looked at Saleh's naked body in awed horror.

"What happened? Were you squashed by a train?"

"It would have been better; at least one dies once, not a thousand times! What brought you over here?" asked Saleh.

"I heard you were in trouble. News travels fast in these parts, and I bring along Zeina's sympathy."

"Tell her I am fine and don't tell her anything else."

Later, when Maamour had left, the two friends exchanged theories of why the Catfish had accused him falsely, and who had forced him and why.

Just before sleeping the Trunk asked in a grieved voice, "I wonder why the estate hates you so much, Saleh . . ."

Next day, Saleh sat alone quietly in the small empty barn of his hut. The Trunk had just left. His mind was void of any thoughts. The door squeaked. He had forgotten to bar it after his friend went out, and his club was in the other room. His heart leaped out of sudden fright. But it was Yasmeen; she filled the entrance of the barn with her body. Her face lit up, rejoicing to see him sitting. With a quick gesture he covered the lower part of his naked abdomen with his rough jute tunic which was lying at hand, his eyes meeting hers in a hard look. He did not answer her smile. She knelt at his feet.

"Hello!"

He kept quiet. With her index finger she slowly followed the lines of his chest and played over his ribs, smoothly, caressing him; it went downwards, wandered lazily on his abdomen. He recoiled suddenly and slapped hard at her face sending it to the ground. His voice hissed sharply between his bare teeth.

"Out! Get out!"

She raised her head from the ground, looked at him and smiled.

His face reddened deeply, then turned pale again.

"I deserve it! Hit again! Come on . . . hit again!"

She curved her long neck in charming coyness, throwing her veil far from her, so that her hair appeared like lustrous curtains on her shoulders. She moved closer, on her knees, but he withdrew from her.

"Are you afraid of me . . ."

"You are crazy . . . you want me killed this time."

"Am I not worth it . . . ?"

And again with her index finger, she caressed him, playing over his ribs. His voice quivered, begging.

"Please . . . go away."

Her beautiful face seemed to melt from sudden tenderness toward him, her finger going down, following the lines of the black imprint of the lash on his skin, that curved from his back, to end on the chest, over the abdomen. His trembling voice pleaded again.

"Leave me alone, please . . ."

Her eyes now sparkled with desire; the smile had gone; her face glowing, she came nearer him, paralyzing him; her lips touched his cheek and she went on caressing his face with her lips, kissing him lightly, as she had done before with her finger.

Her fragrance filled his mind with its sweet yet cunningly overpowering scent. He bit her lips but she bit back, and then he kissed her, in a hungry yearning kiss that craved for the warmth of her lips, which slipped away, then returned again in a whirl. Suddenly with one hand she pressed the back of his head; with the other she unbuttoned her robe while bending her body backward. He embraced her tightly with his powerful arm. Inflamed by an ardent, mad, uncontrollable desire, he took her with all the violent power of youth. He took his revenge harshly, paying no attention to her cries of pain and protest. She had long ago forgotten the effervescence of youth, and its brutal force. She remembered it now with a painful acuteness; her eyes cried because of its delightful sweetness. He savagely took revenge on her and on the estate, and he hit hard again and again with his love, avenging himself for all the sufferings, miseries, and humiliations.

He reclined on his side, panting, drops of sweat shining on his forehead.

"Am I not worth . . . death?"

He approved, with a nod, smiling to her.

"Would you suffer the whip again till death for my love?"

He nodded gratefully, contented. She laughed merrily, her voice ringing like small bells.

"Don't be afraid . . . no one will hurt you now, I'll see to it."

"What do you mean?"

"You betrayed me . . . so I let them have you, tearing you apart, like mad dogs in rage . . . but now it's different, I will protect you. With the movement of my small finger I make Mahrous, the first of them, move like a marionette. But tell me . . . who was the bitch?"

He frowned, so she gently stroked his forehead between his eyebrows.

"All right . . . don't get angry . . . keep your secret . . . but beware from now on . . . don't do it again. Don't ever betray me . . . ?"

The thought of Zeina came to his mind. . . . How different she was from this woman. The wide blue-green eyes full of lust and mischievous desire, against the almond-shaped ones with the color of corn shining under the morning dew. Zeina . . . how very far she had retreated from his mind now. . . . Tomorrow she would leave with her family to the far desert from where she came.

Yasmeen, looking at his misty eyes, got angry and warned sharply:

"I said . . . take care! Do not ever betray me again!!!"

He laughed a merry short laugh.

"Don't be afraid . . . I really have no one but you now . . ."

He was still panting, the drops of sweat still shining on his forehead. So she asked, "You are dead tired, aren't you?"

He said yes, nodding his head.

"There is nothing called being tired when you are with me . . ."

And she started playing again with one finger, caressing his across his ribs, and blood surged within his arteries, deep in his body, his heart galloping madly; an overpowering desire caught fire all over him, surging painfully in its delightful joy.

Just before sunset, for the fifth time, his eyes wept from the tormenting pleasure. His whole body wanted to yell "enough," yet was incapable of stopping.

He heard the door close behind her with a squeak. The Trunk would be there in a minute. He shivered, feeling cold, so he put on his tunic, though its rough jute texture irritated his bruised skin.

He suddenly remembered his mother, sitting in the next room. He felt angry at himself that he had not thought of her the whole morning. Did she hear? Did she understand what happened so near her? It was becoming dark, as night fell quickly in this season when the sun went down. He went to the other room and saw her sitting on the floor, reclining her head against the wall. He lighted the small kerosene lamp, but his tired hand shook a little and its glass shield fell and broke, shattered. He gathered the broken pieces, with anguish in his heart. Was it a bad omen? Under the dancing yellow light of the kerosene lamp he looked at his mother again. She did not move, a quiet silent figure, yet he noticed the gleam of tears, dribbling slowly on her cheeks. She must have heard. He went to her and called softly:

"Mother . . ."

She did not answer. So he passed the back of his hand under her closed eyes, wiping her tears. Her face twitched slightly under his touch; definitely she was not aware of what was happening around her. But deep inside himself he was not fully convinced, doubt still lurked in his mind. He felt an immense sadness. At that moment the Trunk entered with his face lighting cheerfully. He saw Saleh standing in the room, but he became aware of the sad tone in his friend's voice when they exchanged greetings.

"What is it? You don't feel well?"

"No, I am all right."

"Who broke the lamp glass?"

"I did . . ."

"I notice that you tolerate the roughness of your sack tunic now, did you put it on yourself?"

"Yes . . . I felt cold . . ."

"Cold? What is the matter with you? Your voice sounds strange . . ."

"No . . . I am all right . . ."

"I hope you won't become like Hameed?"

"What do you mean? What is the matter with Hameed?"

The Trunk explained by a suggestive gesture: he played his fingers near his temple.

"He went mad?" asked Saleh.

"Yes . . . his father keeps him locked up but one can hear his inhuman yells till the end of his street."

At this moment the door opened; Yasmeen appeared, holding a plate of cooked food and a loaf of bread. She smiled sweetly, and a mocking twinkle shone in her eyes when she faced the Trunk.

His eyes began to bulge, showing the extreme of astonishment. The usual coarse aggressive grumble began resounding in his chest. He scowled taking a step forward.

"Leave her . . . Trunk."

He stopped, completely confused, and turned to stare at Saleh, who looked back with a strange swift glance, a mixture of shame, regret, despair, and even fear. Then he looked down, avoiding his gaze.

Yasmeen entered, pushed herself past the Trunk, brushed her robe against him, scornfully shouted at him.

"What a poison!"

She gave Saleh the plate of food and the bread, then with an ostentatious sweetness she started talking to Umm Saleh.

"Oh! Poor Umm Saleh . . . No one took care of you today. Come . . . my dear . . . let's go and wash ourselves at the canal . . ."

She made her rise, pulling her up from under her armpits, and supporting her, step by step, they left.

"Does that mean . . . that you and her . . . ?" grumbled the Trunk, still disbelieving. Saleh nodded, confessing in shame, but he raised his eyes to the Trunk, appealing.

"You deserve the whip that flogged your back . . . they should have killed you with it . . ."

"You are right . . . now I deserve it . . ."

"How did it happen?"

"She came this morning and I was alone as you left me . . . and . . . well . . . what do you want me to explain, Trunk . . .

for something I didn't do . . . and she is a bold bitch . . . she didn't leave me till sunset . . . we hadn't time even to eat . . ."

Saleh was very pale, with beads of sweat shining on his forehead. He put himself between the door and his friend, facing him, preventing the other from leaving the hut.

"Please, don't leave me . . . don't be angry with me . . ."

The Trunk noticed that the eyes of his friend were suddenly wide open and moved strangely in quick shifts. The yellow glow of the kerosene lamp danced in their depth. He understood that his friend was in the verge of folly. He immediately stroked Saleh's cheek gently with his big paw. The other took his hand and they shook hands.

"Please don't go yet, Trunk . . . have dinner with me . . . ?"

"Why not, with pleasure . . ."

So when Yasmeen came back, she found them happily seated with the plate of food between them. Saleh immediately rose, taking hold of his mother's hand from her. The smiling Trunk was sending Yasmeen merry glances from his seat, fluttering his eyebrows. She turned and violently banged the door behind her.

CHAPTER

II

N ext day, Saleh went to ask for work. Early morning found him standing with the Trunk in front of the estate office building, just below its terrace. Saleh as usual leaned his back on the wall behind him, let his gaze wander in front of him. His eyes narrowed and his teeth clenched when his gaze fell on the mansion, far away, there beyond the empty yard, partly hidden by white morning fog. He pressed harder on his clenched teeth so as not to cry aloud as he remembered what happened. How he bore the mounting excruciating pain for a long time while an astonished look appeared in the eyes of his tormentors. Yet he knew that when his body practically lost its consciousness and its will it cried for mercy, promised to kiss their feet. He gazed at the mansion again. What a strange brutal force was hiding there behind its walls! Was it satisfied? Was it through with him, had it reached its aim? Or did it still lie there in wait for him? Which do you want more, he thought, that I kneel contented on my own accord, or that I become an animal like the rest of them? That I lose my power of thinking, that I give up my freedom, a beast amidst a herd of beasts? His eyes looked around him at the faces of the laborers gathered around him, their hard features, their empty eyes like beads of glass, their furtive glances that turned quickly in cowardly flight.

"You stupid beast!"

Saleh's eyes met those of the Catfish, and he was astonished to receive a smiling nod of pleasant greeting from him. He turned his head in contempt, without answering to the smile or the greeting. He said to himself, of course, with the appearance of dawn the whole village knows but you, that I have become Yasmeen's lover . . . you old worn-out slipper, dirty old rag. . . . Ah! Now here is Mahrous coming, with his head looking small on his huge body . . . twisting the points of his big mustache with his fingers, putting on a show of brute force, and around him a gathering of servile laborers, slightly bent, obsequiously shuffling their feet, opening the way for him to pass. Far off stand the sons of Sheikh Shaban's family grouped together. Like him they are considered black sheep, fear moving their entrails deep in them, though they pretend not to care, aloof, standing erect, their bodies showing their nakedness through the holes of their ragged clothes. They look desperately poor.

Saleh saw Abou Bakr in their midst. Oh, dear Abou Bakr, continuous misery and humiliation are beginning to affect you! Your body is thinner and your head is slightly bent. Where are your past proud looks and the fierce shine in your black eyes? Will they end by acquiring the tinge of empty bottles and the color of dust, like those of the Catfish?

Now comes Hassan Effendi; there is more shuffle of retreating feet, making way for him to pass. There he is, advancing happily, jumping from one foot to the other.

"Hee! Hee!" He laughed the way a horse would do when he saw Saleh, who received the jet of his saliva that merrily escaped from the hole of his missing front tooth. He curved his thumb and index finger, forming a circle to indicate precision with his hand, sending a loud kiss in the air at the same time.

"Beautiful, what a grand beautiful beating . . . exactly what was needed . . . I think you lost the desire to do . . . for ever. . . ."

And with a dirty middle finger he made a shameful gesture to explain what he meant. Everyone laughed in obsequious merriment. But the laughter stopped abruptly as Saleh answered in a loud, grave voice.

"I faced the beating and suffered under it like a man, Hassan Effendi, as long as I was conscious."

The merry face in front of him changed its color, the smile vanishing for a second. But he ordered Mahrous to join Saleh and the Trunk to the team of young men who were hoeing the newly planted corn.

When they returned from work at sunset they found the village in turmoil. The women were standing at the doorsteps of their huts babbling in sharp shrill voices. Hameed in his newly acquired madness had escaped from his father's house and had climbed the mansion's wall. The vast empty square yard which was bordered on one side by the mansion and on the other by the estate office building began to fill with men, their women following. Saleh and the Trunk joined them, running. They all stood at a respectful distance from the wall. Then their faces lighted in a hilarious merriment as they observed from the vast gate, now open, the Chief, Mahrous, Hassan Effendi, all the foremen, and a group of guards gathered around the trunk of a tree at the side of the main alley leading to the mansion. They were shouting at the top of their coarse husky voices every imaginable threat and warning, mingled with the vilest insults, while from inside the tree came the sharp giggling chirrup of Hameed, making fun of the men below, sending them mocking remarks in complete idiocy. The hilarious faces of the peasants lighted up more when they saw Abdullah, the savage tough guard of the mansion, climb the trunk of the tree and disappear in its foliage, which began to shake as if a storm was taking hold of its center. Leaves and small branches flew, while a mixture of shrieking, barking, coarse roars and thunderous grumbles overwhelmed the fierce voices of the guards and men at the foot of the tree. Suddenly the laborers hailed in utter joy, clapping, as the lithe body of Hameed appeared, climbing swiftly like a cat to the slender top of the tree. The guard Abdullah followed slowly. The Trunk fell on his back, legs up, holding his belly in uncontrollable laughter. Many workers could hardly find their breath, tears dribbling down their cheeks, the mirth shaking their very souls. At the same moment, from under the tree, came the chorus of harsh voices, the lion roar of the Chief, the bellowing of Mahrous, the neighing of Hassan Effendi, and the barking of the guards. The top of the tree began to swing. Abdullah stopped climbing and held the tree trunk tight so as not to fall, then Hameed threw away his clothes and appeared naked like a black kitten under the red glow of the setting sun, and directed his organ at the raised head of the guard, sending down on him a continuous jet of urine, the drops of which sparkled under the red light, filling the guard's nostrils.

Abdullah now began a slow cautious descent, retreating. But Hameed increased the swaying pendulum movement of the tree, so Abdullah stuck again to the trunk. The climax of the show came when the chief and his men fled like scared crows from under the tree, followed by the dirty missiles of Hameed, who had emptied his bowels in his hand and threw his excrement at them. They turned on the peasants who were rolling on the ground incapable of arresting their uncontrollable laughter.

"What are you laughing at . . . you sons of bitches!"

They chased them with raised canes, but their faces soiled with brown human excrement were enough to raise more laughter.

Hameed suddenly descended the tree, as swiftly as he had climbed it, slipped past Abdullah, and was out in the empty space. The guards followed him, but he vanished in the fields after circling many times among the groups of men. Late that night the village people were still shaken with bouts of laughter.

The village had lost its first singer but acquired a new jolly village idiot, the last one having died a year ago now.

Hameed did not return to his father's hut. He disappeared for a few days, then took refuge in a small abandoned room in a ruined house at the end of the village. He would roam the countryside all day. The laborers would see him pass on the road, talking to himself in an endless conversation, playing with a long bamboo stick above his head in continuous movement.

His voice, which once had been beautiful, would come to them with the breeze as a sharp chirrup. His face took on a strange ugliness, with hollow concave cheeks and deeply cast yellow eyes. If he noticed Mahrous, he would come at the edge of the field imitating his walk and playing with his fingers like Mahrous rolling an imaginary moustache. The men would hide their mirthful faces quickly in fear of Mahrous. The Head Foreman would take a few steps in the direction of Hameed with his cane raised. Hameed would run rapidly, and disappear, his sharp voice still giggling. It would echo a long time after he was gone. At night they would hear his tambourine beating strange songs which he accompanied with his shrill, out-of-tune voice, the tambourine being the only belonging that he had retrieved from his father's house. His father was the only one that cared for him. The old man would place a plate of food every night just at the door of the half-demolished room. A shaky hand would snatch it from underneath the door. His father was the only person whom Hameed feared and respected. He would tremble when he saw him, stopping as if paralyzed; then he would crawl at his father's feet like a dog. The old man would generally let him go, hiding his tears of sorrow. At other times he would punish Hameed severely if he went too far with his mad jokes. Then he would give him a dreadful punishment, hitting hard on his thin body with his club. One such occasion came on the day Hameed entered Guirguis Effendi's office and tore all the books, then poured the ink-pot on the clerk's head. Guirguis Effendi never totally recovered from his fright. He would turn in an uncontrollable movement of panic all the time, even if there was no one in the room. His wife confirmed that at night he had nightmares, raising his voice, while sleeping, in imitation of Hameed's sharp chirrup.

Hameed would yell but would accept his punishment. He would disappear for a few days, then one night the tambourine would resume its strange beating, accompanied by the shrill inhuman voice singing, and the village people would know then that Hameed was back. Some of them would sigh in sorrow, remembering the handsome fellow with the beautiful voice, who used to enchant them during the corn reaping season.

Saleh quickly regained his strength and health as if nothing had happened to him. It was only a matter of days before all traces of his black bruises and long wounds had healed, leaving only white filaments where the whip had cut deeply. He walked erect again with that springy, well-balanced gait, the shining glow of sunburn returning to his complexion.

Though he still perceived the well-hidden hostility of the estate's men and the village people, he soon got proof of Yasmeen's influence and power, and understood how right she was when she told him that she would protect him. One day during the noon resting period the Head Foreman raised his gruff voice summoning everyone back to work; the labourers protested, since he had allowed only fifteen minutes instead of the whole hour. He had received orders to be hard with the men and punish them because of their attitude during Hameed's show at the mansion gate.

So Mahrous walked on the road, lashing the sleeping men right and left with his bamboo cane as he passed, and Saleh, who was also sleeping, suddenly opened his eyes to see the cane descending with a hiss across his chest; he recoiled, already feeling the burning scorch on his body, when he saw in amazement the cane hesitating a fraction of a second, then catching the body of the Trunk beside him. His friend jumped from its sting and rubbed his ribs, cursing Mahrous, who was already far away. Saleh laughed happily, very pleased, when the Trunk said, "What a lucky chap you are . . . you son of a bitch, the Madam's thighs protect you."

The Trunk and Saleh were not the only two who noticed the quick movement of the bamboo cane and understood its meaning. And as news spread, the men sensed the change of wind and acted accordingly. Now the faces would return his greetings in a gentle polite way, their owners smiling in a friendly fashion. They would even volunteer to shake hands.

The only pair of eyes that turned away were those of the Catfish. When Saleh saw him avoiding his gaze for the first time, he understood that the old man finally had learned the truth, and he could not prevent himself from smiling wickedly at the other face, a nasty smile that carried a message of derision to the betraying cuckold. But he immediately was sorry for it, his conscience pricking him. The old man must be suffering like hell.

The village people were really surprised at the love affair between Yasmeen and Saleh blossoming openly after his deadly punishment.

The secret telegraph spread the most intimate details. But now they were only gossiping to pass time and had lost their dangerous attacking power.

The circumstances having changed completely, the important people concerned, and the first of them Mahrous, accepted the new situation, and so the village people followed, accepting it also, especially since the Catfish had made a terrible mistake that really could not be forgiven. Had he killed Saleh, he would have reaped the respect of the whole village, but to go and report him to the Palace made him a miserable dirty squealer. And after the terrible flogging Saleh acquired certain rights over the Catfish and Yasmeen. That he chose to take them by this method, well, it was his concern. The marks of the whip over his body had more value than a seal on a marital contract. Yasmeen was now his, and it was for the Catfish to leave her to him and divorce her.

The eyes of the gossips twinkled merrily at the detailed news, the hard wrinkled features moved a little in reprobation, the heads nodding; but they said gravely, "The boy is a dirty son of a bitch, it's true . . . but he has suffered a lot . . . and the Catfish wronged him tremendously. . . . He should leave her to him."

The lover gained his official position and became the owner of his marital rights. So Yasmeen ended by having two husbands, an abnormal situation, but the wrong part of it lay with the Catfish. Two husbands, laborers, in utter misery, the first an old man in rags, the second a young man, handsome but having only a rough brown sack that curtained his thighs half-way down and only partly covered his nakedness.

As regarded the sheer commercial aspect nothing was changed; on the contrary, Yasmeen's important clients understood that Saleh was only a mere Catfish, but a younger one, and presented no danger. They found in the cool satisfied Yasmeen a real artist, wishing really to please them with her body in every possible way in an effort to quench their ever-increasing appetite for lust and debauchery.

As for Yasmeen, for the first time in her life she was deeply moved and crying for love with her very soul. She craved Saleh's body with a mad desire that she had never felt for anyone. He aroused in her exactly the same sensations she aroused in others; a burning fire that moved the smallest fibre in her body, yet the moment it was fulfilled, it inflamed her again with an unquenchable passion of love for him.

From an early age she had learned to recognize the signs of desire and its different aspects, up to its madness, but always in others; she felt nothing, even after puberty. She became an artist in the profession of giving love without ever feeling it herself. She learned how to make a man crazy, and giving love to make him revolve his eyes by a tight twist of a muscle in her body here or there. But now it was her turn to feel her face brighten in extreme happiness from the mere sight of her man, as blood ascended to her complexion, burning her cheeks with a rosy red glow. She also wondered at how strange it was that the moment she touched his body even with one finger she felt her body quiver with a joyful urge for love. He, after that first day of love when Yasmeen conquered him, subjugated himself completely. His personality broke into two. One Saleh, deep in himself, observed Yasmeen with a hard look and admitted that she was a wonderful animal, a well-equipped machine for making love. He observed the second Saleh weeping in delightful pleasure. He also admitted that the second Saleh had a tremendous power for making love. He counted his achievements like a referee in a ring, and agreed that this Saleh was also a formidable sexual machine, a special bull of its kind, more powerful than the bull at the estate farm. But he was the special bull of the Madam. And so, while the second Saleh fell on his side exhausted, panting, contented, the other Saleh looked at him mockingly. He warned himself not to fail her ever, or the whip would surely put him straight and teach him his lesson.

Saleh at this moment would look at Yasmeen with fierce hatred, his eyes narrowing, despising himself too. But he usually sighed quickly in surrender, reclining flat on his back, looking at the ceiling in utter despair.

He resumed giving her his daily wages, which were not much, especially since they did not include Friday's wages. Yasmeen treated him harshly whenever they were not making love, hardly giving him more than what was absolutely necessary. He never was really hungry, but she did not give him anything extra. When she realized how much she loved him, her harsh treatment increased; she hid her feeling toward him, afraid that he would dominate her. She emphasized his poverty, the fact that he was only a laborer, a denuded one, and she the lady, and that he should be grateful and contented to be her obedient slave.

Sometimes she would deliberately delay her visit to him at sunset, and he would wait patiently at his doorstep, cross-legged near his mother. Smells of cooked food would come to him from the nearby houses, smells of spices, garlic, hot bread. Hunger would clench painfully at his stomach, yet he would wait in quiet patience. Now the stars were beginning to show, one after the other. He started to feel weary and restless, his hunger increasing. The day had been a long one, and hard; he had eaten a small piece of bread at noon and had had nothing else to eat from dawn till now. She really could have sent the food with Ahmed, her son. He would rise, enter his hut, return with the small pack of tobacco and roll a small thin cigarette. Hot smoke scorched his stomach, twisting it more. He turned his head, searching the darkness for any sign of her. Night had fallen now completely. Long laughter and merry conversations came to him from the neighboring houses, as tongues were set free in happy babbling, after bellies got full. He tried not to think of food, letting his long eyelashes fall over his eyes.

They say that the cotton plantations have been ruined by the cotton worm . . . they say the wages have gone down further. . . . Still no sign of her.

Sometimes many hours would pass this way. Then his face would light up: there she came . . . in a slow, springy, wavy motion, the plate of food and the loaf of bread in her hand. The lights of the open doors fell on her. The heavy gold pendant glittered on her long dress with its design of flowery patterns. The black veil emphasized the glowing white complexion of her face. Yasmeen usually sat down by his mother to feed her. So his anger would vanish and gratefulness take its place.

If ever he asked her, while eating, why she was late, she would casually skip over answering and move the conversation to another subject.

Sometimes her heart would melt when she looked at him, wiping the empty plate with the last piece of bread, making it shine. She knew that he was not quite full yet, still hungry, but she would keep quiet; she would hear him then drink a long drink from the jar, filling his stomach with water.

In general he would take his revenge during love-making,

penetrating her brutally, hurting her deeply with all the bursting power of youth. She would turn her wincing face, moaning of pain, while inside she cried of delight and joy. So one Saleh, deep inside himself, would observe her sternly in hate . . . while the other would weep of sweet, extreme pleasure.

Once he quarrelled with her. She really had come very late, so he shouted at her and insulted her. She slapped him. Terror took her when she saw his features changing in a frightening scowl of hate. He jumped at her, pulling at her hair, beating her brutally in a mad rage. She cringed under the heavy blows, screaming of pain; then she slipped from between his arms and fled to the street.

He was sorry immediately and ran after her, not caring about the neighbors who were coming out of their houses to look, delighted. He reached the end of his street but she had vanished. He came back, shivering, unnerved, his pupils dilated, engulfing most of the iris color. He passed an agitated night and went to work in the morning already exhausted from lack of sleep. She did not show up next day in the evening, so they had to sleep without dinner, he and his mother. He asked himself again and again what was to become of them. He grieved and repented over his sudden madness; how did he come to lose control of himself and beat her? Fear began to take hold of him . . . what would be the repercussions of her anger?

Next day the Trunk noticed that he did not eat at the noon rest. He asked him why. Saleh pretended he was not hungry, ashamed to tell him that he had no bread. At sunset he debated whether he should go to her house. He had not eaten for two days. He took his mother to the canal and washed her and her dirty soiled clothing. He felt nauseated. He came back with her, step by step, holding the old woman, afraid of collapsing before reaching his house. His heart leaped with joy: Ahmed was waiting at his doorstep. He came running when he saw Saleh, whose heart sank as he heard him say:

"Mother . . . sends the rest of your money, twenty piastres. . . ."

He gave him the money but Saleh called him and gave back the money, begging, "Please take back the money to her, tell her I am sorry. . . ." Then he added, hesitating a little, ashamed to tell such things to so young a boy, "Please tell her I'll kiss her feet when she comes. . . ."

He sat at his doorstep, leaning back against the wall. Then he saw the boy returning; but he passed him at a run, shouting with his shrill voice as he passed by him, "Mother said throw the money to him!!!"

He disappeared at the end of the street and Saleh saw in his lap, on the rough jute of his tunic, the piece of money. Despair and fear crept again into his heart. But he raised his head: there was the boy Ahmed returning again, the quick patter of his bare feet preceding him. He shouted again, passing swiftly in the other direction.

"Mother is at home . . . Father went to buy tobacco. . . ."

The small features of the little pimp smiled meaningly. Saleh was quicker than he in reaching Yasmeen's house. He found her milking the cow. She raised her head and turned to look at him. His heart sank; how could he have been so brutal? One of her cheeks was swollen and had a large red-blue bruise.

She hissed, though deep inside she was pleased, "Get out!"

"Yasmeen, please."

"Get out or I'll start screaming."

"Forgive me! It's my first mistake and the last one, I'll kiss your feet, but forgive me."

The little pimp interceded too, with a sincere emotion that made him cry, moved by Saleh's emotion.

"Mother, forgive Uncle Saleh, he is so sad!"

Yasmeen looked at her son and laughed, forgiving. "All right . . . go now to your house . . . I'll meet you there later."

Outside her house, mad with joy, he raised Yasmeen's boy Ahmed high up from the ground and kissed him fondly, gratefully, on both cheeks. She came, fascinatingly beautiful in spite of the marks of the blow, the plate of food and the loaf of bread in her hand. She put them on the low wooden table and laid it just at the feet of Umm Saleh.

Saleh seated himself too, and was preparing himself to eat when she reminded him, "I am waiting . . ."

She stood erect, with a slightly raised head, haughty. He turned, raising his head to her, astonished.

"What are you waiting for?"

"You promised you'd kiss my feet."

His face blanched.

"Are you serious? . . . Do you really want me to kiss your feet . . ."

She made a movement as if to turn to go out.

"No . . . wait . . ."

He knelt in front of her, embracing her legs. Then he said, smiling, begging, "It is . . . a shame . . . don't be serious about it . . ."

"And my beating, was it not a shame? Kiss my feet and don't raise your head unless I order you to. . . ."

He bent his head slowly and kissed her soft slippers. She remained quiet for a while, leaving his head bent. Then she grasped his hair, pulled it backwards, and with all her might she slapped him. He remained silent, closing his eyes. His face reddened deeply to the roots of his hair, then blanched to extreme pallor many times in succession; she slapped him again hard, but he remained quiet, raising his head, his long eyelashes covering the gleam of hatred. Shining drops of tears filled the long slits between their two rows. From that day onward he was careful not to shout at her or anger her in any way. The Trunk was surprised to note that his friend remained quiet all the time. He never gave the slightest hint of his love for Yasmeen, though for him, the Trunk, she represented the Woman, that most strange and beautifully charming animal, from whom he received only a touch here or there in the crowded market. He asked him . . . but wondered at the short sad tone of his friend's voice when he answered, as if he was hiding a deep sorrow inside him.

"You look tired."

"Yes I am."

"Yasmeen passed last night with you?"

"Yes."

"Does she sleep with you every night?"

"Yes, almost . . ."

One day Yasmeen asked Saleh why he never spoke about the little sheep. He looked away so she would not read anything in his face. She told him to bring it back so she could sell it in the market. He obeyed but sent the Trunk in his place, since he could not face Maamour. Once he saw Zeina; she stood in his way and looked at him. There was so much sadness in her eyes that he could say nothing to her. He knew that she must have heard about his relationship with Yasmeen. Meanwhile the Trunk had bought back the sheep and Yasmeen appropriated it.

"The shepherd wouldn't give it to me," said the Trunk. "He insulted you . . . cursed the estate and everything in it. He was choking with rage. . . ."

Saleh flinched but said nothing; Yasmeen assumed that he was distressed because she had said she would sell the sheep.

One evening the Trunk could not believe his ears when Saleh asked him simply, in his grave slow manner, not to visit him any more at his house. Yasmeen did not wish to see him there. And Saleh turned away and entered his street, leaving his friend scowling, boiling with rage.

For the next few days the Trunk deliberately avoided greeting him or standing beside him in the early morning gathering of workers. But he would still steal a glance at him from time to time. There he was alone, leaning, as usual, his back against the wall below the terrace of the estate office building; standing on one foot, with the other leg bent against the wall, his head always looking at the dust by his bare foot.

During the noon rest, the Trunk would laugh loudly in an ostentatious way, so that Saleh would hear him cracking jokes with fellow laborers.

Pretending not to look at Saleh, but actually observing him all the time from the corner of his eye, the Trunk wondered about him. Saleh had never been a talker but now he was always silent. There he was sitting alone under a tree, a little apart from anyone, chewing a small piece of bread carefully, slowly. Although the expression of his handsome face seemed relaxed, he never smiled any more.

His long powerful muscles flowed from the opening of his old jute garment, inspiring respect and admiration in their graceful arrangement. But the old sack that partly covered his naked body gave him a look of utter indigence. The Trunk's heart melted in sympathy for his friend. He could not continue this game of giving him a cold shoulder, so he went to him and sat by his side. Saleh turned slowly and quietly greeted him. The Trunk started reproaching him.

"How could you forbid me from visiting your house?"

He answered in his simple quiet way. "But I did not. . . . It's Yasmeen that said so . . ."

The Trunk understood that he had surrendered, not only his body, but his soul to Yasmeen and that behind his apparent relaxed expression there was despair and grief.

Beginning of autumn. A light breeze passed over the field, making the trees quiver from the rustling of their leaves. The sky took a lovely turquoise colour and in its depth sailed huge ships of white clouds travelling to faraway countries. The men of the field would raise their heads to look at the flocks of ducks flying high up in the sky towards the horizon. They would hear them calling at them when they passed over their heads. Then the wind rose blowing in the valley and the trees cried. The casuarinas wailed, more. . . . But a new life began to burgeon in the small branches under the cool breath of the wind.

At night the full moon poured white shining chalk on the roads, and under its kind touch the cotton balls cracked open.

In one of the days at the beginning of autumn an awful calamity befell the people of the estate. They had been expecting it for some time and yet they were painfully struck by it when it happened.

Saleh was working at the cotton harvest late that afternoon. His job was to carry the cotton bales, huge sacks that the pickers had filled, from the fields to the nearby road, and load them into the trailers that would transport them to the warehouses near the estate's office building. Saleh was listening to the happy songs of the children in choruses emulating themselves, feeling that this crop, the white gold, was goodness itself and and that the beatings of the cane every now and then, their suffering, could not prevent them from making a feast out of the harvesting. Saleh was just starting to run with the huge cotton bale on his bent back, his legs shaking from the heavy load, when the voices of the children came to an abrupt stop. An abnormal, dead silence fell over the fields. He raised his head slightly, still bent, and saw on the main road where he was heading, Younes Effendi tying his horse to the branch of a tree and then coming toward him. He immediately let go his bale and placed himself cautiously behind it, at a good distance from Younes and the short leather whip that dangled nervously from his hand. But Younes's eyes burned with a strange yellow flame. His face had become thinner and paler, giving its moth-eaten complexion a yellow, really ugly look.

"What an ugly son-of-a-bitch face," said Saleh between his teeth.

He was feeling, like the rest of the workers, an awful apprehension that something was about to happen now. Sheikh Shaban had just announced the engagement of his son Abou Bakr to his cousin, Ali's sister Haneya. He had also decided the date of the marriage, hastening it in order to stop all rumors. There were only a few days left before the marriage was to take place. The secret telegraph of the village ascertained that Younes Effendi fell into a mad rage when he heard the news and that there had been some secret rendezvous at the old abandoned water wheel near Sheikh Shaban's land.

They say that Younes Effendi wanted to go to the Sheikh and ask for his niece, but the Chief advised him against it as he would certainly be refused, and then also because that would mean the end of his job at the estate, with unpredictable consequences for him. Old, dreadful, long-forgotten files might suddenly emerge in the open. . . . The Chief also pointed out to him that the girl was still a child, happy to flirt and play with such an important man in the estate; she was flattered, but if it came to marriage she would certainly prefer her cousin.

The mouths of the men around opened in awed fearful anticipation, as Younes Effendi, striding rapidly, came toward Abou Bakr, who stood, erect, pale-faced, but haughty by the side of a cotton bale that he was going to carry like Saleh to the trailers on the main road. No one heard what they said to each other. Suddenly the fist of Younes Effendi landed with tremendous force on Abou Bakr's nose; and he fell on his back. He remained in this position for a split second, stunned, blood dribbling from his nose. Then he jumped at Younes Effendi, but all the foremen and even Mahrous separated them, holding Abou Bakr. He fought with them, but he was held from behind by the others, with his lower belly arched and protruding. Younes Effendi took advantage of this to kick him viciously. Abou Bakr doubled with his knees coming up to his chest and the hands held him as though seated above the ground. But then his head fell and he became limp, losing consciousness completely. All this happened in few seconds, the laborers gaping, paralyzed. Then from the adjoining corn field came some of the relatives of the Sheikh Shaban family running, their hoes raised. All the men in the adjoining fields joined them in revolt.

Mahrous whispered to Younes, "Quick, ride your horse."

Younes turned and began to run. He passed near Saleh who automatically advanced his foot. Younes Effendi fell flat on his face. Saleh was on him, holding him, trying to prevent his escape till the men could join him. They fought fiercely, but Younes managed to slip between his hands and started to run again. Saleh could have caught up with him, but his violent revolt had suddenly cooled down. He was sorry now that he had become involved in a situation that was of no concern to him. He escaped from the lash of one of the foremen and quickly returned to his bale, preparing himself for the task of lifting it again. But at this moment the workers from the corn field had arrived and surrounded Abou Bakr, who was beginning to regain consciousness.

Mahrous raised his cane as usual, bellowing, "Every one return to his work you sons of bitches . . ." And he started to shout his usual mixture of threats and vile insults. But he lowered his cane slowly, turned, began to increase his speed, and then started to run at great speed till he reached his donkey on the main road. After the flight of Mahrous all the foremen vanished in the landscape around, while the laborers gathered on the main road. Saleh joined them, their excitement gaining hold of him. He saw the Trunk in their midst. They all marched on the road like a small army, raising their hoes or their fists, yelling threats at the estate administration. . . . Yet the more they advanced and approached the village the cooler they got. Saleh noticed one of the men ducking into a bush, another leaving on a side road. At the entrance of the village they had melted into a small group, most of them from Sheikh Shaban's family.

The Trunk and Saleh exchanged glances, then they slipped away also, entering the first side street they came to.

Under the terrace stood about twelve guards with their guns in their hands. Younes Effendi was on the terrace beside the Chief, his horse tied to the balustrade. The remainder of the now very cool army yelled, as if in one voice, the ceremonial greeting as they marched past:

"Peace be with you, your Lordship, peace, God's grace and blessings be with you, your Lordship!!!"

Of course the Chief, as usual, did not answer, but Gaith answered bluntly on behalf of everyone present.

"And peace be with you."

In the village most of the men faced the wrath of their women, who wailed, wept, and shouted at them alternately. Some of them started beating their husbands. Was not life sufficiently difficult, that they had to be foolish enough to get involved in other people's business!

Yasmeen was cooking dinner and had a long metal scoop in her hand. When news came to her, narrating in full detail what Saleh had done to Younes Effendi, she galloped in utter rage to his house and fell on him with the scoop; he raised his arms to protect his head, but received a few nasty blows. He begged, "All right I was mad, I know I was wrong. It is a shame, Yasmeen . . . enough, enough . . ."

He slipped past her, running to the Trunk's house. Sounds of blows and agitated screams reached him from there too, so he fled to the little mud platform on the bank of the canal under the willow tree, his little mosque.

Younes was leaving, untying his horse, when Mahrous whispered to him again, "Be cautious Younes Effendi . . . you have overstepped and done what is not allowed. . . . I beg you, for your own safety, starting from tonight, send someone to ask for a peaceful settlement of the quarrel . . ."

Younes did not answer. He shrugged his shoulders and was on his horse galloping again. Late that night Younes Effendi extinguished his cigarette, and the room fell into darkness. He opened the window shutters a little. The moon sent a ray of light through it. A strange gleam in his eyes shone when he placed his face at the slit of the opened shutter, looking at the black masses outside in the middle of the white shining spaces. The village looked quiet. Some dogs barked lazily, unconvinced, at a passing shadow, high up in the air. . . . He took his revolver, opened it in the light of the moon ray and inserted a bullet in its muzzle; then he closed it with a snap. He weighed it in his hand; quite a heavy one . . . but well balanced. He returned to the window for a last look before closing it again. Everything looked quiet. In the dark he felt his way to his small barn. The horse greeted him by neighing and flattening its ears. He saddled it, took it out, and was awed by the stillness of the night. He jumped on the horse, lightly as usual, and started to ride quickly but noiselessly, as if the horse knew that its owner wanted the cover of the night and its silence. He chose to ride in the depth of the tree shadows, cautiously, inspecting the way, often turning to see if he was followed; but he saw nothing.

Once or twice he asked himself if he had not glimpsed the naked shadow of a man disappearing behind a tree trunk.

"Those son-of-a-bitch peasants always walk naked at night so that their white clothes won't point to them."

He stopped listening, inspecting the darkness; not a movement, not a sound.

He resumed his slow cautious ride. He found the old water wheel, lifting its wooden arms from its metal parts. He tied his horse, stood listening again, then pushed his body between the two arms and seated himself. The night was quiet and beautiful.

The full moon gently touched everything and poured its shining light over the fields. A peculiar, unreal sight; as if all things were raised in space, silver colored. His heart felt heavy, full of anguish, sadness and sorrow.

There he was, Younes Effendi, waiting for a mere peasant girl; behind him lay the past history of his life, full of debauchery and utter recklessness, and the present was oppressive and painfully disheartening. The future . . . dark and terrifying. He brooded for a minute about his ill fate.

Then he saw the picture of Abou Bakr filling his imagination, as he had seen him today. Erect, pale, with deep love showing in his eyes. His voice had quivered when he said quietly, "No, Younes Effendi, I cannot leave her. I love her and she is of my own flesh and blood . . ."

Why had he thrown his fist at him in a mad gesture? Pity . . . he felt sorry. . . . He remembered Mahrous's whisper, and he regretted that he had not asked for permission to apologize to Sheikh Shaban. The good man would have received him and pardoned him and then protected him. What a pity! It was always his bad temper that dominated at the end. But he laughed happily inside him when he remembered the vicious kick: how it crushed the soft parts under the thick sole of his boot. A short laugh shook him as he congratulated himself.

"I think the groom will postpone the wedding night forever. . . ."

Suddenly he heard the crack of a twig. He was all attention, his muscles taut. He touched his pistol; Haneya? The horse neighed loudly in excitement. He took out his revolver, half rising, turning and looking in every direction, piercing the dark shadows of the trees around, listening. No one . . . probably a wild cat roaming around . . . he relaxed, pushing himself again into his seat between the two arms of the water wheel, smiling happily at the lovely image of Haneya when it came to his mind. His face kept the smile while his head was suddenly severed from the body at the neck by the sharp edge of the sickle with a terrible blow. The body without its head remained seated, relaxed, pushed in between the two arms of the water wheel.

On the second day, at noon, the corpse was discovered by one of the estate guards in the same relaxed seated position, as if still waiting quietly. The guard was attracted by the neighing of the horse, then he saw the body . . . and for a long minute his mind refused to receive the image . . . not believing his eyes. Younes Effendi sits without his head. Then he understood, and retreated . . . then he turned and fled, running at full speed, terrified. . . .

The Chief looked at the sky, his eyelids drooping, nearly closing them. The palm of his hand opened as if in prayer.

"Poor Younes . . . !!!" Then, smiling widely, he ordered, "Call the police."

He understood that this news meant his victory and the end of Sheikh Shaban. Everyone in the village understood it too, when they heard that the police had imprisoned the male members of his family. That evening, at the police headquarters near the train station, the Chief and his whole staff came to proceed with the questioning.

Men and women stood at their doorsteps, sad, silent. The breeze they received carried faintly the waves of the high-pitched dreadful cries.

It moved their entrails inside out.

Saleh too, sat in silence; the Trunk, for the first time since Yasmeen forbade it, came and was seated by his side at his doorstep. They listened quietly. There was no chant calling for prayer from the nearby mosque.

On the second day the men went to the field exhausted from passing a sleepless night. They would stop working, straightening their bent backs, hearing. . . . Saleh too, at his work lifting cotton bales, would suddenly stop to listen, pale-faced, hardly finding his breath, panting. . . .

On the third day at dawn a terrible quietness took over the whole village. Now the breeze did not carry any other sound but the rustling of leaves, so everyone knew that the investigation had ended. The killers had confessed. Abou Bakr and Ali were found guilty and transferred under escort to the main prison of the capitol for their trial.

Yasmeen asked Saleh that night why he looked so exhausted and pale. He turned his head away from her, answering quietly.

"No, nothing that really matters. . . . I feel fine . . ."—but two small drops of tears rolled down his cheeks.

A whole week passed and the village forgot about Abou Bakr and Ali. Saleh's main concern was to work harder . . . to give more at it than was really asked from him, to please the foremen, so they would say that he was a good fellow, a hard worker, and maybe then the estate administration would forget about his previous attitude toward the late Younes Effendi . . . Yasmeen now came to pass every night with him. She could not bear to stay away from him, even for only one night. But she came very late, after she had given Mahrous or the others what they asked for; and she would leave before dawn.

He usually was fast asleep, lying on the ground of the small empty barn of his house, when she would slip under the rough sack and awaken him by the warm contact of her naked generous body on his skin. However tired he felt, he would embrace her tightly, rolling over her, and violently penetrate deep into her, with a continuous always renewed vigor. In the morning, before leaving his hut, he would notice his mother crying silently. At this hour she was usually already seated under the small window, reclining a shoulder and her head against the wall.

Many times by the grey light of dawn he noticed the tears rolling on her wrinkled cheeks. He knew then that in glimpses of consciousness she had heard and understood what was going on in the next room between Yasmeen and him, and that she was grieving for him, worrying about him. So he would turn back and come to her and kiss her on the forehead, asking in this silent way for her forgiveness.

One morning he felt unusually moved by the tears shining on her face. He came to her and kissed her on the forehead. Though his touch was very light he was most surprised to see her head slide down along the wall against which it had been reclining, and fall to her chest. Then the whole body followed and crumpled down on the ground in a heap. He knew by the abnormal angle of her neck that she was dead.

He went out, gently closing the door behind him, and walked to Yasmeen's house. On his way he crossed paths with the Catfish going to work. He received from him a nasty look from the dust-coloured eyes. He did not care. Yasmeen was really surprised when he entered her house at this hour; she immediately knew that something very important must have happened, and shouted at him anxiously as he stood in front of her, silent, a little pale.

"What's the matter? . . . Come on, say it."

He answered in a cool, matter-of-fact way, "Mother is dead."

She raised her eyes in utter astonishment, disbelieving because he was not even crying, but she saw the pallor of his face. She jumped and ran to his house. He followed her slowly, and before he arrived he could hear her wailing.

The Trunk and some of the men volunteered to bring a coffin from the mosque, and Yasmeen arranged with the women to buy a shroud. The Trunk helped Saleh prepare an awning for the funeral feast, and Yasmeen gave him a garment to wear. The smell of phenol, an antiseptic, filled his nostrils: the garment belonged to Khalil, the male nurse.

The funeral procession started around noon. From his bamboo chair the Chief saw it coming, and remarked to Guirguis Effendi, "I hope God gives you a longer life, Guirguis; Suleiman Hawari's wife is bidding us farewell."

He stood up, and with a regretful glance at his comfortable chair, went to join the procession cortege. Saleh walked behind the coffin as he had done when his father died. He asked himself whether it was his mother in the coffin or his father. Somehow the funeral had the reality of an old dream. The same slow respectful steps; the same mourners chanting, "God is great," the same faint smell of putrefaction.

That evening began the hotly disputed match, the same exactly as he had seen played few months ago. It began with the race between Chief Abdul Meguid and Sheikh Maamoun over the cooked goose and its mountain of rice. Yasmeen had sent two servings on two trays. The Catfish was sitting in front of one of them and of course he was obliged to ask Mahrous to join him. The other tray, a little more generous, was for Saleh, and automatically Khalil the male nurse invited himself and joined him. All the men present nodded their heads in agreement; this was really a very diplomatic way of acting, a smooth compromise between the two husbands, of which everyone approved. The balance of course was a little more in Saleh's favor . . . as his tray was somewhat larger . . . but that also was understandable and correct.

Saleh quickly picked a piece of bread and started chewing it to prevent the nervous laughter that was about to manifest itself loudly when he heard the high loud belch rising from the over-filled Chief's stomach, announcing the end of the match: the same belch he had heard a few months ago.

Then came the same moment of happy digestion, the chanting of the holy Koran giving the mind and the body the necessary relaxation.

Later that night, after the mourners had left, Saleh accompanied Sheikh Maamoun to Mahrous's house where he had been invited to pass the rest of the night. Then he returned to his hut.

In the middle of the room he stopped, hesitating, his eyes swiftly looking for his mother; the corner was empty. He frowned, clenching his teeth hard so as not to cry. . . . He left the room and entered the small empty barn. When he lay down on the floor, his body touched the nakedness of Yasmeen. She was already there. His hands went over her, caressing her. She protested. "No, not tonight."

He agreed and repeated, "True . . . not tonight."

But he was rolling over her and with a quick move threw the phenol-impregnated clothes away from his body, while she protested, "No, by the grace of God, it's not done . . ."

His voice became husky and coarse, rattling harshly, while he penetrated her brutally.

"Yes, you are right . . . by God it's not done."

Her moaning continued, increasing in intensity. . . .

He went to work the next day. When he came back to his house he was struck with astonishment at what he saw: the door of his house was barred from the outside, a heavy new black lock closing it. His few pieces of furniture were thrown on the ground in a heap . . . the small low wooden table, his straw mat, the lamp, the basin, the clay jar, his mother's wooden trunk where she had kept her few rags and some of his old books. He gazed stupidly around him, dazed. An old neighbor volunteered to inform him.

"The guard Gaith came and threw your things out . . . and locked the door."

The estate had reclaimed the hut. The administration built houses for the workers to live in as long as they were working on its land. He understood: they had waited for his mother's death to execute a decision taken a long time ago when his father died.

He walked fast to Yasmeen's house, in panic; jumped over the head of the Catfish; and entered her house, crying out loudly.

"Yasmeen . . . Gaith threw my things out in the street and locked the door of my house . . ."

She frowned, looking surprised and angry; suddenly her expression changed and she shouted at him, warning him.

"Saleh, take care . . . you old fool!!!"

The Catfish, behind him, was raising his hoe. He would have

cracked Saleh's head from behind if Saleh had not turned swiftly and ducked, avoiding the blow. Saleh caught the hand holding the hoe, twisting it. The old man scowled with pain, his short bowed legs kicked the air, not reaching him. . . . He let go the hoe. Yasmeen screamed, "Leave him, Saleh . . . leave him . . ."

Saleh shouted at the old man's face.

"Don't be afraid . . . I won't take your house, but don't try again any of your dirty tricks, I warn you!!! I'll blow your head if . . ."

Then with a powerful push he sent the old man flying backward. He stopped when his back collided with the wall at the end of the room. Dust fell all over him. Saleh turned back, getting out.

"Wait . . . sit at the doorstep," ordered Yasmeen, so he went out and sat, leaning his back on the wall just at the entrance. The Catfish also came silently and sat like him but on the other side. Yasmeen placed a small plate of cooked food and a loaf of bread in front of each man. The Catfish opened his big mouth and began to chew in a powerful regular way, while Saleh did not touch his plate. Yasmeen shouted at him.

"Come on, my boy . . . eat!"

Saleh sighed and began to eat.

Then Yasmeen ordered the small boy Ahmed to go and call Mahrous. After a while his huge stature appeared, his long white robe flying majestically around him, his impressive, slightly protruding belly preceding him. The neighbors sitting at their doorsteps on the other side of the street jumped to their feet, calling him with various "Be my guest . . ." greetings. The Catfish and Saleh stood with their heads slightly bent in respect. Mahrous entered, stooping a little to avoid hitting the top of the entrance with his head, and went to the end of the room to sit on the straw mat. The Catfish obsequiously fetched a cotton cushion and propped it behind his back. . . . Saleh went to sit on the other side of the room, bowing his face. Yasmeen coyly presented Mahrous with tea, then seated herself beside him, laughing, complimenting him, joking with him. Suddenly the smile vanished and she asked, her face angry and hard:

"Why did you take the boy's house . . ."

Mahrous sent her a quick glance which contained regret, a prayer, and even a little fear.

"By God I did not know myself. When I heard about it I sent for

Gaith . . . and he told me . . . the reason. This . . . dirty . . . son of a bitch . . . doesn't know how to behave even now . . ."

The "bitch" whose funeral Mahrous had attended the day before . . . but he pursued:

"Imagine, my dear Yasmeen, that this . . . (a very dirty insult) . . . this . . . hit Younes Effendi and threw him flat on the ground . . . and tore his shirt . . ."

He stopped talking after embroidering his speech with the vilest insults aimed at Saleh, who kept quiet, bending his head in shame, red-faced, because of the shocking insults thrown at him in front of Yasmeen, the children, and the Catfish.

"Younes is dead!" said Yasmeen.

"Yes, but the story was repeated and what he did was reported . . ."

And with a gesture of his hand toward the ceiling he meant that it was reported to the highest authorities at the Palace.

"Orders came from high up to regain his hut and throw him out . . . I went myself to the Chief, who was angry that he had been overpassed; the orders came directly to the head of the guard, so we went and pleaded for this son of a bitch . . . naked ass. . . . We said that he was like a mule . . . an idiot, an animal . . . all muscles with no brains . . . and that it was a pity to make him lose them by obliging him to sleep in the open air . . ."

"And so," interrupted Yasmeen anxiously, afraid now.

"Well, the orders just came to allow him to have the old demolished house at the end of the village . . ."

Saleh raised his head and cried out, outraged, protesting.

"Hameed's hole!!!?"

"Yes, you son of a bitch . . . yes, you . . . the house is crumbling, that's true but there is still one good room. . . . you could put straw on its roof and consolidate its walls with some mud bricks and clean it up . . . it's better than open air. . . . And Hameed has no right to occupy it . . ."

Yasmeen gratefully agreed.

"That is true."

So Mahrous said to him, "In any case . . . you will be someone with a house of your own. . . . Or maybe you prefer to live on the market's garbage and sleep at night in the open air . . . and if you go straight . . . minding your own business . . . hard at work, maybe in a year or two you may be allowed to return to your house. The Chief has permitted you to work at it tomorrow with a laborer of your choice, and he even ordered me to give you some wood and straw and even a door; what do you want more?"

"Yes, you are right. . . . Come, Saleh, and thank your Uncle Mahrous," said Yasmeen gratefully.

Saleh got up and went to Mahrous, knelt, and placed a kiss on the big rough dark hand of the Head Foreman, who in return slapped him with a powerful blow on his naked nape with the palm of his other hand, as a sign of a domineering yet friendly satisfaction.

Saleh passed the night in the street, guarding his few heaps outside his previous home. He could not find sleep; he pressed his almost naked body against the wall, trying to avoid the damp cold of the falling dew.

The Head Foreman allowed the Trunk to be the laborer who would repair the small single room in the abandoned, crumbling house with Saleh.

Saleh and the Trunk worked at it the whole day. At first they could not even enter it, wondering how poor Hameed could. There was a huge nest of big wasps just at the entrance. It was a difficult and dangerous task to get rid of it, but they succeeded by covering their heads with a sack and some rags, then introducing a gasoline-soaked piece of burning cloth attached to a long pole into the nest and burning it. At the end of the day, the filthy, nauseating smell had vanished and the walls were painted with a fresh layer of mud from the canal. The floor was cleaned and sprinkled with dry clean dust. Saleh's old torn straw mat had been washed and laid on the floor.

They added some missing beams to the roof and covered it with dried corn stalks and straw, and above it all dried cotton-wood branches. That roof could not keep out heavy rain but it was all right. There was a door now that could be closed from the inside with a bar.

Saleh smiled when he put his trunk in the corner. Yasmeen came many times to watch what was going on. When the setting sun threw its gentle red rays glowing on the straw roof, Yasmeen was pleased. She even kissed the Trunk on his mud-splashed face, inducing in him such a commotion that Saleh laughed at him, heartily happy.

Late that night Saleh was dozing. He had not locked the bar catch, so that Yasmeen could open the door from the outside. He heard it squeak, opening slowly. He smiled, waiting for her warm body to glide on his. But the sweet warmth was late to manifest itself, just a split second more than it should have been. So he opened his eyes, and by the moonlight coming from the open door he saw the sharp iron end of a hoe shining over his head, descending like lightning with a terrible speed. He recoiled and the sharp edge of the hoe cut his straw mat and penetrated deeply in the ground at the exact spot where his head had been. He jumped at the shadow above him, but the other plunged his teeth into his neck, biting him savagely. Yet he had a frail, weak body and immediately fell on the ground screaming under Saleh's heavy blows.

It was Hameed's voice, crying of pain. He rolled on the ground, trying to escape, but Saleh held him tight, hitting him brutally. The teeth of the madman snapped in the air repeatedly, missing their bite, while Saleh went on beating him harshly. The whole village knew then from the continuous inhuman yells that Saleh was giving poor mad Hameed a terrible punishment.

Yasmeen was awakened by the horrible cries and listened for a while in sadness. When she could bear it no more, she quickly ran to Saleh's room. She begged him but he refused to stop the beating, as if he intended to tear Hameed apart. But she begged again and again of him.

"For God's sake, stop it . . . you shouldn't."

He finally obeyed and she sat beside him. He was shaking all over, panting . . . while the moans of the madman grew fainter and fainter as he went away. She reproached Saleh gently.

"You shouldn't have . . . it's a sin."

She felt his hot palms running over her body, undressing her, caressing her; she abandoned herself, still reproaching and protesting, weeping sincerely.

"You should not have . . . it's a sin."

He was already over her, violently taking her, when his voice answered, getting coarse and husky.

"You are right . . . it is a sin."

She stopped sobbing and groaned loudly.

The bright blueness in the sky took a deeper tone. The flowers of autumn blossomed, the cool breeze carried a reviving green fragrance. The tall reeds along the canal sent their white fluffy seeds to fly with the wind in every direction, making people sneeze.

Days became shorter and nights longer. The cotton picking ended and so did the rice harvesting. The land offered its naked surfaces, and the plows penetrated it, reviving its fertility. Saleh worked behind two great bulls, his muscles knotting in hard round masses as he pushed on the plow with all his force, opening the good black earth, turning up its entrails. Then he worked at the wheat sowing. He marched erect, slightly arched, with his broad chest meeting the wind. He threw the seeds with a great gesture of the arm. The fresh breeze, the smell of the black earth presenting its plowed entrails, the beautiful act of the hand sowing, all that gave him an intoxicating, nearly sexual pleasure.

But the charm ended with the sunset, when he slowly returned to his hut, alone. The Trunk was giving him a cold shoulder because of what he had done to Hameed. Satisfying Yasmeen, pleasing her, loving her, that was his only aim, she was everything to him now. She represented the piece of bread that he received from her hand gratefully and the quenching of his sexual desire that was his only true pleasure.

This Friday, he was lying by her side; they had passed together a whole night. It was nearly noon, he felt happily empty, with a numbness quieting all his senses like the sweet intoxication of opium.

He looked at her, letting his gaze wander over the curves of her beautiful body. The white of her complexion glowed in the soft light that came from under the door, as there was no window in his little room.

He went over her with his big brown hand, caressing her, then he suddenly stopped, puzzled.

She turned and smiled, her cheeks coloring a little.

"It is yours . . ."

He gave a short laugh.

"You are pregnant."

"I swear by God's name it is yours . . ."

"How can you be sure . . . ?"

"I am sure . . . there is no doubt about it."

He kept quiet, so she asked him.

"Are you pleased . . . "

He smiled a really poor smile but he nodded, saying yes.

She caressed the rim of his ear slowly with one finger.

"I wanted always to have a child with such a small ear . . ."

What made him want to ask for such an impossible, absolutely mad demand? His voice quivered as he asked:

"If it's a boy . . . I want you to teach him how to read and write, send him to school; you are rich . . . you can afford it."

Small bells chimed as she laughed, merrily sarcastic.

"You are really crazy. What did you gain yourself? Do you really want him to go hoeing cotton with books under his arm?"

He kept quiet . . . disturbed and disappointed.

From that day onward, he was suddenly gentle with her during the act of love, penetrating her slowly and smoothly, not with deep, brutal, violent embrace. He took his pleasure and gave hers as if she was something most precious that could break between his hands. With time she also did not come every night as she used to, but spaced her visits more and more as time went by.

Now the weather was really cold at night, and Saleh complained of it to Yasmeen. Though there was no window in his small room, the piercing cold found its way through thousands of small holes in the straw roof to his naked body, doubled up shivering in a corner.

His short tunic made of an old sack could hardly protect him, but when he complained to Yasmeen, she only gave him another sack. Yet he thanked her gratefully, crouching like a ball inside it.

C H A P T E R

12

A few days before a harsh cold wind had risen and blown for a day or two; the sky went yellow and so did the people's faces. It returned now with renewed fierceness. Saleh's teeth clattered and his body inside his sack trembled painfully. He was anxious for fear the straw roof might fly away with the wind. A little before dawn it calmed for a while, so he could sleep; but the wind came back again and met him with full force as he was standing in front of the estate's offices, jumping from one foot to the other. Ah! the pain he felt ascending from the soles of his bare feet! The frozen ground pricked them deeply. If he tried to warm his hands by blowing his breath in his palms, the wind would go under his tunic, raising it up, leaving him naked to the waist . . . and a thousand lashes would be of benefit to scorch his shivering body. He would get his hands down quickly, trying in vain to hold the short tunic in place in an attempt to appear decent in front of the other workers who gathered nearby, men, women, children, girls and boys of all ages, who came to beg for work.

Ah . . . the pain . . . the suffering . . . the humiliation . . . when would it all end? His gaze turned to the high walls in spite of himself. What an awful power lay crouching behind them . . . he shivered strongly, and thought: The trees around the Palace are threatening me with their agitated branches like arms moving nervously in menacing gestures. . . . Ah! . . . What do you still want from me? I offer by body and flesh willingly every day and my eyes never let the foremen out of their sight . . . my heart has become hard and pitiless . . . my mind only thinks about you . . . how can I please you more?

His attention was drawn by the shrill voice of Hassan Effendi. His mouth, still smiling, threw jets of white vapor from the hole of his missing front tooth instead of the usual saliva. He advanced with his funny gait, dancing and jumping, but inside a thick overcoat. He was wearing woolen gloves and his head and neck were carefully covered. He picked a man here, another there, . . . the old Catfish, and that was all. He climbed the stairs of the terrace. The men protested, begging "Hassan Effendi . . . and the rest of us . . . ?"

"There is no work . . . is it my fault? . . . I wish you all happiness . . . good-bye!!!" The men scattered, their abdominal muscles contracted like hard square columns in wait for the days of hunger to come. In wintertime there was little work to do at the estate: perhaps a house destroyed by showers of rain to be repaired, or a broken fence. Even January was a cruel and hard month though one could find work in the canals which now were emptied of their water. They had to be cleaned of their weeds and mud deposits, but it was a very hateful job, as the men shivered all day long, naked in the cold mud.

Saleh went to Yasmeen.

The moment she saw him, she shouted at him.

"Go and find work! If you don't, you won't eat!!!"

He protested apologetically. "But it's not my fault . . ."

"I don't care . . . that's your problem! No money . . . no food. I warn you . . ."

He was appalled by her cruelty; his voice quivered with anger.

"You owe me money, where is the price of the little sheep?"

"Go to hell . . . and the price of the shroud? And Sheikh Maamoun's fees? Was it my mother or yours who died . . . ?"

He turned away, afraid to lose his temper, avoiding a quarrel.

Like the rest of the workers, he went to catch fish in the muddy drains, but as everyone else was doing the same, the fish vanished too. He remained long hours in the cold, freezing mud and rarely caught a small fish, the size of a finger. To stop his hunger, he thought of cooking some herbs as some peasants did, but it seemed he was not used to them or was inexperienced in choosing them, since they caused gripings in his intestines, turning them inside out. He passed the whole night running to the empty space behind the village, suffering from severe diarrhea.

Then one night Yasmeen would come with a loaf of bread and a hot plate of cooked rice in her hand. He would nearly weep with immense gratitude. His face radiant, he would then give her pleasure . . . carefully . . . gently . . . as her pregnancy showed more and more.

That was why if Yasmeen had asked him to kiss the ground she treaded on, he would have done it willingly. Now he understood why the work at the estate barn was so much appreciated by the peasants. How right had the Trunk been when he told him so; it was a prison . . . one suffocated in it because of lack of freedom . . . but at least a daily meal was guaranteed.

One night the wind rose again, but this time the darkness was shattered by lightning and thunder, and the skies poured tons of heavy rain. Yasmeen remembered Saleh. She had excessively neglected him and left him without food for several days, now. She ran to his hut, carrying the loaf of bread under her dress because of the rain. The room was dark, as Saleh had no more fuel for his small kerosene lamp, but she knew the room well. It had been more than a week, but she knew that Saleh was there though he did not answer to her call.

"Saleh?"

By the sudden flash of lightning she saw him shrunk in a corner, shaking all over, his eyes wide with terror.

She quickly went to her house and returned with a little kerosene and lighted the small lamp.

"Are you ill?"

"No." His teeth chattered when he answered.

She asked him, "Are you afraid?"

"Yes." He nodded, confessing his fear of the thunderstorm and the lightning, trembling all over.

"Poor crazy fellow . . . mad. . . ." She knelt beside him and took him in her arms, rocking him gently as if he was a baby, until he went to sleep near dawn.

The sun was bright again. He sat naked at the doorstep of his hut receiving the warmth of the sun. He had laid his wet tunic on the roof to dry. Yasmeen saw him eating a good piece of bread, joyfully closing his eyes in utter satisfaction.

"Are you always afraid of the thunder?"

"Oh no. . . . It was the first time."

She smiled at him, moved. "What a crazy fellow you are. . . ."

This was the only day he did not run at dawn to ask for work in front of the estate office building, though he usually returned home a few minutes later, disappointed. One day Mahrous asked him, along with quite a big group of men, to go and fetch their hoes. They went and returned quickly, wondering what job it was that needed a hoe at this time of the year. They were gaily marching behind Mahrous when their hearts sank and their faces scowled in sad alarm, as the Head Foreman took a side road that led to Sheikh Shaban's house.

The house was empty and abandoned; the men started hitting at its dry mud walls, destroying it, obeying Mahrous's orders. Saleh's legs refused to carry him, and he fell on his knees, bent as if he was giving way under too heavy a load pressing hard on his back; sobs shook him. Mahrous quickly went to him, angry; and as if a little afraid for him, he lashed him with his cane. "Up you go . . . I chose you because I thought you needed a job . . . a real occasion in this time of the year . . . but take care . . . don't harm yourself stupidly." Saleh, still sobbing like a big child, rose, took his hoe from the ground, and like everybody else started digging at the walls to destroy them.

Judgment had been passed on Abou Bakr and Ali. They were found guilty and were to be hanged shortly. . . . Sheikh Shaban had tried with various court orders to delay the hanging; he had been obliged to sell his land so as to be able to pay the court expenses and the fees of the lawyers.

At sunset Saleh was sitting on his doorstep when Yasmeen came with a nice plate of cooked food and the usual loaf of bread. She was smiling, she must have learned that he had found work. She could not believe her eyes when she saw him scowl with a frightful grimace, his eyes moving to and fro rapidly, madly. . . . Then he jumped at her, threw the plate of food at her face, and punched her brutally, shouting at her, "Go away you bitch. . . ."

She fled in terror, but he pursued her, catching up with her just at the entrance of her street; and there he threw her on the ground and kicked her and punched her hard.

Neighbors fell on him to force him to let her escape.

The village people expected her to abort, but she did not, as if Saleh in his mad blows had had mercy for the child and spared him.

Late that night there rose from Saleh's house the inhuman yells of a madman. The village heard them in awed astonishment. But when the noise went on and on without interruption, they smiled: they had gained another mad idiot for the village. The Trunk thought at first it was Hameed; but his father told him that it was Saleh and he went hurriedly to his friend's house, immediately forgetting his grudge.

The door was locked from the inside when the Trunk knocked, asking him to open. The yelling stopped abruptly but the door remain closed. The Trunk begged for a long time at the door but Saleh would not open.

Near dawn the strange inhuman yells sounded again, went on for a while, then stopped. The villagers heard them, merrily smiling again, hoping that Saleh in his newly acquired madness would entertain them with some idiotic gay incidents. The Trunk, out of all the village men, cried sadly, lying awake on the ground near his sleeping brothers and sisters.

Yasmeen, too, was sobbing, blaming herself for his madness. She wailed, "It is my fault . . . I made him go hungry . . . I humiliated him . . . what a terrible misfortune. . . ."

So when she saw him in the early morning, dragging himself, exhausted, to the door of her hut, begging for her pardon, falling on his knees and then trying to kiss her feet, she was filled with immense joy. She forgave him and forgot his blows, and took his face between her hands, making him rise from the ground. He left her suddenly, and turned away, running down the street.

Mahrous and his team were already at work when Saleh joined them at the abandoned house of Sheikh Shaban, which was already half destroyed. Mahrous gave him a hard look, evaluating the degree of his madness, but he saw him digging at the walls with his hoe in such a regular fashion and with so much energy that he was convinced that Saleh was not completely mad after all.

A week later the estate trucks were working on the land where once stood the gay bunch of palm trees and the house of Sheikh Shaban, and the plows were turning the earth. The Sheikh's family was allotted a small house in the upper village by the estate, but the Sheikh himself had departed and was never seen again, even after the village heard that his son and nephew had been hanged.

Another week in November passed, warm and full of sunshine. Saleh was lazily lying on the ground in front of his hut. He had been sent away again this morning by Hassan Effendi. There was no work. What could he do but bake his body in the sun, appearing in his short rough tunic in the dazzling light like a huge lizard with a brown belly. He gazed at the enormous white clouds that glided high above in the blue sky, changing their shapes with their slow movement. Who knew to what strange countries they were heading?

A dog passed by slowly, yellow, dirty looking. Saleh, with an automatic gesture, threw a stone at him. The dog twisted his body and quickened his steps, his tail curved inward between his hind legs. But before disappearing he turned his head and looked at Saleh reproachfully, as if he was saying, "How could you be so cruel as to send a stone at me, on such a beautiful day?"

Then Saleh saw a man coming his way, dressed in white

clothes that shone under the sun. Long pants covered the legs to the feet; a tunic fell to just below the knees, with a short vest over it. It was the Bedouin's dress: Maamour. Saleh jumped, attempted to reach for his club, but let himself fall on the ground again. He would refuse to fight.

"Peace be with you."

Saleh was on his feet again. His face brightened gratefully because Maamour had greeted him.

"Peace be with you! Peace, God's grace and His blessings be with you . . . Maamour . . ." But Maamour ignored Saleh's outstretched hand, which remained in mid-air, hesitating; then Saleh let it drop down alongside his body, ashamed.

"I see that you are all right. You are not mad as I heard you were. . . . In any case I came to deliver you a message. . . ."

And Maamour explained that this was their last day in the estate. . . . The rains which had fallen a week ago had also reached the desert, which would be covered by vegetation in a few days, and so the Bedouins with their families and their sheep were returning to it. Zeina was leaving too with her family. She had asked Maamour to deliver Saleh a small present, and he presented now to Saleh a leather necklace with a small leather sack as a pendant. Saleh opened it; there was a small hard piece of rounded leather like a coin and on it there were embossed in gold letters a few verses from the Koran. The present was a token meant to preserve him from madness and evil. It read:

"In the name of God the all merciful I opened for you a clear lighted road. Whereby God will pardon your present sins and your past ones, and will touch you with His grace and guide you on the right path."

Maamour suddenly jumped to his feet and took a few steps backward in astonishment, as he saw Saleh's face change in a savage scowl. Strange powerful sobs shook him. His head was violently thrown backward, and an inhuman cry rose from his mouth, like a wolf's howl in the night.

He's mad . . . definitely mad, said Maamour to himself in sorrow and somewhat afraid. Saleh fell on his knees and slowly went to the ground, his face touching the dust, still shaking with horrible strong sobs. He raised his head from the ground and looked at Maamour, his face still wet with tears, but having regained its gentle beauty. Then Maamour saw him bend his head again, kissing his feet, trembling all over. He thought, my God . . . what a terrible sight . . . the poor crazy fellow; but he heard him say, "For God's sake, Maamour, take me with you on your journey, far from this place; I will be your servant . . . your slave. Without any pay . . . just give me a piece of bread."

Maamour raised Saleh's face by gently pulling up at his chin.

"Come on . . . get up, don't do that . . . you know that I am a servant myself. I work for Sheikh Kataan. I am a paid shepherd."

"You can tell him that you bought a slave. I promise I will be faithful."

Maamour smiled a gentle smile, his eyes wet with contagious tears.

"All that for Zeina's love."

"No . . . I swear to God. . . . No . . . I promise. I won't try to see her. . . . If you take me out of this estate, I will follow you forever as your slave. . . . If you leave me they will kill me or drive me to madness. . . ."

Maamour frowned, puzzled . . . then his face showed a sudden determination.

"All right, I will take you with me. . . . I will try to convince Sheikh El-Kataan. I don't think he will mind. Tomorrow night follow the train tracks to the west, don't stop. You will find me waiting for you."

A blazing sun could not have lighted Saleh's face as did this immense joy that made all his features smile happily. He rose quickly and with arms raised above his head, on the tip of his toes, hardly touching the ground, he danced merrily. Villagers gazed from far and laughed. With quick gestures of their fingers at their temples they signed to Maamour that Saleh was crazy: after crying and howling the madman was dancing. Maamour himself was puzzled and bewildered and a little worried; but Saleh said, "Let them believe I am mad. . . . They won't try to search for me when I am gone. . . ." Maamour laughed, reassured, and departed, while Saleh went on dancing and making faces at the villagers who gathered, looking from far, not daring to approach. He showed them his tongue, a really crazy twinkle dancing in his eyes.

Late that night Yasmeen came. She had heard the news that Saleh was howling and crying, then dancing in front of the Bedouin in a crazy show, and she came to see for herself. She found him unusually excited, with his eyes rolling away from her all the time, incapable of sustaining her attentive questioning gaze. He was afraid she would see through him, but she was convinced that he was not normal any more and was slowly drowning in mental folly. She grieved for him and started to stroke his face gently and caress him. Her hand followed the curve of his neck and went to play with the fluffy hair on his chest—and suddenly stopped. She had discovered the leather pendant. She opened it . . . angry.

"It is the bitch that sent it. . . ."

He laughed loudly in nervous agitation.

"Oh no, it's the Bedouin shepherd, Maamour, that gave it to me, as a token of his friendship and as a farewell present. . . ."

And he quickly kissed her, choked on her lips the cry of anger and protest, and with a sly flexible turn of his body was over her, tenderly loving her. She melted in his arms, forgetting the leather pendant.

Near dawn she was sleeping, contented, her beautiful face lodged in the curve of his arm, rosy with satisfied desire. He passed his hand over the smooth round mass of her belly. . . . He felt a movement inside, like a kick. . . . He talked to himself: Well, you won't see your son growing, Saleh boy. . . . You won't see him running with his little feet . . . a small pimp like Ahmed . . . then become a big powerful young man, handsome . . . all muscles . . . but brainless, a beast in the midst of a herd . . . and his mind a toy in the hand of a tyrannical despot. . . . Then Saleh smiled, hearing the sigh of contentment as he gently stroked Yasmeen's belly. What a beautiful woman . . . with such a generous wonderful body. . . . You are fertility, the mother, the earth that receives the semen of life. You do not care to whom belongs the hand that sows it . . . but love grows generously, giving back its fruits.

Later in the morning, with dawn, he went to ask for work as usual and waited for Hassan Effendi with the other workers gathered in front of the estate's management offices. Hassan Effendi did not show up. So he returned slowly home. On his way the Trunk approached him. "Saleh . . ."

He rebuked him, refusing to make peace with him, and hardened his features. "Good-bye, I can't talk to you now. . . ."

"Please, Saleh, talk to me . . . I know you are not mad . . . I was angry because you hit poor Hameed brutally, but now I know that you suffered from it as much as I did. Please forgive me."

The Trunk's ugly face was so pitiful to look at that Saleh's heart melted. He could not leave his friend this way, so he asked him, lowering his voice unconsciously, "Come, I have something to tell you."

They went and sat at Saleh's door; Yasmeen had gone. Saleh was astonished to hear the Trunk insisting that he would follow him. He tried to persuade him, but the other would not hear of it, saying that Maamour would have to do with a second obedient slave.

While they were discussing it they heard the sharp whistles of the Bedouin shepherds reaching them from far. They leaned to see them pass the edge of the village. There on the estate's main road moved the flocks of white sheep under the trees. Maamour and his colleagues drove them fast ahead, with shouts, whistles, and movements of their arms. Then the camel caravan with their baggage and belongings appeared, with Sheikh El-Kataan leading, his gun on his shoulder, gleaming in the sun. Then the big camel litter with the women. Zeina was not with the litter but was following, riding on a camel of her own: a small figure, moving slowly in the midst of the sheep column. Saleh felt a pang at his heart. He got the impression that she was looking at him from afar. When the caravan passed away, they resumed their discussion.

The Trunk convinced Saleh by pointing out to him that the estate would turn its wrath on him because he was known as Saleh's friend. But they agreed that if Maamour refused to take the Trunk he would not create any trouble and would return without letting anyone know. When night came Saleh took his club and a small sack in which he gathered his small belongings: his razor, the broken mirror, a few rags, his old copy-books, the Holy Koran, a pencil. . . .

The Trunk joined him with his club and a sack on his shoulders. . . . Saleh was worried and asked if his father, Ali Keilani, had noticed anything.

"Yes, he noticed . . . and understood immediately. He did not say anything or ask any question, but he kissed me tenderly on my forehead, bidding me farewell, wishing me luck quietly. Don't be alarmed, he will not divulge our secret. . . . He is a good man." They walked hurriedly, taking side roads to avoid passing by the mansion and the main road, their hearts pounding. They felt like escaping thieves who were not sure if they could get away with their loot. The night was dark and cold, clouds obscuring the stars. They followed the railroad tracks. Saleh knew then that Maamour had not lied and that the sheep did in fact pass along these tracks: they could smell the pungent smell of sheep urine in their nostrils. Also they could feel the small balls of feces lodging between their bare toes as they went on.

When dawn finally broke they had walked so long that their feet were bleeding from the sharp stones between the railway tracks. A dense fog obliterated the view in front of them.

Suddenly they were in the midst of the sheep. The dogs attacked them, fiercely barking. But Maamour ordered them away, rising from the ground where he was lying, enveloped in the special wool blanket which the Bedouins always carry on their shoulders.

Maamour welcomed Saleh and turned to the Trunk with a smile.

"I was sure you would come too, and I asked permission for two instead of one. The Sheikh accepted, partly because I insisted and partly because of his anger at the estate officials and their manners. But he warned me that you were under my responsibility. He went ahead with the camels and part of the sheep to reach the nearby main town in time to buy a few necessities. We will meet him there."

The Trunk's and Saleh's faces lighted up happily, and Saleh knelt and tried to kiss Maamour's hand but immediately received a powerful slap.

"I told you before never to kiss my hand. . . ."

But Saleh turned towards the Trunk and ordered, "Come, you dirty dog . . . kneel in front of your new master. . . ."

The Trunk threw himself at the feet of Maamour, who got angry.

"Get up . . . that's a sin! . . . Do you believe you're still on the estate's land . . . ?"

Maamour led them to a small dancing fire and they sat around it. He offered them bread; it was a different, sweeter tasting bread. Maamour baked it daily from desert barley; for them it tasted as if it were the angels' special bread.

They drank goat's milk, which passed down their throats smoothly and went to their heads like wine, making them drunk with pleasure. Then they drank tea. . . . Maamour in their honor flavored it with pieces of dried carnation flowers. Then Maamour told them to sleep until he was ready to leave.

They slept immediately. Maamour gave them only two hours; he knew they were exhausted, but he wanted to put as much distance as possible between them and the estate. The minute he mentioned the estate their expressions changed, but he reassured them. Maamour was careful like all Bedouins. He avoided the main roads, choosing the less-travelled ones among the fields, and constantly made allowances for Saleh and the Trunk during the journey. They began to adore him; they had never known anyone like him before. He was as pure and gentle as his fair handsome face, with its white bright complexion, suggested. Even the animals seemed to recognize his good nature. The dogs came to him from time to time for an affectionate pat or a caress, and the sheep rubbed themselves against him. In the evening, he measured the barley flour, added some water to it, made dough, and baked it on top of the fire. When the Trunk and Saleh offered to fetch some dry twigs for him, he would thank them with a smile, but he never ordered them to do anything. At mealtimes he gave each of them an equal portion and afterward fed his dogs with the same care.

At noon they noticed that he left them and went a little farther away; stood, his face turned toward the east; and prayed. He would do the same in the afternoon and at sunset, again at night, and at dawn. They observed him from far, and they felt their abasement. There was no difference between them and the dogs that also watched Maamour. Yet they did not dare to join him in his fervent prayer.

Once Maamour asked Saleh, "Why don't you pray?"

"I will if you order me."

"No. . . . Never pray because you are obliged to, you must believe in God first . . . know Him, then pray of your own free will."

"I am afraid He won't accept my prayers. . . . He will discover the lies that come from my dirty, soiled heart."

"Don't say that, Saleh. . . . He is the all-merciful, and you must believe in His mercy."

Saleh put a miserable smile on his lips, nodding in sadness. "His mercy! I lost my belief in it when He remained silent, when He did not answer my cries and my calls . . . and I suffered and suffered and He wronged me again and again. He would not even allow me to die when I begged for death from my very soul."

"Shut up . . . that's blasphemy . . . are you not afraid of His punishment?"

"I lived in hell . . . and I believe that hell is for people like me.

It is their fate, and I will enter it again when the time comes, at peace with myself, because I don't expect anything else. As for now, I am not ambitious and I don't want to be more than this dog you are feeding with your own hands."

Maamour patted Saleh's cheek gently.

"Don't say that . . . have faith."

Saleh did not answer and remained with his head bent, frowning. So Maamour turned to the Trunk.

"And you, why don't you pray?"

The Trunk shrank like a cat caught stealing a piece of meat, and from his large chest rose the usual coarse mumble as he tried to explain his perplexity and fright. Maamour laughed, waved his raised arms, and whistled, ordering the sheep to move.

On the third day they had arrived at the outskirts of a big city. There they found the rest of the sheep, the camels, and the big litter. Saleh saw Sheikh Kataan coming their way. He felt a strange solemn respect for the man, as if he were a saint or a prophet of some kind, and truly his appearance now suggested it. He advanced erect and the dust at his feet was raised in golden waves by the sheep that took the color of sunset.

He looked handsome, with his short grey beard and his white clothes. Behind his head the town glittered with many colors reflecting the setting sun in thousands of glass windows, as if the Sheikh was wearing a crown of precious stones. Maamour ran to him and kissed his hand, then he made a gesture to Saleh and the Trunk to come nearer, but the Sheikh raised his hand, stopping them. They gaped in astonishment. Saleh immediately understood that something was wrong. Something awful must have happened, to prevent the Sheikh from allowing his hand to be kissed by them. Then Maamour came back, frowning when he explained to Saleh what was the matter. He could not believe his ears—though he had expected something of the sort. A great theft had taken place at the estate. A detective from the police had come to Sheikh Kataan during the market in the morning to ask him if he had seen Saleh and the Trunk. The police suspected that they had joined the Sheikh's caravan; but as they did not find them they went away.

The big safe in Guirguis Effendi's office had been found opened, and all the money that was in it was gone. It was a large sum. A back window was broken; and Guirguis said Saleh was the only one who knew that he concealed the safe's key in the drawer of his desk, which was broken, too, and the key gone.

Saleh used to spy on him a few months ago when he entered the office, every now and then, with the excuse of asking for work. Furthermore they found Saleh's hoe inside the office; all the villagers recognized it and the fingerprints would prove it. They assumed that he must have left it there when he retreated in a hurry, afraid to be caught.

The Sheikh advised them to return the money and to give themselves up. The coarse drum in the Trunk's chest began to resound its grumble, but it ended in a loud sob. Saleh's eyes filled with tears and they rolled down on his cheeks. He looked at Maamour in despair and his voice quivered when he said, "That the estate's men, when they learned at the break of dawn of our departure, planned the theft and put the blame on me, that is a logical thing to believe. But that Sheikh Kataan, and especially you, Maamour, believe that I did it; that is awful."

He opened his sack and overturned it, letting everything in it fall to the ground: his few books, the tea kettle, all his few belongings, scattered in the dust. With a quick gesture he removed his tunic and stood naked, only the leather necklace showing around his neck, and he shouted:

"Where could I hide the money? You, too, Trunk, remove your clothes and empty your sack. . . ."

But Maamour stopped him by saying, "No, Trunk, don't. I am sure that you are innocent, Saleh. . . ."

Maamour turned back to the Sheikh, who had not advanced an inch. He stood there in the colored light as if he had grown taller than nature, an illuminated halo around his head. The Sheikh was looking at Saleh from afar and their eyes met. Saleh felt a strange sensation taking hold of him; as if he was now in front of God himself, naked as he was created, with all the ornaments, lies, and coverings having fallen around him, and he was waiting judgment. Though the distance was great, he caught a glimpse of a twinkle in the Sheikh's eyes, and a smile. The Sheikh spoke; Maamour turned happily, waving to them to come nearer; Saleh put on his tunic, then slowly approached the Sheikh. He let one knee drop to the ground and kissed the hand of the Sheikh, who said, gently patting his bent head, "Get up, my boy . . . get up . . . don't be afraid, you will find peace and security with Sheikh Kataan. . . ."

Sobs shook Saleh as he recovered from his strong emotion, his lower lip trembling still, like that of a child wanting to cry. He made a sign to the Trunk, who stood there, bewildered. In one or two jumps the Trunk was at the Sheikh's feet; he did not dare to kiss the Sheikh's hand but crouched on the ground till his head touched the dust in front of him.

"Get up, my boy, never prostrate yourself to the ground for a man . . . do that only to God."

Then he laughed, saying to Maamour, "Don't you think that this wild animal may frighten the sheep?"

Maamour answered merrily, "That's true, but wolves, too, will run away the moment they smell the odor."

Later at night, Maamour brought them Bedouin clothes, which stretched at every seam, as they were made for slimmer bodies; but they were proud of them nonetheless. They slept happily, as if they were sailors on their last night before leaving the port for a long journey of adventures and hardship: afraid, but still feeling the ship's keel giving them a feeling of security.

Before dawn they went to kiss the Sheikh's hands once more, bidding him farewell, as he was leaving with his family, part of the flock, and the camels for the desert, leaving Maamour with the rest of the sheep.

The Sheikh advised his shepherd to travel slowly, using side roads between the fields and avoiding police stations at the entrances of cities.

The young men saw the last camel disappear in the darkness of the night. . . . A thin thread of light appeared at the horizon. The dawn star glittered there; so the whistle of Maamour rose sharply and the sheep rose also from the ground and started moving. The two new shepherds copied his gestures and waved with their arms, enveloped by the wool blankets that covered even their faces.

For the first few days, Saleh was ill at ease with his new clothes, in spite of the cold weather. He was too warm and often stopped, sweating. Maamour refused to let him take off the blanket and ordered him to wear it like a sash even at noontime. It was also difficult for Saleh to live in the open, without the roof he was used to. He kept wishing he could find some wall to lean on. During the day the sun stared at him constantly. At night it was the stars. The wind stroked his face, sometimes as a soft breeze and sometimes as a strong gale that stung his eyes. But little by little, he got accustomed to this new hut which was his blanket. He learned to twirl it around himself and lie curled up in it like a snail in its shell.

Gradually the sheep got used to him and would stop when he

stopped, march on when he did. Maamour taught him to tie his leg to the leg of the leader of the flock when he slept so that the sheep would not stray at night without waking him.

There were days of rain, and Maamour taught Saleh to cover himself with his blanket in such a way that no drop would touch him. Fields followed each other in different patterns, yet Saleh was astonished to discover that the countryside was the same everywhere, as if he had not left the estate. The same bamboo stalks on the banks of the canals; ponds here and there, with dirty water, in front of black little mud huts. Small villages; the same children playing; the same piles of dung left to dry, and very often clothes were also spread over the huts to dry. Once they saw a terrace in front of an office building that looked so much like the one they knew that they gaped at it, astonished. Near it was the high wall of the mansion surrounded by a dense forest of casuarina trees. . . . They fled in terror. The chest of the Trunk echoed the usual rumble and grumble. Maamour shouted at them, "Don't be afraid," that it was not the same estate. But still they did not stop before they had left it far behind, and all the sheep followed them.

During this week, the Trunk and Saleh reached the peak of their happiness. They lived days that they could never have imagined possible. If someone had told the Trunk that death was waiting for him if he pursued his journey, he would have shrugged his shoulders and gone on, smiling, not minding in the least, his large bare feet trampling on the warm dust.

What added to Saleh's and the Trunk's belief that the desert was the promised paradise were the signs that appeared on Maamour's face. He would make a grimace of disgust if they passed near a village, with all the nasty smells of the rotting humanity who piled on top of each other in these small mud huts, the smell of dung, the fetid odor in the back yards of the houses, the pungent smell of rotten muddy ponds; he would then drive the sheep hastily away. At other times he would stop to smell the breeze, and joy would light up his face.

"The desert smell is beginning to reach us . . . let us go to the west. . . ."

West was always his guide . . . however the side roads he took turned or wound alongside the fields, he went westward. The land began to change. The dust had a whiter color, and then slowly, very slowly, after a few days, the sand began to be part of the earth.

The fields were an endless expanse of orange and yellow. There were many gardens and groves of orange trees. The dry wind carried a new variety of fragrances. The sheep knew they were nearing the desert and they hurried, lifting their heads from time to time to smell the flowers. Maamour took pains to find the right grazing grounds to please and satisfy them. He often went to the guard of a plantation with a smile, a joke, or a gift of money, to ask permission for his flock to graze. Frequently, after dinner, he entertained his friends with folk tales and old legends. Sometimes he played the flute which always hung at his waist, lovely, poignant tunes. He played only when he wanted and not when somebody asked him.

"Don't ask me to play for you. The flute does not take orders. If it wants to talk to you, it will in its own time."

One of those days the rains came back, but this time in short, light showers, as if the sad grey sky was brooding and crying quietly. As the morning went on, the grey clouds vanished, leaving flocks of small white balls that looked very much like sheep running in the blue bright sky. The day turned out beautiful, sunny, radiant.

Suddenly a terrible disaster fell on them and caught them by surprise, at a moment when they least expected it.

They had just arrived at the steep bank of a large, deep canal. Maamour merrily shouted, "That's the last canal you will meet before the desert. . . . We will only see water in the wells from now on."

The canal was nearly empty except for a small running brook that gaily sparkled in its depth. The sheep stretched their necks at the bank, asking for water.

Maamour found on the bank a sort of stair formed by big blocks of white stone, where they could make the sheep go down, drink, and come up again, one at a time, a difficult, tiresome job. When they had finished with it they sat on the edge of the bank, panting, sweat shining on their foreheads. They lighted cigarettes. It was one of those lovely days of early winter so familiar in the valley.

The sun's rays were gentle in their warmth, and a cool breeze caressed their faces tenderly. The sky was beautifully blue and bright. Everything sparkled with light and far things appeared nearer, close enough to be touched by the hand.

At a distance a dam crossed the canal. Its big metal doors were closed, allowing to escape only the small brook that ran merrily in the depth of the canal. Maamour said gaily, "Fellows, you won't see such lovely water for years . . . for anyone who wants to bathe, this is the right time."

In a moment they had removed their clothes and were naked in the golden light. The Trunk could not prevent himself from laughing at the sight of Maamour's nakedness. His laughter increased as he pointed his finger shamelessly at a certain part of Maamour's body.

"How strange is your body!!!"

Yes, Maamour's body was very different from those of the two peasants, who had large powerful bodies, covered with strong heavy muscles which had been built layer by layer by the steel weight of the hoe. The sun had given their skin a golden brown color, and the constant attacks of bilharzia worms in the canals had made their organs burgeon into enormous instruments, as if nature, to combat the disease, gave them a renewed, more powerful vigor. Maamour, on the contrary, had a shepherd's body, lithe and delicate, fashioned by the desert wind.

Maamour blushed deeply like a cock's comb. The redness got down even to his chest. He shouted at the Trunk jokingly, but rather angry, too.

"Because you are an animal, a bull, you dark peasant . . ."

Saleh was mad with rage. He fell on the Trunk, slapping him hard on his naked body. The Trunk cried out with pain, apologizing loudly, but still went on laughing. He ran to the stairs and quickly went down the steep bank to the water. Saleh followed him, slapping him harshly. They circled, in a whirl of sparkling water, till the uproar of the Trunk appealed to the mercy of Maamour, who ordered Saleh to stop the punishment. He went down and placed himself between them.

There was little water. Their bellies touched the sand of the bottom as they lay flat on the surface; they splashed the water with their outstretched arms, raising fountains of colored drops.

Their eyes reflected happily the blueness of the sky. Maamour was the first to shiver from the cold water, so he went out. . . . Saleh joined him. They sat at the top of the steep bank, drying themselves in the sun. They gazed smiling at the Trunk who, like a big child, was playing with the water in delightful joy.

Saleh started to roll a cigarette, and Maamour too. So for a second their attention was taken away from observing the Trunk.

Suddenly the sand underneath them shook and a frightful uproar thundered. The dam's door was now wide open and a mountain of water was rolling towards them at full speed. Saleh and Maamour cried in one voice.

"Trunk!!!"

He rose from the water, standing, paralyzed, terrified, looking at the huge mountain of a river that rolled and boiled menacingly toward him. He had already drifted farther away from the stairs.

"Trunk!!! Trunk!!!" yelled his friends at the top of their voices.

The Trunk got over his paralysis and swiftly moved to the bank, but it was too late to reach the place with the stairs, so he climbed the steep bank. He was just going to touch Saleh's outstretched hand when the sand under him crumbled, throwing him into the bubbling, foaming water. He disappeared in its depth. An arm appeared, then a foot. Saleh ran on the bank and threw himself at him; he managed to reach him and embrace his limp body tightly. He struggled fiercely against the current that was rolling them, got hold of the hanging branch of a small bush which grew on the bank, and stuck to it. He took a deep breath and raised the limp body of the Trunk out of the water, which in effervescent rage was rolling all around him, pulling at him. He dared not try to climb the bank because of its steepness and its quickly crumbling sand.

But he heard Maamour calling above him. He looked up and saw a dangling rope coming toward him. When he was sure he could catch it, he let go of the bush and quickly grasped the rope, his muscles painfully strained. Maamour had tied the rope to the donkey that carried the flour and their belongings during the journey. So he pulled them both out of the water and up the bank.

They laid the Trunk on his back, and Saleh started to compress his chest and release it, while Maamour moved his arms up and down, following the movement of artificial respiration. A bloody froth appeared at the Trunk's gaping mouth. Saleh cried out at his friend to respond, begging him to revive, but his features remained fixed in the same horror-stricken scowl. An hour passed. Maamour stopped the movement of his arms and closed his eyes. He stood up, raised his hand to his head, and touched his temples with his fingers.

"Great is our Lord. . . ." Maamour chanted gravely the prayer of the dead, while Saleh sobbed, falling on his friend's chest, embracing him tightly.

Then Maamour looked around; no one had seen what happened. The place was deserted. With a sharp voice he ordered Saleh to leave the Trunk and stop weeping. They should depart quickly. As Saleh did not obey but tightened his embrace, Maamour's voice got angry and quivered as he sharply reminded him of his oath.

"You promised to obey me. I said leave him. . . . Stop crying. . . . Put on your clothes. . . ."

Saleh obeyed slowly but watched in dazed astonishment, his eyes wide, unbelieving, when Maamour took the Trunk's body in his arms, dragged him, and threw him over the bank into the canal. He quickly dressed, then whistled sharply, calling the sheep. As Saleh stood dazed, as if paralyzed, he went to him and with all his might slapped him in the face.

"Move!!!" shouted Maamour at him.

Saleh's face reddened deeply but he remained still, so Maamour slapped him again, hard. "Move, I said!!!"

That did it . . . he became attentive and began to dress.

They drove the sheep fast and crossed over the bridge on the dam. Its guard, who had opened the gates, was sitting on the other side talking to a fisherman. Neither of them could have seen what happened from where they were. Yet they sensed that something was wrong, as they noticed the agitation of both shepherds and the speed with which they were driving the sheep. They followed them with a suspicious gaze till they disappeared in the desert.

A young sheep fell, dying from the effort of running in the sun. Maamour stopped, and from the small sack that was always dangling at his side he took a knife, opened it, and with a quick gesture, cut the sheep's throat mercifully, saying gravely the usual sentence.

"In the name of God, the all merciful. . . ."

Saleh, from a distance, fixed his gaze on the blood pouring on the sand, fascinated. Maamour did not resume his march, afraid for the sheep. He planted his long club in the sand and spread over it his blanket, making a small tent.

He crawled under its shade, and from his sack he took out a small book, the Holy Koran, and began chanting the verses in a loud, sad but beautiful voice, mourning, while Saleh remained standing, incapable of turning his gaze away from the remains of the small pool of blood that was quickly being absorbed. One of the dogs came near; smelling the blood, advancing his muzzle cautiously; then looked at Maamour as if asking for permission. When Maamour went on chanting, he licked the wound with a rosy red tongue. Another dog approached. The first dog got hold of the sheep by a big bite at his neck and dragged it, growling. Saleh went on looking at the red stain on the sand. Behind a sand dune the dogs were fighting a fierce battle over the sheep's body. When the sun went down, Maamour prepared the fire and cooked the bread and ordered Saleh to eat. He obeyed. Then Maamour resumed chanting the Holy Koran verses. Late at night he closed the book and ordered Saleh to envelop himself carefully with his wool blanket and try to sleep. He did, and his shocked, dazed mind drowned in deep sleep.

Just before dawn Maamour woke him up, and they resumed their journey.

Maamour was justified in longing for the desert. In this season it was really so beautiful that it was beyond description. The orange-colored dunes followed each other with their smooth shapes so quieting to the mind. Between them the valleys were covered with germinating bright green sprouts of herbs, inter-mingled with little flowers that had the loveliest colors imagina-ble. They formed exquisite patterns of mauve, green, blue, yellow, red, and rose.

The dazzling light played over all, changing its character all the time. Quiet and gentle over a smooth dune, it shone and glittered over a sharp rock which rose from underneath the sand. Then it smiled again on the flowers in the valleys.

Water was present everywhere between the high dunes after the heavy rains, and Saleh quickly learned how to differentiate the real small lakes from the sparkling mirages which vanished when he came near. The breeze was dry, stimulating, carrying the various flower fragrances that went to the head like wine.

Two days elapsed, and Saleh succumbed to the attack of all this beauty. His mind recovered from the confusion and shock, and he began again to perceive and feel with all his senses. That did not mean that he forgot the Trunk. On the contrary, his grief took a new dimension; he was too familiar with suffering to be tricked by this charming nature that did its best to anesthetize his senses.

As for Maamour, the moment he closed the Book his heart felt at peace. Sorrow left him. His deep belief in God protected him from every possible grief. The Trunk died; well, what of it? Let it be! It was God's will. The Trunk was surely tramping happily with his large bare feet in his Eden.

Yet Maamour was preoccupied; he noticed the deep grief that was concealed behind Saleh's apparently placid face. It showed in the darkness and width of his eyes, in a tightness at the corners of his lips that was not smoothed out by time.

Once Maamour opened the subject of the Trunk's death with Saleh, trying at the same time to give him faith in God. Saleh listened without interrupting him. Maamour talked for a long time, reasoning with him gently, presenting argument after argument. When he finished and stopped talking, Saleh slowly turned his face toward him and gave him a stern, hard look.

"Dear Maamour, that you order me around as you please, that is your right. When you ordered me to leave the Trunk, I obeyed immediately because you reminded me of my promise; and I did not object when you threw him in the canal like a dog without a shroud or a tomb so that he might rest in peace; I did not move and I did not utter a word. . . ." Maamour blushed deeply, trying to answer and justify himself, but he stuttered, ashamed. "Well . . . I . . . I only meant to protect us from the police and give us time to reach the desert."

Saleh raised his hand in protest and said with the same cold, even voice, "Do not misunderstand me, I am not reproaching you for anything, I will never allow myself to discuss your actions. What I tried to say is that I am your obedient slave but only with my body.

"I will follow you like your faithful dog. If you want to punish me for any reason I will present my bare back to you and you will find me kissing the hand which has flogged me. If you want to kill me and get rid of me like you did with the small sheep that you slaughtered . . . well . . . I . . . will present my neck to your knife. But my mind is mine, my ideas . . . the way I think, this is mine. Don't every try to impose your opinions . . . you won't be able. . . ."

Then Maamour saw his friend speaking as if in a trance, his eyes misty, the black iris nearly filling them, his voice trembling.

"Yes, you won't be able. . . . The palace before you tried and failed . . . and they never forgave me . . . they are still after me. . . . The Trunk was killed because of me . . . because he followed me . . . oh! dear Trunk . . . my gentle friend . . . how right you were when you warned me that the estate's land is everywhere . . . that its domain extends far beyond my village."

Maamour paled and asked in astonishment.

"What palace? . . . What do you mean . . . ?"

Saleh recovered his attention and apologized in a sweet gentle voice. "I am sorry, my master . . . I neglected you for a minute . . . do you want to punish me?" Maamour's eyes filled with tears and he answered sadly.

"Never call me master . . . I am Maamour, your friend. . . ."

Saleh answered in the same even voice, as if in surrender.

"All right . . . Maamour . . . thank you. . . ."

This discussion defined once and for all the limits of their relations. Maamour never tried to talk about the Trunk or to impose his views. He also avoided hurting Saleh's feelings in any way. Saleh, on the other hand, carried out his promise, promptly obeying any suggestions from Maamour, always attentive to his friend's wishes, doing his best to serve him, hiding carefully his sadness. For instance, he knew that Maamour, after dinner, liked to tell stories and tales, so he would encourage him by coaxing, "Please, Maamour . . . tell me a nice story. . . ."

His friend's face would light up with joy and he would embark on a long tale about the Arab warriors and their adventures. Saleh would listen, empty-minded, not even hearing; yet when his friend ended it, he would thank him and ask for another one.

"It was a beautiful story, Maamour, can you tell me another one?"

The only thing that Saleh enjoyed without pretending was when Maamour played the bamboo flute. He would then remember the coarse features of the Trunk, that melted the moment he heard the flute. Tears would roll on Saleh's face, his heart aching from sorrow as the tune sadly whistled on.

Days passed along and the journey went on. Maamour always kept in the northwestern direction.

C H A P T E R

13

O ne morning they approached the desert wells known as Kataani wells. These dated back to Roman times and had been discovered in the middle of the desert by Sheikh Kataan's tribe. They were small wells, walled with white stones and surrounded by about a thousand tents. As Maamour's caravan drew near, dogs barked to announce their arrival and women ran out of the tents, hailing them with a peculiar "you, you" sound.

The young men of the tribe rushed to Maamour and Saleh and welcomed them. Saleh enjoyed the friendly reception and smiled with pleasure. The scenery was attractive: golden sand, white sheep, black tents, loud "you, you" singing, smiling faces, cordiality. A crazy hope overtook him; could this place really be his haven where he could have peace at last, and where the long arm of tyranny would fail to reach him. Sheikh Kataan stood in front of his tent to welcome them. They kissed his hand while the women went in, but he kindly bowed his head and embraced them both. But an instant's astonishment flickered in his eyes when he noticed they were only two. He kept quiet and with a gesture invited them to follow him inside the tent.

Saleh never thought that the tent could be so vast, so luxurious and comfortable. A colored curtain divided it in half. Behind it, women were whispering and giggling. The ground was covered with sheepskins embroidered with bright colors and topped with silk cushions. The bottom edges of the tent were raised above the level of the earth and allowed a reclining person to glance at the desert landscape, the orange-colored dunes, and the blue horizon beyond. The Sheikh sat cross-legged and bade Saleh and Maamour sit down beside him. The curtain opened, and a young boy put in front of them a tray of bread, cheese, yogurt, patties, honey, and black olives. For the first time in his life, Saleh happily ate such delicious food.

A few minutes later the young boy returned with a metal bowl and a jug. He washed their hands and took away the tray. Next he brought some tea in an elegant kettle which had the shape of a tall angry goose, and added some small dried carnation flowers to the tea. The silence in the tent was broken only by the sound of the water boiling in the kettle.

"Where is our monster?" asked the Sheikh softly.

The tea in Saleh's mouth tasted bitter as Maamour related the story of the Trunk's death.

"Maamour," advised the Sheikh in his grave voice, "leave tomorrow morning with the sheep and travel to the valley of the caverns."

"That is a very far place . . . wild and dangerous, my Lord . . . full of wolves."

"Take a rifle with you. Don't you think the protection of your friend is worth the danger?"

"But why run away? No one saw us, and I threw the body in the canal. It surely drifted with the current."

"There is a possibility that someone may have seen you and informed . . . you will find the mounted police here in no time. But they would never go so far as to search for you at the valley of the caverns."

Saleh opened his mouth to thank the Sheikh but stammered a few unintelligible words.

Sheikh Kataan patted him on the shoulder.

"Don't be afraid. No harm will come to you. As for you, Maamour, you will come back every twenty days to get news and flour and other necessities. You will leave the sheep and the rifle in the care of Saleh. Teach him how to use it. Go, my son, in God's peace."

Saleh and Maamour were welcomed outside the tent by another group of men. Maamour whispered to Saleh.

"Don't try to talk to them. You might give yourself away. I will tell them you are a Bedouin and that you have joined us with the Sheikh's permission. They may not believe me, but even if they don't they will respect my secret. We are not at the estate here and these men would rather have their tongues cut than divulge the secret of a fellow tribesman or a friend."

Saleh sat next to Maamour all day while the men surrounded them, talking and joking, avidly curious about the newcomer.

"Where do you come from?" asked one. Saleh mutely indicated the horizon. Each in turn used his own subtlety to try to discover the secret of the enigma that was Saleh, but in vain. Saleh remained silent.

"Do you plan to stay with the Sheikh, among us?"

Once more Saleh answered with gestures.

In the evening a group of tribesmen rode on their horses toward the sand dunes which bordered the barley fields. They raced at tremendous speed, stopped abruptly, and came back over the dunes, jumping on and off and over and under the horses at full gallop.

"Those are our young tribesmen. They are practicing horse riding. Soon the day will come when they will march forth to get back our stolen land." Maamour explained.

The next performance was target practice. They were all excellent shots. Saleh's attention was attracted by a young man who acted as their leader. He was hideous, his face having been ravaged by a fire or an accident. He also looked dangerous. He stopped his horse in front of Saleh and asked, "Where do you come from?" Saleh's face reddened. . . . He was going to answer and commit a mistake . . . but at the last moment kept quiet. He was so annoyed by the haughty disdain with which the horseman spoke and looked at him that he looked back with the same disdain. He just took out his hand from under his wool blanket and made a gesture towards the west.

Annoyed, the ugly horseman kicked his horse fiercely and rode off.

"He is the Sheikh's nephew, Massoud; avoid him. He has a ferocious, nasty temper," said Maamour.

"Can that be the cousin to whom Aysha is promised?" asked Saleh.

Maamour nodded.

"What happened to his ugly face?"

"A mine exploded in his face. It is said that his body is disfigured as well . . . and that he can't do . . . you know what I mean."

"Good God, why does he want to marry Aysha, to make her suffer? Why does the Sheikh want to sacrifice his daughter to him?"

"The Sheikh hates Massoud, but traditions are much stronger than even Sheikh Kataan. Massoud is Aysha's first cousin and has all the rights. Also, he is a brave freedom fighter. Every now and then he crosses the border with his friends until they reach the mountains of their country, and puts mines under the railroad tracks at strategic places. He has gained the tribe's respect."

Night fell quickly, and as the colors faded from the dunes, Saleh and Maamour ate and prepared to sleep, but in a quiet sadness. Maamour played his flute, while his friend faced the cool night air and watched the sky. The moon seemed to be hurrying along with the clouds around it forming a protective shield. From the flute came a last cry that rattled like a sob.

In the morning the Sheikh himself told Maamour to take all the food and supplies they needed for the journey and to tie everything on the backs of three donkeys.

The journey went on slowly and at leisure; as they crossed each valley the flock would disperse among the flowers and the green sprouts. Saleh followed, feeling disheartened and sad but not knowing why. Was it because he understood the tyranny and cruelty that lay hidden behind the smiling faces of the seven wells he just left? Was it because he felt the danger that lay in wait for his friend, just by looking at the ugly face of Aysha's cousin Massoud?

His uneasiness reached its peak on the fourth day, as evil looking black clouds hurried in the sky, agitated as if they quarrelled fiercely with each other. The wind rose cold and whipped their faces with the sand that it threw at them in continuous whirls.

Saleh got frightened and sat curled in his blanket. Maamour did the same and the sand streamed under them and between their bare toes. Suddenly the sky darkened. Saleh trembled, his teeth chattered, while the wind howled around him like attacking wolves. Maamour quickly rose and started gathering the sheep. He was amazed to notice that his friend did not rise to give him a hand. He called to him but his voice was lost in the wind, so he gathered them alone, all around Saleh: hundreds and hundreds of sheep, their muzzles touching each other. He got hold of the leader's horn and dragged her till he reached Saleh and sat beside him, then tied the leader's foot to his. He bent to do the same thing with his friend's foot. When he grasped it his astonishment increased: he felt Saleh's foot shaking severely. He pulled at his friend's blanket, exposing his face, and was shocked: the frightened eyes rolled in all directions and a yellow glow danced in their depth, though no light filtered through the dark clouds. Maamour shouted close to his ear.

"What is the matter with you . . . ?"

Saleh nodded many times, admitting he was all right, but at this moment the sky burst into a terrible thunder, its echo resounding in the whole desert. By the light of the lightning Maamour saw Saleh's face grimace strangely in an expression of profound terror. He shouted again at his ear, "Are you afraid?"

He nodded yes many times. So Maamour smiled and said tenderly, in a whisper that was carried by the wind, the same phrase that Yasmeen had said once in the climax of a storm at the estate, "You poor crazy fellow . . . mad . . ."

Maamour passed his arms around his shoulders, holding him tight against him to comfort him, and enveloped both their bodies in one blanket. He heard him say with a sigh, "Thank you."

Maamour tied his free foot to Saleh's as he had done with the ewe . . . and its warmth went to his friend's heart. He stopped shivering and smiled. He was no longer afraid, though the wind howled and the storm thundered.

Heavy rains poured over them at night as they lay crouched under their blankets; but at dawn the cold wind quieted and the mad black clouds fled away, leaving soft grey ones to replace them. The sun, hesitantly, threw a weak silvery ray through the clouds to look at the two young men who were shivering, their teeth chattering, not from fear now but from severe cold. Then a powerful ray found an opening between the clouds and joyfully played on everything. So the leader of the sheep jumped, running, pulling at Maamour, who pulled at Saleh too and dragged him for a short distance. They laughed and detached themselves. The sheep quickly scattered to eat the wet flowers' heads, and immediately got drunk from their fermented nectar.

The crevasse between the grey blocks of clouds widened and revealed a whole window of blue bright sky. That allowed the radiant sun to enter with its warmth. The two young men removed their wet clothes, laid them on the sand to dry, and ran to the top of the dunes and met there in the wonderful golden light. They came back, still running and jumping, and massaged their bodies and fought the cold in every possible way. Their naked bodies shone like the flowers, and the small sand crystals bloomed with fiery joyful colors.

From that day on Saleh's heart opened up fully to enjoy the beauty around him. He eagerly tasted the special sweet nectar of freedom. It went to his head and made him drunk with pleasure while he was filling his lungs with the cool reviving desert air. He forgot about the humiliation, the oppression, the miseries, the grief. How could he not forget? From now on, his master was also his friend and colleague who happily smiled at him, and, all the time, merrily turned his radiant lovely face toward him. The vast, colorful, beautiful desert was his playground; the soft sand his bedmat; the ever-changing wonderful sky his roof.

Maamour, from the night when he rocked Saleh between his arms like a frightened child while the storm raged around them, acquired a deep affection for him. His heart would melt with tenderness when he saw Saleh move fast, escalating a high dune, far away, and meeting the sun; then turn back and roll along its slope and twist; then jump again, speeding back, laughing happily, or dancing crazily, his hands clapping above his head.

Saleh's freedom was not only to play, jump, and run as he pleased. It also included performing a most interesting task, which called for a continuous, tremendous effort to fulfill it; the care of the sheep. It was a difficult job but a fascinating one, as it was linked with life itself. Every day a ewe would give birth to a small lamb, and with the advance of winter more and more were born every day. Maamour taught Saleh how to help in the actual delivery and then how to care for the mother and the lamb. Very often he had two or three deliveries at the same time. His eyes would mist with joy when the little lambs fell quivering between his hands. Some of the mothers refused to feed their lambs and it was his responsibility to discover that quickly, before the lamb died.

During their march, as they went from one valley to the other, Saleh would often carry two or three lambs in his arms.

He learned to discover the right valley, full of green sprouts. More important still, Maamour taught him to discover the presence of snakes or scorpions in a wide area around them, before allowing the sheep to graze.

The most difficult lesson, yet the most important one that Maamour taught him every day, was the art of the shepherd in knowing the desert, and how to find one's way in its vast wilderness. They would sit for hours and Maamour would explain the secrets of the stars, how to use them so as not to get lost: the position of the sun, the comparison between light and shade, the movement of one's shadow. Saleh quickly learned that everything had a significance in the desert. The dunes, the shapes of the rocks, their color, their texture, even the sand and its infinitesimal crystal beads carried a message.

Water was plentiful among the rocks in this season, but it rapidly evaporated under the breath of the hot wind. The desert was treacherous and often dangerously harsh. The sheep did not mind very much, as the desert plants retained their water, so that they seldom had to drink, but the danger lay for the poor weak human beings. Maamour taught Saleh always to refill the skin water-bags that were carried by the three donkeys, and always to travel from one well known point of water that never dried, even in the summer, to another.

Saleh remembered his old copy-books and he was immensely pleased when he found them with his few belongings in his old sack over the donkey. He thanked his friend for bringing them along. Maamour was really surprised to discover that Saleh had learned to read and write. He would watch in utter astonishment as he wrote down the names and positions of the various water wells and how to reach them. Sometimes Saleh would record any idea that crossed his mind just for the pleasure of letting his pencil run on the paper.

One day big mountains appeared at the horizon. Maamour pointed to them and announced that they had finally arrived at the end of their journey. In front of them lay the valleys of the caverns.

The valleys were vast and beautiful . . . full of flowers and rich green herbs. But Maamour was uneasy; he inspected the sand with a frown on his face. There were a lot of sand prints showing the passage of running wolves, and fierce bloody battles had left their traces all around. The proximity of the mountains and their numerous caverns made it a perfect dwelling place for wild animals.

At night Maamour lighted several big fires at the corners of the valley. He sat with the rifle in his lap. Saleh sat by his side, gazing at the darkness of the night beyond.

The sheep turned their heads nervously. In the middle of the night they heard the frightful howl of a wolf calling from far. The echo resounded for a long time. Others answered from various parts of the desert. The dogs barked fiercely. Maamour pulled the trigger hammer of the rifle back, ready, his voice hissing between his teeth as he said:

"Damn it . . . what a nasty place, I shouldn't have obeyed the Sheikh . . ." Two green dots glittered in the dark beyond the fires. Maamour pulled at the trigger. The shot echoed loudly and the green eyes vanished. A minute later Maamour cursed again between his teeth.

"Damn it!!!"

The green pair were back again, dancing. Saleh went out of his wits when his gaze discerned the black bodies of the wolves, their green eyes dancing beyond the fire. Terror gripped him as he remembered his dream. He whispered to Maamour.

"Ah . . . the black dogs . . . the eyes . . . I saw them in a nightmare . . . a long time ago . . . at the estate . . . I saw them. . . ."

Maamour answered, hissing.

"Damn it!!!"

The dogs barked fiercely but hesitated to attack. Eventually they did, and the fighting animals growled and snarled and snapped their teeth and the wounded dogs cried. Maamour jumped with the rifle in his hand, but Saleh caught him and cried out, begging.

"Don't go, they mean death . . . I saw them . . . they were in the cemetery . . . between the tombs."

Maamour got free from Saleh's grip and jumped again and ran. He aimed and fired when he came near the scene of the battle. The shot was followed by a horrible howl that cried out many times as if it was human. It ended in a choked rattle. The wolves fled. The dogs followed them, snarling and barking at them. Maamour fired another shot in their direction but higher up, afraid to wound a dog. He called to them, and called them back by whistling. They came, panting, trembling on their legs, yet they went on barking fiercely. They gathered around the wounded wolf that tried to bite and rise. Saleh raised his club and cracked its head with a terrible blow. One of the dogs lay on the ground with his throat opened, his body still quivering.

Maamour and Saleh increased the height of the fire with dried herbs and twigs they had gathered in the morning. They had a lot of difficulty in keeping the terrified sheep together. They called and whistled at the dogs all the time to prevent them from attacking the wolves again, keeping them around, afraid for them.

The wolves came back, the smell of blood increasing their wrath, but remained far away, not daring to approach. Only their glittering green eyes could be seen, coming, then vanishing, jumping and dancing in the dark.

Maamour fired shots in their direction every now and then to keep them at a distance. A crack of dawn light appeared at the eastern horizon, and everything suddenly went quiet in the valley. The dogs stopped barking.

The friends glanced at each other, sighing deeply. They nodded their heads as if saying together, silently, "Thank God!"

Saleh prepared tea on the remaining coals, while Maamour baked some bread. After they ate, drank, and fed the dogs, they went to see what had become of the dead wolf. They were horror-struck. Both the wolf's and the dog's bones were shining clean, not one piece of flesh left attached to them. They hurriedly gathered the tired sheep, pushing, shouting, and whistling at them to speed them.

They fled from these valleys as fast as they could. They marched the whole day, as Maamour wanted to put the maximum distance possible between them and the valleys of the caverns. At sunset they let themselves fall on the sand, exhausted, their heads aching with a continuous pulsating drumbeat.

A little after midnight the dogs barked fiercely. Far away glittered the green eyes. Maamour fired his rifle.

"Damn it . . ."

He whistled to the dogs, calling them around him to prevent them from attacking. Saleh quickly lit a small fire and another night passed with continuous sharp whistling, firing the rifle from time to time, and keeping the small fire alive.

At dawn they slept; before noon they had already resumed their march.

At sunset they stopped and gathered enough twigs from the scattered bushes of the desert to keep the fire going all night. They arranged turns between them. Maamour would sleep while Saleh was on guard duty. Nothing happened. After midnight a wolf howled from very far, the dogs barked a sporadic, not very convincing bark, then kept quiet. Maamour, who had gotten up, took his turn and Saleh slept. Nothing happened.

They resumed their journey but in a more leisurely manner. Maamour headed north for a few days, then turned to the east, aiming for the Sanjara wells.

They did not hear the wolf's howl any more, at night. Yet they were uneasy. They felt that the wolves were still silently following. They could not see them, but many signs pointed to their presence. The dogs did not jump or run or quarrel behind the dunes, as they had before, but kept around the herd as if they were afraid. They would sit quietly, then raise their heads, smelling the breeze, troubled, ill at ease.

Even the sheep looked worried; they would not scatter, happily grazing, but kept grouped, raising their heads, too, as if they smelled something. Maamour noticed all these signs and was amazed. These parts of the desert were a crossing path for flocks. Very near the Sanjara wells, every day they would come across fresh balls of sheep's dung, proving that some had just passed. Yet the wolves were following them and only them . . . Why? He felt frightened and puzzled, but kept his anxiety to himself. So at night he never closed his eyes, sitting from sunset till dawn with the rifle ready in his lap. He would say to Saleh:

"You take my turn to sleep. . . . I feel wide awake. I'll wake you when I feel sleepy."

He never did. Saleh used never to discuss a word or a wish, considering them as orders, so he would lie down and envelop himself carefully with his wool blanket, pretending to sleep.

Yet he himself would not sleep either, but he would observe his friend or gaze at the darkness around, opening his eyes every now and then.

He would take advantage of a brief moment in the morning, when Maamour would rest and sleep for a while, to run quickly behind the dunes, and there his heart would sink. His eyes would open wider as he saw, unbelieving, the traces of three wolves on the sand.

One day the tents around the Sanjara wells appeared. The sheep dogs barked happily and the Sanjara dogs answered them loudly. Maamour sighed in relief, his face brightening. Saleh, too, smiled, his mind suddenly at rest. Here lay civilization, where people and animals lived in harmony. Here was peace and security.

The women were gathered around the wells. Their flexible, lithe yet well-fashioned bodies bent and rose in quick gay movements as they filled their urns. The reel purred merrily as the bucket went down, then up again and threw a fountain of sparkling water that splashed with a sweet sound.

Some Sanjara tribesmen left their tents and came to greet them.

"Hello . . . how are you. . . ." Sweet words, comforting to the heart. They welcomed Saleh with warm cordiality. When they came to him, he saw a flicker of curiosity in their eyes. He escaped their questions as he had before, at the Kataani wells, amused. One of them even asked Maamour:

"Is your friend dumb?"

Saleh laughed but he did not answer.

They went to pay their respects to the Sheikh of the Sanjara, who courteously received them at the entrance of his tent.

He was a short old man with a small wrinkled face like a brown date dried by the sun, but his narrow black eyes sparkled with intelligence. He threw a keen evaluating glance at Saleh. The wrinkles on his face showed a faint smile that vanished immediately.

He asked nothing, as if his glance had given him all the answers needed.

Maamour asked him if he could leave Saleh under his protection, as he intended to travel back to the Kataani wells the following day. He had to report to his master about their journey and bring a few essentials from there. He asked their host if he needed anything from Sheikh Kataan.

"Oh yes, congratulate him on the wedding of his daughter Aysha. . . . I will attend the wedding."

If a mine had exploded under Maamour's feet, it could not have produced such a commotion in him. He stuttered.

"Wed . . . wed . . . wedding . . . ?"

"Of course, my son, Sheikh Kataan sent me a message a week ago; Aysha's wedding will be on Tuesday two weeks from now."

After a prolonged, heavy silence, Maamour rose and thanked the old man, trying his best to pull himself together, afraid to collapse and make a fool of himself. They went out of the tent and walked a few steps quietly, though he was swaying a little like a drunk. Suddenly he ran and disappeared behind the dunes. Saleh stopped for a little while outside the Sheikh's tent, bewildered; then he quickly followed his friend's footprints on the soft sand of the dunes. He found him. Great sobs shook him heavily. Saleh touched his shoulder, saying tenderly, "Don't get sore, my Lord. . . . I'll kill the man. There won't be any marriage . . ."

Maamour lifted his handsome face, wet with tears, and smiled a miserable smile.

"What a crazy fellow you. . . . No. . . . First of all, I am not your Lord and you are not my slave. I don't approve of murder or any offense. . . . I always knew that this day would come, but I didn't expect it to be so painful, that's all. . . . What must be . . . let it be."

They passed a difficult night of restless brooding, but in the early morning they departed. Saleh followed Maamour with the sheep at a certain distance.

"I'll feel lonely, my Lord . . . please don't stay too long, and take care of yourself . . ." said Saleh, his lower lip unvoluntarily quivering.

Maamour, too, felt like crying when he gently patted Saleh's cheek. "I have told you so many times, don't call me my Lord."

Saleh grasped the hand that touched his cheek and kissed it. Maamour remained paralyzed for a moment. If he made the slightest movement, it would trigger his complete collapse and allow the repressed sobs in him to burst out. He remained silent, immobile, for a while, then he removed the leather belt of the rifle from his shoulder and presented the weapon to Saleh. He advised him never to wander farther than a day's distance from the Sanjara wells. Then he put his hand in the little sack that was always dangling at his side, and got out the small bamboo flute.

"Take the flute, Saleh, you need it more than I do now; learn how to play it . . ."

He smiled and hesitated a little, then said, "You have my heart with you now . . . if you blow in it I'll hear you from far . . . from wherever I go. . . ." He quickly turned his back, jumped on the donkey, and rode off as fast as he could. After a while he vanished behind a dune.

For the first time Saleh was all alone. He felt acutely the dreariness of being lonely. The desert around him extended endlessly. One dune followed another monotonously. If he cried out, only the echo of his own voice would answer him.

The Trunk was dead, and Maamour had left him, and Zeina . . . he had no right even to think of her. He was alone . . . utterly and completely alone. He shook his head as if he wanted to shake away the gloom, and became attentive. He still held the rifle in his hand; the other hand was holding the flute. He smiled at it and went to the donkey that carried his small belongings, found his sack and took out a few rags, the sewing needle, and the cotton reel. The sun was setting rapidly while he was still busy fashioning a small sack which would dangle from his shoulder at his waist like Maamour's sack and in which he would carry his flute. He got annoyed with himself. He had forgotten his duties. He jumped to his feet and went to the donkey, put his things back and quickly started to gather the grazing sheep, whistling loudly. He left them grouped and started to milk the few goats that always accompany a flock of sheep to provide milk for the shepherd and his dogs. He picked dried bushes and twigs all around, running like a madman, going and coming.

It was already night and he was still baking the bread, the dogs sitting around him looking at this crazy shepherd quietly, attentively, but with a reproach in their eyes for his being late in feeding them. Yet from time to time they also looked at him fondly, pardoning him, wagging their tails. Late that night he wrapped himself in his woolen blanket. His eyes closing, he was falling asleep when he felt the moist touch of a muzzle gently awakening him. It was the big ewe, the leader, reminding him that he had forgotten to tie her leg to him. He smiled, suddenly happy, and did so.

A little after midnight he raised his head, awakening, oppressed. The night was pitch dark. Suddenly he was tense; his very soul shook from terror: the echo was sending back the howl of a wolf far away. He grasped his rifle. His heart was pounding madly in his chest. The small fire near him was almost extinguished. He revived it, then he waited, listening carefully; another howl came, from very far.

He hissed between his teeth, "Impossible . . . it's impossible. . . ." Could the wolves have been waiting for the sheep outside the Sanjara wells all this time . . . in an area crossed every day by several flocks of sheep? Why his sheep? . . . No! It did not make sense! Suddenly his eyes widened in horror as he noticed that his dogs were not barking in answer to the howl. They were quietly seated around him near the fire; some of them even wagged their tails at him, as if the wolves presented no danger. He listened again, all his nerves tense, wide awake. The howl was getting fainter, but he cried aloud and jumped up, holding his rifle, untied his foot from the leader ewe, and started to run. The howl was coming from the direction Maamour had taken: they were following him. The dogs started to run after him; some passed him, barking. They were afraid because their master was. But he stopped, panting. The night was really dark, Maamour was out of reach. He was at more than a day's walking distance by now and Saleh could not leave the sheep.

The dogs stopped immediately too; some of them barked at the night in different directions but in an unconvinced manner. Saleh came back to the fire, weeping and sobbing loudly. The dogs looked at him, a little nervous but astonished. What a crazy shepherd! They wagged their tails. He got mad at them and started beating them with the iron muzzle of his rifle, tears dribbling on his cheeks. They fled howling. He calmed down and sat by the fire and looked at its dancing flame, fascinated by it. He imagined that eyes were sparkling in its center.

Dawn peered at the horizon and sent its light on the sand. The moment Saleh could differentiate the marks left by Maamour's donkey he ran along their track. After a long time he stopped.

The traces left by wolves' paws crossed the path. They seemed to have hesitated. The marks were all around, as if the wolves had been smelling the sand to find their way. Then they followed the donkey track; he was now sure that three wolves were following Maamour.

He came running back again, gathered the sheep, and started his rapid journey, following the track again, whistling and pushing them to speed the sheep. At about noon he discovered where Maamour had rested and got down from his donkey. There was the place of his small fire that was now extinguished. Saleh carefully looked around. The wolves had followed Maamour but then had stopped at a distance from him. They had not attacked him. The tracks showed where Maamour had resumed his ride. The wolves, too, had resumed their pursuit, patiently but slowly. This was strange, incredible. Yet Saleh realized that at no moment had the wolves tried to attack or approach him. Maamour, in any case, had a club, a long heavy shepherd's club. It was reinforced with an iron tip and could be a dangerous weapon.

The sheep behind Saleh scattered now. The place was beautiful, full of flowers, mauve and yellow amidst the green of herbs and young sprouts. The dogs were smelling the wolves' tracks, but they looked quiet and reassured. Saleh's features relaxed. He planted his club in the sand and spread his blanket on it, erecting a little tent; and slipping under its shade, he rested.

The days passed quietly as Saleh lived and slept with the sheep. He had initially thought the solitude would drive him insane, but found himself continuously busy with one thing or another . . . a ewe giving birth, a lamb that needed extra care, the search for suitable grazing grounds, hunting for enough dry twigs to make a fire, baking bread, feeding the dogs, disciplining them when necessary.

He learned to play Maamour's flute, and composed melodies so sad that they brought tears to his eyes. He kept in mind Maamour's advice about not straying too far away from the Sanjara wells, and circled within a reasonable radius. A week later he returned to the Sanjara for news of Maamour, but there was none. He left word of his location and went back to the flock.

That night he lit a fire and tied his foot to the leader's as usual. Just as he was about to fall asleep, he heard the dogs barking fiercely. All of a sudden their bark changed, it took on a happy note. He untied his foot quickly. In the glow of the fire the shape of a camel with two persons on it emerged from the dark night.

"Who's there?" he shouted, the rifle in his hand.

"Friends," answered a familiar voice. Saleh placed the gun on the sand and was overwhelmed with an intense emotion, acute joy and gratitude; he went quickly to the side of the camel.

He received Maamour in his wide open arms. They embraced each other tightly, hugging each other cheek by cheek. Then they shook hands many times, each giving his hand to grasp the other, tightening the grip, then returning it to his chest, his palm on his heart, and again going to shake again.

"How did you know where I was?"

"I saw the light of your fire," said Maamour. "Listen, Aysha is with me."

"Aysha?"

Maamour seemed both happy and apprehensive. "She came to me at dawn when I got back and begged me to take her away or she would commit suicide. I could see that she meant it. Saleh, what could I do? I decided to come to Sanjara and put myself under the protection of its Sheikh; he is a good man, and Sheikh Kataan respects him and avoids his anger. He was also a good friend of my father's, God have mercy on his soul, and I am positive he will not refuse my plea. Anyway, if Sheikh Kataan refuses to allow us to marry, I will be put to death. It doesn't matter, because Aysha means to kill herself for my sake; so we will die together."

Saleh stood looking at his friend, who seemed to be asking some kind of forgiveness for his deed.

Maamour turned toward his camel and made it kneel so Aysha could come down. Aysha was taller than Zeina, and much darker, but very attractive. She covered her face with a veil and left only her eyes bare. She stared at Saleh with lovely dark eyes.

"Bring the Holy Koran, Saleh," Maamour said trembling.

Saleh fetched it and told Maamour and Aysha to stand in front of him. Then he read the prayer of the blessed Fatiha and married them.

At dawn Maamour and Aysha left on the camel for the Sanjara wells. Saleh assembled the sheep and followed them.

When he found Maamour, he learned that the Sanjara Sheikh had agreed to give him and Aysha his protection. Maamour was jubilant. He explained that no one would dare to harm either one of them as long as they remained in this sanctuary. In fact, the Sheikh had departed to Sheikh Kataan's encampment to inform him that his daughter had already married Maamour and that he must respect her wish.

"He whipped us both but he gave us his protection as if we were his own flesh and blood. Who would have believed this old man had such strength?"

One week later, Maamour came to Saleh with good news. Shiekh Kataan had sent his blessings. The only problem was with the cruel cousin, Massoud; but after some persuasion by the elders of the tribe he had accepted three hundred pounds as compensation, and the Sanjara Sheikh had paid the amount on the spot. Massoud had demanded such a huge sum to make it impossible for Maamour to pay it, but Sheikh Kataan himself had secretly given the money to the Sanjara Sheikh to protect both Aysha and Maamour from Massoud's revenge. Both Sheikhs and Massoud had read the prayer of the Fatiha in front of the assembled tribe as a sign of peace, and it had been decided that Aysha would eventually come back with Maamour to live near her father.

In the meanwhile, Maamour accompanied Saleh into the desert with the flocks. That night they really made a joyous feast around a dancing glowing fire, chatting merrily, happy about their good fortune. Saleh even delighted Maamour by playing for him with the flute a few notes of a melody he had tried to compose, having learnt the art of playing the flute in the past few weeks. But Saleh suddenly stopped, his face darkening. The dogs who usually gambolled behind the dunes were suddenly gathered around them, near the fire. They raised their muzzles to smell the breeze, worried. Maamour, excited and absorbed in his overwhelming joy, had not noticed anything; he asked in good faith:

"Why did you stop?"

"No . . . no . . . Nothing at all . . ." and Saleh resumed his flute playing.

Late that night they were laying enveloped in their blankets. Saleh had promised himself to remain awake and keep watch, he was worried . . . yet he felt tired and was just dozing off, when he jumped up, sitting in panic, terrified. . . . It was too late; he heard the snap of his forearm, that had been raised in an uncontrolled last gesture of protection, cracking. His mind suddenly darkened and lost consciousness, as the heavy club, after breaking his forearm, fell across his raised face.

He regained consciousness. Acute, terrible pain filled his mind. Then he heard distinctly the repeated inhuman cry that rattled every time near its end. He understood that it was Maamour's voice screaming. He panted and gathered all his strength, disregarding the increasing violent pain, tightening his muscles. Only one arm and one leg responded. The other leg and arm were broken. The heavy club which had smashed across his face had squeezed one eye out of its socket. It was dangling on his cheek attached by its nerves. He heard the snarls of the wolves as they quarrelled, their teeth snapping, and the repeated calls of Maamour screaming. He braced himself up in a tremendous effort, dragging himself on the sand by one arm and one leg, suffering like hell. He reached his rifle; its metal was shining in the faint glow of the fire. He raised it and pulled the trigger. The shot resounded in his brain with its echo and the excruciating pain. The wolves fled and he resumed his crawling slowly, dragging his inert leg and arm. Every step was like a whole year of suffering. It was dawn when he perceived the loud panting and rattling of his friend.

The screaming and yelling stopped a long time ago. He realized that he was now near his friend. He raised his face again, turning his head a little to look with the only eye left.

Maamour sat in the air naked, with his arms tied behind his back. The long club with its iron tip kept him pinned to the ground. It passed through him from between his thighs to appear in a fountain of torn red intestines in the middle of his belly, where pieces of flesh had been bitten off by the wolves. His face alone was free of any injury, pale like a white handkerchief shining under the light of dawn. He relaxed when he saw Saleh, and a smile showed on his face, gently greeting him, his eyes looking at Saleh tenderly.

Saleh let himself fall on his broken arm but raised the other to grasp the horrible club. But he stopped midway. Maamour had screamed an inhuman loud cry. His face was distorted in a dreadful manner. Light rosy bubbles appeared around his lips.

Saleh let his arm drop and raised his head, Maamour's features relaxed again and the gentle smile illuminated the beautiful white face. He heard him whisper.

"Shoot me, Saleh. . . . Shoot with the gun . . ."

Saleh shook his head, crawling a step backward, his injured eye dangling from its bloody attachment on his cheek. The eyes before him begged tenderly, and he heard the soft whisper.

"Please . . . set me free . . . free . . ."

Tears mixed with blood rolled down Saleh's cheeks, but he shook his head, refusing. So he heard Maamour whisper again.

"Remember your promise . . . I am your master . . . obey . . . set me free . . . free."

Saleh refused again, half his face frowning, blood and tears dribbling on it. The whisper begged again, coaxing him.

"Obey . . . please . . . set me free . . ."

He raised the muzzle of the rifle and pulled the trigger. The shot went off and the handsome face fell backward, facing the sky, shining white, fixed in a beautiful, relaxed smile that thanked tenderly.

The red hole in his forehead looked like a red rose blooming with all its petals.

CHAPTER

14

T hree days later Sheikh Kataan found them. One of Massoud's colleagues who had taken part in the murder had informed on him, repenting.

Saleh was on the verge of death, unconscious, delirious. The Sheikh was aghast at the cruelty of the horrible crime. He buried his shepherd Maamour. He had great difficulty in rounding up the sheep with the help of the whole tribe. They had scattered in the desert and a great many of them were lost, killed by wolves. The dogs had fled, returning to the wild life.

A few months later Saleh's bones healed. One leg was shorter than the other, but he could walk, limping. His pale face was disfigured by a long scar which crossed it from the forehead to the chin. He had lost his right eye; his eyelid fell over the pit where it should have been, like a slack curtain.

He would have died if it had not been for the continuous care he received from Sheikh Kataan's family, especially Zeina. It also helped that he was a peasant with a body which had acquired the power to resist the stress of shock, diseases, and miseries of all kinds.

After another few months Aysha gave birth to a son, a small bundle of flesh who laughed at times or cried at others, but who looked very much like Maamour.

Massoud had vanished and nothing was heard about him. Some said that Sheikh Kataan had arranged for his killing, some that he was in the desert. No one was really sure. Some assured that he was dead; others that he had crossed the border and escaped from the Sheikh's revenge.

As for Saleh, after his recovery he did not return to a normal life. On the contrary, he acted very strangely. At dawn he would disappear beyond the dunes in the desert, and return at sunset to eat a little food which he gobbled fast without even looking at what he was eating, like a dog. Then he would sleep outside the tent in the open air, wrapped in his blanket. He would never talk to anyone; he was silent all the time, frowning. Even Zeina could not draw his attention, and she tried, like every young woman who sees her lover deeply hurt. When she crossed his path intentionally, he would blush, and the white scar in his face would bulge more, but he would quickly bend his head and avoid her glance. Zeina used to pass the night crying for his love, yearning for the mere sight of him, and then grieve all day because he always escaped from her presence. For her he was still the handsome young lad she had seen at the estate's canal, with a lovely face that shone with innocent desire. She did not care about the lost eye or the scar; she saw the Saleh she knew beneath them.

Some young tribesmen tried to approach him in the hope of gaining his friendship, others out of mere curiosity to know what he was doing all day long in the desert.

They followed his tracks on the sand and discovered him, far away, behind a dune, playing with his flute strange, enchanting melodies. They were awed and amazed at their beauty. But when he became aware of their presence he rose in a violent fury, his face scowling in a frightening grin. They fled, really shaken, terrified. He pursued them, yelling loudly, savagely throwing big stones at them with all his might, wounding some of them.

From that day he was left alone. Tribesmen avoided him, afraid of him; they said that he was completely crazy, a dangerous mad man.

One day he was sitting alone behind a sand dune, far away from the tents, when a young tribesman came near him. The moment he saw him, Saleh raised his club and his face became purple with rage, scowling.

The youth fled, crying out, "Sheikh Kataan ordered me to call you, he wants you right away."

Saleh entered the big tent and stopped at the entrance. A man was seated beside the Sheikh on the colored carpet, reclining on a silk cushion. He was a rather old man but dressed beautifully in the most opulent of Bedouin clothes. On his head he had a red fez with a blue tassel dangling on its side.

Sheikh Kataan invited Saleh to come in and meet his guest. Saleh advanced, knelt and kissed Sheikh Kataan's hand. He knelt again and kissed the other man's lean hand, which wore a golden ring with a big stone.

Saleh hesitated, then sat on the ground when he was asked to do so by the Sheikh. He squatted at the far end of the tent, bending himself, hiding his bare feet underneath his dress, making himself like a ball, the smallest possible one.

The guest turned his big nose like a crow's beak and showed a row of golden teeth when he smiled widely at Saleh.

"So you are Saleh Hawari. . . ."

If it had not been for the presence of Sheikh Kataan he would have run out of the tent and fled, but instead he bent his head lower in silence.

Sheikh Kataan's grave voice assured the guest,

"This lad is very dear to me, and please consider him my son . . . Chief. Listen Saleh, His Excellency, the Chief, came specially to bring me some news that concerns you. . . . Tell him."

The man with the big nose spoke, but in a thin smooth voice that did not match his coarse features. He narrated how a sentence of life imprisonment had been passed on a criminal called Saleh Hawari for stealing seven hundred pounds and murdering his partner. He had killed him so as not to share the money, and thrown the body in a canal. It was discovered much later because it drifted with the current and got jammed at the mouth of a large water pipe. Though the body was in a very bad state of decomposition, the doctor charged with the autopsy swore in court that he could detect signs of a fight just before his death. Saleh's escape was a further proof of his guilt.

Evidence in court showed that he was acquainted with a woman of bad reputation, a village harlot, who had made a considerable sum of money out of her trade. She had had a son by him. After the theft she disappeared, taking her son and her money with her. She could not be traced and it was believed she went to join him in a hiding place. The Trunk's father came in court and pleaded for Saleh. It was the only voice in his favor. He swore that Saleh could not have committed the crime and that his son died in an accident because he did not know how to swim.

The Trunk's father's testimony saved Saleh from the rope and the court passed the sentence of life imprisonment on him.

Now police investigations led to a fisherman who had become suspicious at the passing of shepherds, not very far from where they found the rags of the deceased.

That was why the police had come to him, as he was the government's appointed Chief of all the desert tribes of this region and represented them in dealing with the authorities. The police had asked him to conduct some investigations of his own.

Saleh remained seated, his head bent, a silent squatting form that took the curves of a big ball. Deep inside him he sighed in relief, his mind at rest, resigned to his fate.

Ah! The Palace had caught up with him at the end and reached its long arm across the desert to seize him. There was no escape from its high walls, but he was pleased by what he learned about Yasmeen; she must have understood why he had fled from the village. He smiled; she took his son with her. She would educate him properly as he had asked her. He would learn how to read and write. Saleh laughed aloud, a gay hysterical laughter, forgetting himself. The Chief of the tribes was startled, afraid; but Sheikh Kataan reassured him.

"My dear Chief . . . Saleh is a gentle boy with a good-hearted nature . . . an unfortunate accident has made his mind rave at times . . . but please consider him as my son. . . . Don't tell anyone or inform about him."

"I am afraid things may go out of my hands."

"No. . . . Tomorrow he will leave with part of my sheep to a far place in the desert and I will prepare some identification papers in the name of Saleh Kataani as if he was one of my tribesmen and just came from the west; of course I am expecting your help, Chief.

"Certainly . . . but the matter will require a few expenses . . ."

A merry twinkle danced in Sheikh Kataan's eyes. He said to Saleh gently, looking at him fondly, "Go now, my son, and leave me with His Excellency, the Chief."

The following day Sheikh Kataan sent a messenger to a young shepherd who was driving over grazing grounds not very far from the Kataani wells a flock of sheep owned by the Sheikh. He ordered him to hurry back. When the young shepherd returned he turned over the flock of sheep to Saleh, who departed immediately. The Sheikh accompanied him, mounted on camel.

After two weeks of a nearly continuous march the blue hue of the terrible mountains loomed on the horizon: the valleys of the caverns. A smile appeared on Saleh's face for the first time in more than a year. The Sheikh gave him a rifle and a sharp dagger. He promised to come every month to see him and to renew the provisions of flour and other goods. Then he left him.

When night came Saleh did not prepare himself to sleep, but removed his clothes completely and lit a big fire, then vanished in the dark.

He took only his dagger with him. He crouched not very far off under the breeze. At midnight the dreadful howl resounded menacingly all over the valley. The sheep dogs barked fiercely, and then Saleh saw the dancing glitter of green eyes. Like a wildcat, noiselessly, he darted and rushed upon them, plunged the dagger deep in many throats, choking the ascending howls of pain and terror. . . . A terrible savage battle followed in the dark. Then Saleh returned, limping, to the fire, happy, victorious, bleeding from many small wounds all over him from the bites of the sharp teeth and the scratches of the curved, acutely sharp claws.

That night Saleh slept quietly, happy for the first time in many months. In the morning he hurried to see; on the sand three wolves lay dead. He danced around their bodies, raised his hands above his head and snapped his fingers in the air, punctuating the gay rhythm, in a crazy gambol. His face twitched merrily and he laughed aloud. Then he cut the wolves into small pieces of meat and fed them to the dogs.

From now on hunting wolves became his pleasure. For days and nights he would follow their traces in the sand and track them to their own dens in the many caverns of the mountains, which gave their name to the valley.

He would remain crouched under the wind, lying in wait for them. Then he would jump. And at the moment of this flexible powerful movement of his taut body, when his fingers clawed at the bloody necks of the wolves, he could feel a sweet happy elation, like a crazy drunkenness.

The wolves fled the area, leaving the mountain caverns for good. They never came back to the valley.

Saleh then turned his attention to the sheep, caring for them fondly again. They grew fat on the rich grazing grounds of the valley. When the Sheikh Kataan came after a month he was delighted, and returned with a number of fat sheep ready for sale.

So now the Sheikh spaced his visits, coming only every two to three months, with the full load of provisions on a camel; and he would go back with some of the fattened offspring. They did not talk, or hardly did, as the Sheikh understood that Saleh had lost the power to communicate with words.

Summer came and with it the danger of thirst, but Saleh found in the mountains a small spring that never went dry. The desiccated flower heads in the rich valley provided a wonderful grazing ground for the sheep. So Saleh asked the Sheikh for permission to remain in the area even in summer.

One day he was looking through his belongings and discovered in his old sack with the Holy Koran and his old copy-books. The white scar on his face bulged when he smiled.

That evening at sunset he prayed for the first time in the years since the days of the estate. His only eye cried hot tears while he was giving thanks. After he finished praying his body shook repeatedly in a long, nearly sexual quiver.

From that day on he entered a new period of his life full of mysticism, thanksgiving, and prayers. For hours he would communicate with God, begging for his pardon, explaining how he had come to falter and sin.

He would then remember Maamour with his beautiful face brightened by the happy glow of faith when he prayed. He would remember his words when he gave him the flute: "Saleh, you have my heart with you now. If you blow in it I will hear you wherever I go. . . ." He would then play strange melodies for his lost friend. Sometimes he would remain for hours, immobile, gazing at the grains of sand running between his bare toes in the wind.

Often he would lie on his back, observing the flight of clouds in the sky. Days followed each other. The sky would change from turquoise blue to light grey. White bright clouds followed black crazy ones. Then the sky would change to a colorless, hot radiant emptiness, like the gleam of a steel blade; shining bright days would be followed by dark black nights, or nights lighted by the glittering stars or the soft gentle touch of the full moon. Cold winds would blow. His body would shiver in their whirls. Then hot winds would come, desiccating everything, parching his throat, raising the sands in dangerous storms. At other times a gentle breeze would console him, carrying with it all the mixed fragrances of blooming flowers.

The desert was always on the move, creeping slowly along its dunes, rolling under the blowing wind.

Days, months, and years passed.

How many years? Saleh would not know exactly. Ten perhaps. He was always alone, yet he never felt really lonely. The Palace was somewhere, looking for him, but he felt safe from its dreadful reach. Here it had lost its claws and sharp menacing teeth.

Suddenly he was reminded of its presence acutely. Whatever he did, however he prayed, however he begged or implored, it would catch up with him and crush him! He heard, dazzled, unbelieving, the roaring of a car engine. He fled terrified behind a dune, taking his rifle with him, crouched behind its top and looked in horror: the car stopped near his frightened sheep. His dogs barked fiercely, but retreated back while barking, also afraid. A strange car, square, grey, with a loud horrible engine growl. Saleh behind his dune began to tremble, yet he was fascinated, and turned his head a little to look with his only eye which widened with terror. His teeth chattered, his whole body shook with violent emotion. Inside the car he saw the white young man with the pink and white fat face that looked like the face of a newborn baby, but a newborn baby wearing gold-rimmed spectacles which shone and gleamed under the radiant sun: the same face that he had seen years ago in the black car at the estate. Beside him sat a dark young fellow. Both wore European clothes.

"Ah . . . ! The Palace men!!!" His eye gleamed and narrowed as he scowled. He aimed his rifle at the fattish young man, having great difficulty steadying his gun with his shaking hands. He pulled the trigger; the shot went off.

"Damn!" he hissed between his chattering teeth. He had missed. He was amazed to see the two young men getting out of the car with hands raised above their heads. He hissed again, "Damn!!!"

He steadied the rifle again, aimed, and grumbled in fierce disappointment when the muzzle of the gun quivered at the last moment, sending the shot astray.

"Damn!!!!"

The young men now had vanished behind the protection of the car.

The long arm of the Palace deviated the shots. It was useless to continue fighting and fleeing . . . better to surrender once and for all.

He stood up and slowly, trembling all over, glided down the sand slope, as if he was pushed down from the back against his will. He stopped a few steps from the car, laid the rifle on the ground, knelt and bent his head till his forehead touched the sand, and remained in this position, shaking all over, frightened beyond imagination.

The young men came from behind the car, amazed, not believing their eyes, looking at this poor Bedouin kneeling, his forehead touching the sand, shaking severely. The dark one stooped and grasped the rifle. Feeling secure, he shouted at Saleh in a strange voice with a queer accent.

"Hey . . . ! Hey!!! What came over you? Are you crazy!!!?" Saleh raised his head, imploring. Tears rolled from his only eye.

He stuttered, still shaking, addressing the young man with the white baby face and gold-rimmed spectacles.

"Forgive me, your Majesty . . . forgive me . . ."

They gazed at him, still dazed, then the dark young man, feeling now completely secure with the rifle, pointed at Saleh.

"What a fool! You really are a Bedouin!" And he laughed loudly. But the other young man reproached him in a gentle voice, full of pity for the Bedouin.

"Shut up, Ibrahim! Don't laugh at this fellow. Don't you see that he is afraid of us? These Bedouins often go years without meeting another human being."

Then he addressed Saleh, but with a friendly, soft voice and a queer accent.

"Come up . . . stand up, man. Don't be frightened, we are now friends. My name is Moustapha, he is Ibrahim. . . . We lost our way . . . we are employees in the desert development and building project. What's your name?"

Saleh's face brightened immediately and he smiled widely. He stood up. "Really? You lost your way? Oh!!! My name is Saleh. . . . Welcome!" Saleh shouted at the dogs which now wanted to attack, recovering from their fright. He offered his hand to shake their hands; he offered it again and again, touching his heart, the palm flat on his chest every time, till the dark young man protested.

"Don't you think it is enough of shaking hands!"

Saleh laughed and laughed merrily while he lighted a small fire. He prepared tea and baked bread. He was so pleased to see them eat avidly his hot bread moistened with cool goat's milk.

Then he rode with them in the car, amazed and a little afraid; but the young men gave him confidence with their gentle voices.

"How will you get back to your sheep. . . . ?" asked Moustapha.

"Oh! I'll walk back . . ."

"But you'll take days . . . two weeks, maybe."

"Oh no . . . not more than four days if I walk at night too."

"You are not afraid for the sheep?"

"Oh no, the place is now safe. . . . The grazing grounds are rich, they won't move a lot. I'll quickly find their traces . . ."

"Why did you fire at us? Why were you so much afraid of us?"

He did not answer; his face darkened a little, suddenly suspicious and afraid again.

Moustapha insisted gently. "Do you never go to civilization?

What is your full name . . . don't you have any address, if we want to find you again . . . ?"

There you are, you cunning fellow . . . you want to hurt me, said Saleh to himself. He glanced at Moustapha sideways in a stern, hostile look . . . but the other's face appeared kind, with no hidden cunning. Saleh hesitated once more, then said, giving his new name, "Saleh Kataani . . . from the Kataani tribe . . . at the Kataani wells."

Moustapha took out from his pocket a small notebook and wrote the name.

Saleh's face blanched, the scar bulged.

"Do you really wish me well . . . ? Please, my Lord Moustapha, do not hurt me . . ."

Moustapha smiled and said kindly, "Tomorrow you will know."

Ibrahim, who was driving, asked in a worried voice, "There is no more gas . . . Do we still have far to go?"

"Oh no, we are very near now to the Sanjara wells."

After a while some yellow lights danced at the horizon. Saleh asked them to stop.

"Straight ahead are the Sanjara wells. Even if your car stops you can continue walking, you won't lose your way, and the Sanjara Sheikh will send a messenger to the nearest frontier guard station for your rescue."

Having said this, Saleh jumped out of the car like a lithe cat and vanished in the night.

A whole year passed after this incident. Saleh was a little excited and worried at first. He had talked too much, and his nerves were so shattered that he suffered from a continuous headache and insomnia for several days. But with the passage of time he forgot the incident completely. He quickly found his sheep, and the dogs barked joyously at him; they were hungry.

Once more Sheikh Kataan came to him as he usually did. The camel knelt and Saleh hurried to him and helped the man get off. He kissed his hand with a profound respect.

The Sheikh had become very old and his formerly grey beard was completely white now. His face was emaciated and wrinkled. Yet he still stood erect. The Sheikh smiled a kind, wide smile at Saleh, who looked at the camel amazed: there were no provisions.

"Gather the sheep. You are leaving with me."

"But my Lord, the place is safe, I won't find a better place."

"Never mind. . . . Gather the sheep . . . you are going to leave my service."

A bomb exploded in Saleh's brain; he gazed at the Sheikh with his only eye, unbelieving; his face blanched, the long scar bulging. But the Sheikh opened his arms widely.

"Come, my child . . . come, let me kiss you and congratulate you, come, my child."

Saleh went to him, dazzled, bewildered still more by this embrace, which was allowed only between equals.

The Sheikh tightly hugged him, then he explained:

"You remember, Saleh my child, the Chief of the tribesmen who came to visit me. He came again. The name that I gave you, by which you are known now, Saleh Kataani, was on a list he received. You have been granted a small plot of land with a little house and a wind-propelled water pump. Congratulations my son . . . how did this happen? . . . No one knows. Even the Chief of the tribesmen did not know. He was really sore; his liver hurt him and he was ill for three days because he had no part in the deal."

Saleh's only eye suddenly wept one tear, then he burst into a loud laughter and then cried again. Then he jumped and whistled nervously, rounding up the sheep.

Saleh stopped at the doorstep of his house. He had just received a guest, Sheikh Kataan, who had come to visit him. He looked at the great Sheikh riding slowly away, erect, majestic, beautifully handsome in his floating white Bedouin clothes.

The setting sun placed a halo of bright light around his head against the turquoise blue sky, which was now invaded by golden red rays. Saleh's face was lit up also with the same bright golden glow. He jumped suddenly and went running as quickly as he could to the end of his garden, from the north border to the south, then again from the east to the west, meeting the sun. He stopped at the water pump and raised his head at the wind propeller, high up, which looked as if it laughed at him with its turning arms. He heard the singing of the water, falling over the white stones. He felt thirsty, so he bent and stretched his neck and drank a long drink of the sweet water, happy, contented.

Moustapha and Ibrahim had visited him earlier in his newly acquired garden. They had brought with them some cuttings of peach trees to be transplanted on his land.

A little while ago Sheikh Kataan had visited him, and they had a very pleasant conversation, most of it silent but very expressive. Saleh understood from the start what the Sheikh meant without really saying it, and he cried out of mad joy inside himself, without showing it. His old crazy dream was about to be realized. The Sheikh had looked at him meaningly, smiled, then said:

"You are now a landowner, Saleh. There is no one who wouldn't feel honored if you proposed marriage."

Their eyes met, and Saleh returned to the Sheikh the same long gaze, thanking him silently. Zeina till now had refused all marriage proposals.

Tomorrow, Sheikh Kataan, I will be at your place proposing, said Saleh to himself.

That night it drizzled a light rain. Saleh raised his head; an anxious expression loomed on his features for a second. No . . . he had forgotten. The roof of his small house was made of reinforced concrete, not of straw or mud.

Zeina pushed herself against him, so their naked bodies melted together again, and Saleh plunged into her warmth. The drizzle tapped all night on the window glass. Thousands of small feet pattered over the roof above their heads, trying to find an opening. They relaxed . . . panting . . . the sky grumbled and growled, thundering, but they smiled to each other, feeling secure.

Zeina's eyes became languid, sleepy; Saleh glided over her, whispering, "You won't sleep with me . . ."

So the eyes like corn wet with dew gleamed in the yellow light of the small kerosene lamp with its wick burning low. Zeina's cheeks colored rosy and her lips parted a little. Elated, she turned her head, shy of showing so much emotion.

At dawn they stopped once again, panting. Light loomed gently at the window, so Zeina said reproachfully, yet smiling happily, before she dozed into sleep, her heart full, satisfied, "You are a terrible peasant . . . brutal . . ."

The rain had stopped, it was a light spring drizzle. Dawn slipped into the garden, scattering away the mist. Saleh too slipped out of his house, hurrying to the enchanting spring. The reel of the pump murmured and the propeller laughed, high up in the air, turning with the breeze. The fountain bubbled, showering his naked body. He shivered once, but he felt the pleasure of the cool water. He massaged his long muscles and then smelled the different fragrances coming from his garden. He smiled as he perceived in the midst of the various odors the special scent of the young peach trees.

Near noon he was hoeing around the small trees. Zeina was standing at the door, feeding the chickens which crowded around her, pushing each other. From time to time he received from her a sweet smile and saw in her eyes the glitter of the goldern corn stalks wet with dew. At the basin of the fountain his little son was fighting and playing with the big goose. His naked little body already had the shining color of red brass; he was a small peasant like his father.

The leaves rustled and communed with the passing breeze in a soft murmur. The reel laughed with the propeller, and the water giggled, gushing in colored bubbles over the little child, his laughter tinkling like small bells.

Saleh had planted deep roots into the earth. There was the small child, playing innocently, not knowing yet that it was his turn now to act. . . . He smiled at him . . . as he suddenly imagined him a bigger boy, running holding his copy-books in his hand. Then he saw him a handsome young man, with a cheerful face, driving a car in the desert, prospecting . . . why not? . . . His heart fluttered just for a second.

Had he not another son, who at this moment was running along to school?

Yasmeen's son. And the roots plunged deeper. He had sowed the seeds and the trees were now blossoming . . . and he smiled.